PRIDE TO PACK

MOUNT ROXBY SERIES: BOOK ONE

AIMIE JENNISON

CONTENTS

PRIDE TO PACK

MOUNT ROXBY SERIES: BOOK ONE

AIMIE JENNISON

DEDICATION

To Nana June.
Thank you for always being my cheerleader.
I will miss you and I will never forget you.

A NOTE FOR THE READER

This book has been written using UK English and is set in Australia. I apologise if there are words or phrases you do not understand. Please feel free to contact me for further explanation, or to discuss the meaning of a particular phrase or word, via my email or any of my social media.

PROLOGUE
ROSABEL - SIX YEARS AGO

"**B**el, get your butt down these stairs now," Uncle Jack bellows from the basement.

"I'm coming. Geez, am I not allowed to even eat breakfast?" I answer, not bothering to shout, knowing he'll hear me clearly, with his were-lion hearing, even if I whisper. Were-animals have extra sensitive hearing.

Aunt Lily pats my back as I pass her, heading to the basement door. "He doesn't want to lose you in this duel, sweetheart. It's your first duel and he knows how strong Jerome is. It has him worried."

I take a deep breath before opening the door and heading down the stairs. The next few hours are going to be painful. Uncle Jack will push me, hard.

Uncle Jack started training me the day after I arrived, at the age of ten. He knew I needed it because as soon as I reached the legal age of duelling—which happened to be eighteen—I would be challenged, time and time again until one of them killed me. The lions just don't think a wolf deserves to be part of their pride. The thing is, I don't even want to be part of their stupid pride.

I just want somewhere to call home.

My home was taken away from me when my parents died. My legal guardian, Aunt Lily, is the only tie I have to my parents. At eighteen, I'm old enough to go off on my own, but my Aunt, Uncle, and cousin Benji, are family. I love them and don't want to leave them.

The basement is set up like any high-end gym, with all the equipment and weights anyone could ask for. The floor is covered in mats to soften the fall when I am sparing with Uncle Jack. I appreciate those mats because I do hit the floor—a lot.

Uncle Jack is standing in the middle of the mats ready to spar. He's trained me in all kinds of Martial Arts, so I'm not limited and won't get stuck if someone fights in some unusual form.

I take hit after hit knowing that this time tomorrow, I will be fighting to the death. This torture Uncle Jack puts me through is for my own good.

The Pride is assembled in the arena, which is basically an open field surrounded by the forests of the pride land. I call it a field but there is nothing there. It's just packed dirt. It has seen many duels over the years; the red dirt the Northern Territory is known for is almost black from all the blood spilled on it.

The lions are circled around the outside of the arena.

Jerome is already waiting in the centre for me.

Humans aren't allowed, it's too dangerous if the fight spreads towards the spectators. Aunt Lily and my cousin Benji are both human so I only have Uncle Jack, who is one of the lions, there to support me.

The crowd parts to let me in.

Uncle Jack gives me one last pat on the shoulder as he stops to stand with the crowd. "You can do this, Bel. Remember your strengths. Forget everything else."

I take a deep breath and face my opponent.

Jerome has a good foot on me in human form. He easily outweighs me. He's smirking at me like he knows he has this fight in the bag.

That's it, Jerome, you keep thinking like that. Let the overconfidence take you that step closer to the body bag.

Grigori Dorfman, the current Leader of the Pride, steps up to stand between us. "Jerome, you have challenged Rosabel to a duel. Does your challenge still stand?"

Jerome nods. "Yes."

"Very well. Rosabel, since you are the challenged party, you have the choice of whether you want to fight in human or animal form."

"Human," I answer immediately. When fighting in animal form, you only need a tooth or claw to connect in the wrong place and you're dead. Fighting as a human may take longer and be harder, but you can control your opponent more. Fighting in animal form isn't a viable option.

Grigori's loud voice booms around the arena. "You both must remain in human form at all times. If either of you shift, or even partially shift, your opponent will be declared winner and you will immediately be put to death. This duel is to the death. Do you both understand the rules?"

"Yes," we answer together.

Grigori throws his arms wide and bows his head. "May the best animal win."

Jerome and I start to circle each other, weighing each other up. Neither of us willing to make the first move.

"Come on Jerome, she's only a little girl," a male voice shouts.

Jerome turns, chasing the voice; I take the opportunity to strike him in the side of the head with a round house kick. He hits the ground and shakes his head. I move in with a kick to his jaw. He seems to anticipate it making a grab for my foot; he was a second too late and only manages to knock my foot away.

I step back and start to circle again as Jerome stands up.

He jabs his fist at my ribs and connects, causing a crack that I have no doubt means something is broken. He follows with a second jab to the same area.

Lapping up the attention as the audience cheers, he smirks. During his distraction I grab his outstretched arm, pulling it against the bend in his elbow. It cracks louder than my ribs, and I see some of the spectators flinch at the sound. I can see the shift cross his face, but he fights it off. Pain can be a trigger to shift, just like it's a trigger for nausea in humans. He did well to fight it off that quick.

The fight goes on for at least twenty minutes, which believe me, when you are fighting to the death *is* a long time. Both of us have been throwing punches and striking with kicks and neither of us is getting the upper hand.

Uncle Jack trained me for at least four hours every day. I have the endurance to handle this fight, but Jerome is getting tired. I can see it and so can the Pride.

"Come on, Jerome. End her," someone shouts.

He tries to execute a roundhouse kick to my face in retaliation to those comments. Fortunately, for me, he's sluggish. I let the momentum in his poorly executed kick take him to the ground before I pounce on his chest and grab his head between my hands.

I snap his neck.

The audience is outraged. Not only have I won, I'm still

breathing. A wolf. A female wolf just beat one of their strongest male lions in a duel to the death.

Grigori walks into the arena and states the obvious by announcing me—the only one still standing and breathing breaths that feel like a hot brand being jabbed into my side—the winner.

The crowd gets louder. He tries to calm them down but it's no use. He nods to Uncle Jack, signalling him to come and take me home so he can try to calm the pride without my distracting presence.

I only manage to hobble a couple of steps before Jerome's brother, Daniel, pushes his way through the crowd.

He gives me a murderous glare as the crowd falls silent.

"I challenge the wolf." He steps into the arena and removes his shirt, preparing to fight.

No way can I survive another duel so soon.

I shake free of Uncle Jack's vice-like grip and settle my feet to show I'm not going to run.

"I accept," I reply officially, as required.

Uncle Jack is red in the face, holding his rage back as he rants at Grigori.

Jared Dorfman, Grigori's oldest son and the next in line to be Pride Leader, steps in front of me. I didn't see where he came from, probably because my eyes are swelling shut and didn't spot his stealthy approach. He gently holds my face between his hands, assessing the damage.

I suck in a breath at the concern I see in his golden eyes. My heart pounds a little harder at his soft touch. None of the pride have ever been concerned about me. I start to think I have read him wrong and he's more concerned about the fact that I'm still breathing, that is, until he speaks.

"It's okay, Rosabel. They can't make you duel again so soon. It's Pride law. They have to give you at least a day to heal."

My stomach plummets. As good as a day reprieve sounds,

it's nowhere near enough time to heal and be fit enough to win another duel. They are just going to prolong my suffering and death.

***

My day reprieve passed in the blink of an eye. It could've had something to do with sleeping through most of it. My body's natural urge to heal while I slept took over. I wanted to train but my body was having none of it.

I gingerly walk in the kitchen to give Benji and Aunt Lily a last minute hug goodbye. I'm not feeling very confident today knowing it might actually be the last hug I get to give them.

Aunt Lily dashes across the room the minute she sees me, taking me in her arms, surrounding me with her floral scent. "It's an abomination. Making you duel when you are still recovering from the last one. I feel like storming down to that arena and giving them a piece of my mind."

"You can't do that. It will only cause trouble for Uncle Jack. I've trained all these years. I can handle it." I pull away, putting on my brave face. I need to leave now before I crack, causing her to do exactly what she wants—no doubt writing her own death warrant in the process.

Benji stands from his seat at the table. "Come on, Bel, you don't want to be late. I'll walk you down the road. Uncle Jack said he'd meet you at Grigori's. There was a meeting this morning." He walks straight out the door without making eye contact with Aunt Lily or me. I can smell his tears so I know the reason why. It's the same reason I follow him out silently, neither of us want to make Aunt Lily any more concerned.

Neither of us speaks again until we reach Grigori's drive, both lost in our own heads. I can't help looking at all the gorgeous houses, seeing the picket fences and beautiful flower beds, only to think people passing through this town have no idea the very people who keep these houses so beautiful would be trying their damnedest to have an eighteen-year-old woman killed just because she's another species.

"Bel," Benji's whimper pulls me from my thoughts.

One look at his blotchy face covered in tears makes me pull him into my arms. "Shhhh. It's okay, Benj."

Grigori's door opens. Jared, Uncle Jack, and Grigori file out. Grigori walks out the gate not even acknowledging we are here. But then again Benji is a lowly human and I'm a wolf; we already know what the lions think of me. Why should he bother acknowledging us?

I watch Jared, expecting him to follow his father but he stops in front of us with Uncle Jack.

I release Benji, holding his shoulders firmly with my hands. "Go home and give Aunt Lily a hug. I'll see you in a little while." I don't care that there's no conviction behind my words. It isn't like I can say, 'Have a good life, I won't see you again.' It's probably true but it would just hurt both of us.

Uncle Jack pulls a sobbing Benji into his embrace, looking at me over Benji's dark hair. "I'm going to take him home. You head down with Jared, I'll catch up." With those parting words, he walks off in the direction of home.

I watch them walk away for a second before turning back towards Jared, who's still standing in front of me. In fact, I'm certain he moved in closer because there's barely an inch between us. I can feel his lion's energy crackling against my skin.

"How are you doing, Bel?" He asks as he stares intently into my eyes. The stare goes all the way down to my toes. *Holy hell.* I feel a flush pulsing through my body.

"I'm fine," I answer curtly. Why would I answer any differently when his pride is trying to kill me?

He growls. That growl does something to my body. I can

honestly say I have never heard a growl come from a lion before; it's quite disturbing…and arousing.

His hot breath is almost in my face. His nostrils flare as he barks at me. "Now. Answer that again, but without the bullshit this time." I can sense a power blazing from his lion. What's going on?

"Fine," I snap. "I feel like shit. It hurts to move. It hurts to breathe. It hurts to think about the fact that I'm being sent to my death by your whole goddamn pride and no fucker seems to give a shit! There. Is that what you wanted to hear?"

"Not exactly, but it's much better than the first answer." He turns and starts walking towards the arena. "Come on, you don't want to be late."

The closer we get to the arena, the calmer I become. It's like a cloud has descended over me, nothing matters but the fight I'm about to face. No amount of worrying or complaining will change a thing. I've got to duel no matter what; I can't ask anyone else to fight for me.

The pride is already circled around the arena, ready to watch the duel.

Jared grabs my hand and pulls me through the parting crowd.

Great, everyone is going to think I was about to run and needed escorting by the leader's son.

Once we get through the crowd, I pull my hand away from Jared's.

"It's about time you turned up. I thought you must have run off scared," Daniel says snarkily.

That growling noise comes from Jared again but he doesn't follow up with a comment.

Grigori steps between us, stopping any verbal diarrhea from spewing out of my mouth. "Daniel, does your challenge against Rosabel still stand?"

"She killed my brother. Too fucking right it does," he snaps.

"A 'yes' will suffice, Daniel," Grigori says with a smirk.

Is this really a time for jokes? One of us is going to die in a minute. Looking at Daniel's muscular body, I have no doubt it's going to be me.

"Rosabel, choose a form." Just like that, no formal wording.

"I challenge Daniel," Jared shouts from next to me. I had actually forgotten he was there. I flick my eyes to him in surprise and our eyes connect. My heart stutters in my chest at the emotions I see burning in his. Murmurs run through the crowd as people question why. Others are questioning if it's even a legal move on Jared's part.

"Daniel, being the challenged party, you are required to choose a form. What do you choose?"

I'm too shell-shocked to take in what's happening around me after that.

Jared's fighting for me and Grigori is letting him. *Why? Have I been sucked into the twilight zone or something?*

Someone's hand grabs me, pulling me out of the arena and towards the spectators. They're not attacking me, so I assume it's Grigori. I can't tear my eyes away from the two lions in the arena long enough to see who belongs to the hand. All I can see is one mass of golden fur. With the roars and yips I can hear, it's clear someone is winning.

It's only a matter of minutes before it's all over, the fur separates into two. The lion that's moving shifts and a naked Jared is left standing in the centre of the arena.

I manage to breathe a sigh of relief before Grigori drags me back towards the centre. He clears his throat before speaking. "Jared, as the winner, do you wish to take on Daniel's challenge towards Rosabel?"

"No," is all he grumbles, as he picks up his clothes off the ground and stalks out of the arena.

Grigori passes me off to Uncle Jack. I have no idea where he came from, or if he was even there through the fight, but he's here now and leading me home.

The Pride didn't seem to know what to do after Jared took on Daniel. It was a week before I was challenged again. I fought that time, but when I was immediately challenged again Jared jumped in and challenged my opponent right back.

Jared joined in on our training sessions the day after his fight with Daniel, not because he needed the training but so he could help me.

It wasn't long before we became a couple; which really didn't help on the fight front.

They didn't want their future leader married to a wolf.

1.

NEW BEGINNINGS

ROSABEL - PRESENT DAY

I take a deep, cleansing breath as I pounce off the bus. Twelve hours sitting in a metal container with a bunch of sweating strangers is not the best idea for someone with a strong nose like mine. And that was just the last bus journey. I had been on three more of around the same duration. It takes a long time to drive from the desert of the Northern Territory, all the way southeast to central New South Wales. I could have flown but it's bad enough travelling in a box that's on the ground, there was no way I was going to travel in a big metal box that floats in the air. Were-animals might be extremely indestructible, but I don't think even I could survive a plane crash. My cousin, Benji, isn't like me and even he warned me about the smell.

I should have listened.

Jared will know I have left by now. Uncle Jack promised he would keep him distracted long enough to give me a good head start.

I didn't tell anyone where I was heading because I hadn't really known myself. I'd just closed my eyes, threw a dart at a map of Australia and chose the nearest town that had a were-wolf pack. I burnt the map to ashes afterwards so there wouldn't be any clues. So even if he does come looking he isn't going to find me.

I know you're wondering why I left. If I was in love with the man who saved my life by duelling for me for the last six years, why would I up and leave? Well let me tell you, that is exactly why I left. Jared didn't deserve to fight every week to save his mate, or wife, from being killed. He deserves a mate that his pride actually likes and accepts. I didn't want him to resent me and that's all our future would hold; resentment.

I only told Aunt Lily, Uncle Jack, and Benji about my plan to leave an hour before my first coach left. Aunt Lily was heartbroken and Benji wasn't far off, but once I explained my reasons Uncle Jack agreed it was for the best. We managed to calm Aunt Lily and Benji down in the end, but I think it will take them a while to fully come to terms with it.

I am hoping to find a werewolf pack that will welcome me. From Pride to Pack, I'm dreaming of finding somewhere to finally call home.

So here I am in Mount Roxby, thankfully off that stinking bus, with a back pack crammed full of my belongings, two hundred dollars in my pocket, and no idea what to do or where to go.

As I stand on the pavement of the main road, taking in my surroundings, I find myself being drawn to a building across the road. It doesn't look special; it's a corner building and has a midnight blue facade, two double doors of the same colour, and a bright purple neon sign - Misty's. There are no windows that I can see, making me think it's a bar or club of some kind. I can't help but go take a closer look.

There's a piece of paper taped to the door. 'Cocktail mixer needed. Apply within.' *I'm going to need a job.* I had worked in the only bar back home for the last couple of years, so I'm used to the bar atmosphere. *Okay, cocktails weren't ordered very often, but how hard can it be?*

As I push the door open I get a really strong sense of dread. It makes me want to turn my behind around and leave in a rush. I take a deep breath and ignore my senses. Once the door shuts behind me the dread goes with it, as if it's just connected to the door in some way.

The smell of cleaning fluid hits me immediately, along with a whole mix of people's personal scents. In the big rectangular room, the solid wooden floorboards under my feet aren't sticky like you expect to find in a bar. The first thing I see is the bar's counter, which is directly opposite the entrance, stretching about eight metres in length from the right hand corner of the room, to the left. There's a door next to the bar and then there are four booths along the wall; a stage— with a beautiful, glossy black piano on the right-hand side—is positioned in the far left of the room along that side wall.

In front of the stage is a large open area which I assume is used as a dance floor. Covering the rest of the floor space is a mixture of circular and rectangular tables, with booths against the other wall until you come to the door again. Every available wall is covered in floor to ceiling mirrors, which makes the whole place look twice as big. Even though there are no windows it isn't dark and dingy, the lighting is used well. The space between the bar and the door is open apart from a few stools along the bar.

There aren't many customers; a couple sit at the right corner of the bar, a guy sits to the far left side, and another couple sit at one of the circular table's right next to the dance floor. It doesn't look very busy but it is only five in the evening; most people will only just be leaving work. It probably won't get too busy for another couple of hours.

I walk over to the bar where I can see a tall, at least six-foot, slim brunette serving. She looks a little puzzled as she stares at me and I start to panic thinking how bad I must look as I have just stepped off the bus, but as I channel her emotions I sense she is feeling confusion. Surely that can't be related to my looks!

"Welcome to Misty's. What can I get ya?" she says in a cute British accent. I can easily sense the lie. The door must have been warded, that's why I felt the dread. A witch's ward! A human shouldn't be able to walk in and she probably knows all the supernatural beings in town. She must be wondering if it's broken.

"Hi, I'm Bel. I'm new in town. I thought I'd try my luck with the sign on your door," I tell her, whilst holding my hand out for her to shake. She glances down at it warily but takes it in hers as she plasters on a welcoming smile. I know the minute she senses my wolf energy, her smile turns genuine and she raises her brow in question. I nod. "I'm a lone wolf...for the time being."

"I'm Misty, nice to meet ya, Bel. Have ya worked in a bar before?"

I look behind the bar which looks just like any other bar, spirit bottles lining shelves and work surfaces, and fridges with beer bottles and premixes in it. "Yeah, I worked in a little bar back home for the last three years, I can give you a number and name for a reference."

Misty screws up her face and shakes her head. "No, I don't really like getting references; I prefer to see for myself. Are ya free tonight?"

"I just stepped off the bus, I haven't had chance to make any plans yet. So I'm all yours." I grin. How lucky is that, a job from the first place I walk into? Now, let's hope finding somewhere to sleep works out just as easy.

"Okay. Get ya self 'round this side of the bar then and I'll give ya a paid trial tonight. Thursday's aren't very busy, so I should be able to keep my eye on ya." She takes me in from head to toe as if she's weighing me up. I must meet her standards because she walks over to the little flap and raises it to allow me behind the bar.

By the looks of things there isn't much room behind the bar, just enough for three or four people to move around and serve comfortably. There's no shelving with personal items on it, just glasses under the bar, fridges and spirit bottles behind it and the draught levers on top.

"That will be great, thanks. Is there somewhere I can leave my bag?" I show her my backpack as I pull it off my back.

She points to the door between the bar and booths. I notice there is a toilet sign on it, which I didn't see during my observations before. "My office is through there, the code for the door is seven-two-five-nine."

I nod in acknowledgement chanting the code to myself over and over, and head through the door into a small, narrow corridor decorated in wooden cladding on the bottom half of the wall which is finished off with a dado rail. The walls above it are white, but you can tell they are well overdue a fresh coat. There's a door to my left with a beautiful Barbie-like woman painted on the full length of the door, and a couple of metres further up the corridor there is another door with a hot guy painted on it.

I walk over to the guy's door and find myself wondering if he is based on a real guy. *He must have girls coming at him from all angles, if so.* I meet his eyes and decide it can't be a real person because his eyes, they look like emeralds and no one has eyes that green.

On the right hand wall about halfway down the corridor there is a steel reinforced door, which has an electric code panel next to it. *They must get some bad types in here if they have security like this. I didn't see any bouncers.*

The only other door is a fire exit at the end of the corridor, which is painted a charcoal grey and has one of those, press-to-release bars across it.

I enter the code Misty gave me and watch as the light turns from red to green as I hear the lock click.

When I open the door, I see the room is small; one wall is covered in filing cabinets, and there are a few hooks on another wall with a coat and bag hung up. Next to the hooks is another door which must lead to a storage room of some sort because the hallway was too long for there not to be more room.

I place my bag on the floor under the hooks, not wanting the weight of my bag to pull the hooks off the wall.

The office is finished off with a metal desk in the middle of the room with a wooden chair from the bar. The walls are painted a cold grey/blue colour. It isn't a very inviting office.

I go back to the bar to find three more customers.

Misty shows me how things run behind the bar; explaining the customers mostly order cocktails since they're mainly werewolves. I know better than anyone that we find it hard to get drunk. A big mix of alcohol like you get in a cocktail gives a little buzz at least.

The guy from the couple that has been here since I walked in, waves me over to the far side of the bar to take his order.

My first order, here goes nothing.

I give him a big smile as I reach him. "Hi. What can I get you?"

"Can we get two Russian Roses, please?"

I look at him puzzled, wracking my brain to think of what that drink could be, with no luck. *Why couldn't he have picked something simple like a Cosmopolitan?*

Noticing my predicament, Misty shouts the ingredients across the bar as she points each one out. "Shaker, vodka, triple sec, pink grapefruit juice, rose syrup, basil, and the juice of two lime wedges."

"Thanks, Misty. I haven't heard of that one before." Great,

my first drink and I don't even know it. What kind of cocktail mixer do I think I am?

"No worries, Bel. You'll probably get a few ya don't know. You'll get used to them eventually. There's a book in the office in case we get a real obscure order but most of the customers know what they are ordering. If in doubt, ya can always ask them. Although ya might get a sneaky customer or two trying to catch ya out on purpose. We have some jokers like that around here," she says, mixing drinks for one of the new customers.

I'm just squeezing the limes into the shaker for the Russian Roses, as I get a whiff of werewolf. I barely get a chance to register the scent before I am hit with a rush of power that can only come from an alpha. The alpha's power wakes the wolf inside me; she starts to stir, making my skin restless and my heartbeat raise. I knew there was a large werewolf pack here but I never imagined I would meet the alpha within the first couple of hours of arriving. *I thought I'd be able to meet a few submissive wolves first; instead I get the most dominant of them all. Great!*

I place the lid on the shaker and start to shake it. I turn around to get a glance at the alpha and can't believe my eyes. He's the gorgeous guy from the men's toilet door painting. I am doing everything possible to not run off to check he's not just stepped out of the painting. He's got a lovely muscular body—but most weres are in good shape—he's about five-foot-eight, with strawberry blonde hair, and he's wearing dark jeans and a baby blue t-shirt.

I pour the drinks out and take the guy's money. I hope he gave me the right amount because I can't concentrate enough to count it, or even think about change. He's started a conversation with a new customer next to him so I don't think he is waiting for change.

I can't stop glancing at the painting guy.

Just as I'm about to take the painting guy's order, Misty beats me to it. "Hi, Theo. How are ya today?"

Smoking hot is how he is! While I'm admiring him I realise he is looking at me, as if waiting for me to answer a question I didn't hear him ask. I look at Misty hoping she can clear it up.

"This is my new cocktail mixer, Bel. You could have warned me there was a new were in town. I thought the wards were down when she walked in here," she says in jest.

Painting guy—Theo, Misty called him—holds his hand out for me to shake. As our hands meet, a tingling sensation shoots from my hand through every fibre of my body. I jump and try to pull my hand back but Theo is just staring at my hand, like he's never seen a hand before.

What the hell was that? I've felt other weres test power but it's never felt like that before. A test of power feels more like a pressure against your skin but then I've never had a werewolf test my power before, maybe they feel different to were-lions.

His gravelly voice breaks my inner dialogue, "I'm Theo. It's a pleasure to meet you." He lifts my hand up to his mouth and places a gentle kiss on it. I notice his nostrils flare as he takes in my scent. *Okay...Weird!!*

As I look into his alluring emerald green eyes, that look just as much like real emeralds as the ones in the painting did, I distractedly reply, "The pleasure is all mine." *Did I really say that out loud?*

Oh my goodness. Please let the floor open up and swallow me. Any time now would be nice.

He stares at me as he rubs his thumb over the top of my hand and slowly pulls his fingers away from mine. I instantly miss his touch. He smirks, like he knows a secret, and winks at me.

Nice one, Bel. You look like a bloody idiot.

I notice Misty is back at her end of the bar again. Thank the angels she didn't witness me act like an idiot.

Okay. Ask him for his order already. He's only a guy.

"What can I get you?" I can't seem to wipe the embarrassed look off my face. I can feel the flush in my cheeks.

"Do you know what a Johnnie Black Sazerac is?" He's still smirking, like the cat that swallowed that dumb tweety bird. Thankfully, it's one of the cocktails I actually know. I have made enough of a fool of myself for one night.

"That's Johnnie Walker Black and Pernod, isn't it?" I ask with a questioning look.

Better to be safe than sorry, or embarrassed again in this case!

As I bring my eyes up, I feel the urge to reach out and touch him. I want to feel that power again. I stop my hand before it moves towards him.

"You're good; I usually always have to list that one up when someone serves me for the first time." He seems like a nice guy. I'd expect an alpha to be more serious and commanding. I don't feel at all intimidated by him. I just want to rub myself against him. I'm glad the bar is between us, because it's the only thing that's stopping me.

"The last place I worked was full of men, and that's a man's drink, so to speak."

As I'm mixing his drink, I realise there's a picture of a wolf howling at a full moon on his t-shirt. "That's fitting," I say with a chuckle.

His chin drops and his eyes stare down to where my eyes are looking and gives his own hearty laugh, "I like to state the obvious," he says with a shrug. "Did you put a request in to come into town?" he asks, as I'm admiring the shape of his body through the tight fitting t-shirt.

"Request? I didn't know I had to," I say, with a worried face.

"Any supernatural being that wants to come into town—whether it be for a long or short stay—needs to make a request to me or the leader of the Mount Roxby Vampire's. He likes to be called the King." He raises his eyebrows in exasperation. "I'd recommend me, I don't bite, unless you ask me to," he jokes.

"Oh. I'm sorry; I didn't know anything about it. I'm from a small town that didn't get many newcomers; it's mainly just the pride that lives in the town." I catch the confused look on his face as I say the word pride and quickly clarify, "I was brought up in a were-lion pride."

"A werewolf in a were-lion pride. That's new. I can put you in the system if you want?"

"That will be great, thanks," I say, as I pass his drink over. He gives me some money and I place it in the till like Misty showed me.

"How did they react to you leaving? Being brought up with them; they would have seen you as one of their own, wouldn't they? I wouldn't have thought they'd be very happy to see you leave," he asks.

"Far from it. No, they were glad to see me leave. They had never really accepted me; even though my Auntie was married to one of them." I stare off into space, thinking about how I was treated by the Pride.

"Once I turned eighteen I was challenged every week, and I didn't even want to be classed as Pride. It was duel after duel, I needed to get away." I snap out of my memories, realising I'm telling my life story to a stranger. He's so easy to talk to, I feel like I've known him all my life. Realistically, I've known him ten minutes, if that!

"I'm sorry. You don't want to hear all that," I say, as I shake my head.

"Can I get another?" A customer down the bar waves me over, thankfully before Theo gets a chance to comment on me blurting all that out to him.

The bar seems to have filled with vampires and werewolves whilst I'd been distracted by Theo. I better get back on with the job or Misty will be firing me before I even really got started.

2.

UNWANTED ENCOUNTERS

THEO

I can't stop staring at Bel, the new barmaid. I can't believe it…But I felt it. The tingle when we touched, my wolf nearly burst out of my skin. That shouldn't happen.

Unless…No.

She can't be.

There's no other explanation though.

I'm dying to touch her again to see if it happens a second time. It's taking every ounce of concentration to stop myself from vaulting the bar to get to her. Her floral scent is making my mouth water and other bodily reactions, completely inappropriate in public.

A heavy hand on my shoulder pulls my attention from my staring. "Who's the hot new barmaid?"

A growl leaves my throat before I can stop it. I catch my energy before it flares. I don't need the whole pack's attention. I turn to face Eddie, who is standing with his hands up in a gesture of surrender.

"Whoa, obviously someone I shouldn't be looking at." He sits on the empty stool next to me.

"Sorry Ed, she's called Bel. New wolf in town," I say, as Bel walks past to serve someone further along the bar. I watch as Ed's nostrils flare when he catches her scent.

"Fuck, she smells good."

As much as my wolf wants to rip his head off for even scenting her, I hold it in. I have no claim over her. I'd only just met her.

My wolf disagrees. *Mine*, is pulsing through my head as he pushes against my skin trying to get to her.

"Did you track the vamp down?" I ask Ed.

Ed is one of my enforcers, or soldiers as some people call them.

Ed grunts. "I couldn't find anything to substantiate the reports we received. Not one person I spoke to has seen any evidence of a rogue vampire. Sorry, boss, but I think it was a time-waster." He waves at Bel as she glances in our direction.

"Hey guys. What you after?" She flashes Ed a friendly smile.

Ed reaches over the bar and offers her his hand. "I'm Ed. It's nice to meet you. I'll have a Jack on the rocks, thanks."

I watch in anticipation as their hands touch, my eyes flashing between them to see if they have a reaction.

"Bel. Nice to meet you, Ed."

I let out the breath I'd been holding when she walks away to get Ed's drink, with no sign of reaction.

"Hey, Theo!" I turn to chase the voice that belongs to someone I usually manage to avoid. Unfortunately, I was too distracted with Bel and didn't even feel or smell her early enough to make a run for it.

I plaster on my best fake smile. "Hi, Chloe. How are you?"

She stops in front of me, trailing her fingers up my forearm. "Much better now I've seen you."

I force myself not to cringe. It's not like Chloe is repulsive—with her beautiful blonde hair, legs up to her armpits, and bright, baby blue eyes—she's far from it. She turns plenty of heads. Unfortunately, she likes to go for the guys that aren't interested, and never takes no for an answer.

I've never casually dated a pack member and I don't intend to start now. Being an alpha, I'm stronger with a mate. A wolf knows his mate when he meets her—I'm pretty sure I found mine tonight. Just imagine the hassle my future mate would have when she joins the pack if it was full of my jealous ex-lovers.

I'm not celibate; I have been in relationships—just not with pack members. I gave up on finding my mate and married a human when I was young, stupid, and wanting to settle down. My marriage ended when she cheated on me. To be honest, the failure of our marriage was my fault. I hadn't told her about being a werewolf, yet I expected her to give me children.

"Can I buy you a drink, Theo?" Chloe asks in a seductive tone.

I glance at my watch to make it look like there's somewhere I need to be. "Actually, I'm just about to leave; I've got a meeting to get to."

Chloe mirrors my actions, glancing at her own watch. "It's a bit late to be having a meeting, isn't it?"

She has no right to question her Alpha, but I don't want her turning up at my house later so I answer her, "Vampires."

Bel makes her way over to us placing a drink in front of us both with a shrug. "I saw you were empty, too."

I pull the glass towards me and pass her some money, making sure to brush her hand with mine. I feel it again; almost like an electric shock shooting from where we touch through my body to my wolf. He jumps up; alert and ready to claim. There is no mistaking it this time. She's my mate. I look into her eyes as they change from chocolate brown to her wolf's amber eyes. She feels it too.

Her wolf knows.

"Thanks, darlin."

She snatches her hand back, looking at it like it was an alien. "Sorry about that. Must be static electricity, or something."

"Or something," I growl, as she rushes off to serve another customer.

After downing my drink, I say my goodbyes and leave quickly; to make my meeting look genuine. My wolf is antsy enough as it is, I can't handle any more Chloe tonight. He doesn't like that I am leaving Bel behind. He's already calling her 'mine.'

I only get a block away from Misty's when I scent a vampire. They have a bloody scent. Werewolves suffer bloodlust. We love the smell of blood and meat, but vampires don't smell like fresh blood. They have a sickly rotting scent. They have strong noses, too. I don't know how they can handle their own stench.

Hoping the vampire I can scent is the rogue we've been hunting down, I follow the smell. I could do with a good fight to distract my wolf from leaving someone he already considers to be our mate, in a bar full of threats.

It's not long before I realise that fight isn't going to happen. I can feel the vampire now and I recognise this one's energy.

Dominick Draconis. The King.

Yeah, he wishes.

"Well, well, well," Dominick quips. "If it isn't the daddy dog himself."

He may be old and he may act all high and mighty, but he ain't nothing but a mosquito to me.

I tell myself that every time we are in each other's company and I still end up at his throat by the end of the conversation. I'm not going to let him get to me. "Dominick."

"What no happy greeting? No wagging tail?"

Try as I might, I don't manage to contain my growl. My wolf might get his fight yet. "What do you know about this rogue vampire I'm hearing reports about?"

"Touchy. Fine. Let's get straight to business then. I'm following up on the reports too, but none of my men have found any leads. He seems to be good at hiding." His phone chimes in his jeans pocket, he reaches his hand in and pulls it out, but on glancing at the screen he ignores the call by angrily shoving it back in his pocket. "Have your men found anything?"

"Not a thing. My guys are calling it a time-waster, but I have a bad feeling about it and I don't like it."

I'm not a fan of Dominick, but this rogue is his kind and if anyone is equipped to find him, a two-thousand-year-old vampire leader is bound to be better at it than I am.

"You're right to be concerned. He's a threat and we need to find him. I have no doubt that in time we will," he proclaims, with the confidence of a leader.

"Yes, we will," I declare, walking away. I'm not concerned about turning my back on the vampire—even when I know our scent is intoxicating and highly addictive to them. The total opposite of how their revolting stench affects us; werewolves and vampires have a pact, of a sort. We can live comfortably in the same town without a war breaking out. Neither of the species can attack the other without serious punishment. I won't lie and say there aren't 'incidents,' but we stay on top of them and our pact helps keep them far and few between.

I reach into my pocket for my keys, unlocking my Pajero as I approach it. I get in and head home.

My home is the pack's home; which means, any member is welcome at any time. I just hope that Chloe finds someone to entertain her tonight because I'm still not up to dealing with her.

3.
VAULTING BARS

ROSABEL

I'm distracted as I serve two or three customers. My mind is still on the reaction to Theo's touch. No matter what bullshit I said about static electricity, I know that isn't what caused it. It has to be something to do with our wolves—I'm just not sure what. It didn't happen when I came in contact with the other wolf he was with, so I am leaning towards it being an alpha thing.

I glance along the bar to see if any of my customers are empty. When my eyes reach Ed, I notice Theo is no longer with him. My wolf reaches out to feel for his power but can't. Realising he must have left whilst I was serving; I search the bar for Barbie girl who was coming onto him earlier. My wolf relaxes when I see her plastered all over another guy. *It didn't take her long to move her affection on to someone else.*

It took all my will power not to jump the bar and drag her away from him when I saw her talking to him earlier. I had to remind my wolf that I had no claim over him. I had spoken to him for a few minutes and that was all. He was the local alpha; she was probably pack, and had more right to lay a claim.

*M*idnight comes quick and fast. It feels like no time has passed when Misty rings the bell for last call. As the last customer leaves, I head to the office to get my bag, realising a little too late that I haven't organised anywhere to sleep tonight.

Misty enters the office and hands me an envelope with some cash in it. "That's for tonight's shift. If ya enjoyed it, I'd love ya to come back same time tomorrow?"

"Yeah, that'd be great. Thank you," I answer, placing the envelope in my bag. "You don't know any hostels that will be open at this time, do you? I came straight in here off the bus without organising anywhere to sleep."

She looks me up and down, weighing me up. "No. They'll all be locked up now. Ya can stay at mine for the night, if ya want?"

"Really? That'd be great. Thanks. I'll go straight to the hostel in the morning."

"No worries. We'll sort it out. I saw you chatting to Theo. It looked like you got on well." She seems excited at that thought. I'm guessing she's a bit of a matchmaker.

She shows me out of the office, locking the door behind us.

"Yeah. He seems like a nice guy, not to mention easy on the eyes." We both giggle as we leave through the fire exit at the end of the corridor.

There is a top of the range purple VW Beetle parked in the deserted alley. *How come it didn't get stolen or stripped for parts during the shift? It's not as if this alley is a high traffic area.*

As we approach the car I feel that sensation of dread again, which answers my previous question...*Wards!*

I wake up to the smell of bacon, eggs, tomatoes, *ooh* and fresh coffee. My nose is great with smells. It's not such a good thing when the smell is unpleasant, like when I got on that bus full of smelly people. *Ugh.* Times like that I wish I had a human nose. Today? Today I am happy to have an extra sensitive nose. It feels like a week since I had a cup of coffee. I'd even be glad for a bad one at the moment. I can't function without a coffee in a morning, and this coffee smells divine.

I dive out of bed, or should I say off the bed since I didn't manage to get under the covers last night. After quickly washing and changing, I follow the lovely smell of food and coffee; after entering two empty lounge rooms I finally find the source. Sitting at the granite breakfast bar in the kitchen is Misty, eating the best looking full English breakfast I have ever seen. Seeing only one plate makes my stomach grumble and decide I need to find a diner as soon as possible.

"Good morning, Misty. Thanks for letting me stay the night. I'll get out your hair now and see you at five for my shift."

Misty slightly spins her stool to face me. "How'd ya sleep?"

"Great. That bed is fantastic."

"Good. There's a plate of breakfast in the oven keeping warm for ya, and there's some fresh coffee in the pot on the side." She waves her hand in the direction of the oven and coffee.

"Oh. You didn't have to do that. Thank you." I grab the tea towel hanging off the oven door and remove my plate from the oven, sitting at the bar on the stool next to Misty.

After eating my breakfast and drinking the best coffee I've ever had, I reach over and pour myself a second cup from the jug on the table.

Misty puts her cup down for seconds too. "I was thinking,

since ya don't have anywhere to stay and there's just me in this big place, do ya wanna stay on a more permanent basis?"

Misty's apartment is actually four apartments knocked into one. She has the whole floor to herself.

"What? Like rent one of the rooms from you? Are you sure? You don't really know me." I can see what's coming; I should have seen it last night when Misty invited me to stay, even though she had only known me for a couple of hours.

I'm an empath. I can feel people's emotions. According to my Aunt, my mum was an empath, too. It's the empathy that's making Misty feel like she can trust me. For some reason, people feel at ease with me. I even get strangers coming up to me on the street and pouring their heart out. Their trust in me isn't false. I'm trustworthy because I feel people's emotions. I don't want them to feel bad, so I do anything I can to make people feel better. I would never do anything to hurt people; for one thing it would hurt me twice as much as it would them.

Misty jumps off her stool and walks over to the sink to rinse her plate. "I know, but I trust ya. I get a good vibe from you and being a witch, I'm all about vibes."

"If you're sure, that would be brilliant. Thank you." I walk over to the sink to rinse my own plate and cup, before placing them in the dishwasher.

The day goes by pretty quick. We just chilled out, drinking coffee and filling each other in on our lives. I got through my life story in no time. I told her about my empathy; which Misty had heard of. Thankfully, it didn't alter her feelings towards me.

Misty has been practising witchcraft for the last ten years. She moved in with her gran when she found out she was a witch at sixteen. Her gran taught her everything she knew. Unfortunately, she passed away last year. She bought the bar and apartment when she was twenty-one with some inheritance money she received from a distant relative she had never met.

We opened up the bar at four in the afternoon and by six thirty it was heaving. There must've been about sixty people spread throughout the bar. When I say people, I mean witches, weres, and vampires. I even think there were a few fae, too. Not a plain ordinary human in sight, thanks to Misty's ward. It's nice to be able to relax and not worry about someone spotting a side effect of a supernatural being. I can see why Misty's is so popular.

I'm having a break in the office at eight when I realise I haven't been in touch with Benji since arriving. When I left he had demanded I ring when I arrived. I retrieve my bag from the cubby hole behind Misty's desk and dig my phone out to find ten missed calls and panicked messages getting more aggressive with each one.

The first text being. 'What the HELL has happened?'

The last text is all caps and I definitely get an urgent vibe from it. 'WHERE THE FUCK ARE YOU, BEL?' He even ended it on a growl that would do any werewolf proud; which is a feat for a human.

I hit call.

When he picks up, I'm expecting a hello to start the conversation. Instead, I just get garbled rambling. I hold the phone away until I think it's over.

It isn't!

It finally goes quiet on his end and I put the phone to my ear.

Now the begging starts. "Benji. I'm sorry I haven't rung sooner, but it's been hectic since I got off the bus. I found a job and a place to rent."

"You should've called, even just to say you're alive. I've been sitting here thinking you must be dead in a gutter somewhere and waiting for the police to come around and ask us to identify your body."

Just then Misty comes in, which means that my break is over and hers has started.

"Look, Benji, my break is over. I have to get back to work but I promise I will send you a huge email giving you a second by second report." I hang up before he can argue about how I don't know how to send email from my phone.

I put the phone and my bag back in the cubby hole, whilst grumbling away to myself. When I look up, I find Misty laughing at me.

"It was, Benji. He was going mental because I haven't rung him to tell him I'm alive," I say, rolling my eyes.

I walk back behind the bar and notice that at least another ten customers have entered since I went on break. The mixture of emotions throughout the room hits me like a brick wall. I take a deep breath and try to focus on my safe barrier that protects me from them. With that breath, there's a smell I recognise from last night.

Theo.

He must be here somewhere. I look around to find him, but come up empty.

"Hey Bel, can I have a Rusty Nail?" yells Theo's lovely gravelly voice from the other end of the bar.

I laugh and nod my head hoping he can see me. I put his drink together—scotch whiskey and Drambuie—walk over to the other end of the bar and place the short glass in front of him.

He takes a test sip. "I'll stump you eventually," he jests as he passes me his money.

"Bring it on."

I serve a few more customers and notice Misty is back out

and Lucy, the other mixer, is missing; probably having her break in the back office.

Misty is laughing with some customers when a vampire comes to the bar. He's the most intimidating vampire I have ever met. The energy coming from him is fierce and wild.

He's at least six-foot-four inches tall with jet black hair in tight curls against his head. His eyes are black and endless. He asks for a Siberian Fizz, which thank my angels I know.

I wouldn't like to ask him how to make it; he's likely to bite me.

I pass him the drink and take the money he offers in payment.

"Are you new here?" he questions

I put the money in the till before answering him. "Yes. I started last night."

As I turn away to look for another customer to serve, he throws his hand in front of me. "I'm Dominick Drake."

As I shake his extremely cold hand, he grins at my shudder. "Do you have a name?"

"Rosabel McGuiness. Nice to make your acquaintance," I say insincerely. I don't know if vampires can feel a lie like werewolves can, and to be honest, I don't care. I just want to get away from him. He gives me the heebie-jeebies.

"The pleasure is all mine, darling," he says rather creepily. He's even looking at me, as if wondering how my blood would taste.

"Quit thinking about what she tastes like. We have a deal—you don't touch werewolves," says the gravelly voice that's becoming ever so familiar. He must have made his way over for another drink, but when I look at his glass, it's still full.

"Oh. Is she a new one of yours?" asks Dominick, looking rather disappointed.

"No. She's a lone wolf. Before you ask, she's on the supe census. I saw to it myself."

"Well. If she isn't part of your pack, she's not included in our deal. I haven't tasted a werewolf for over a century. You taste so much better than humans." He licks his lips while staring at me intently, even hungrier than before.

Brilliant. Why do I have to be something tasty?

With that reply, I feel extreme anger and regret coming off Theo. My wolf bristles at the feel of the alpha energy coming off him. The whole bar falls silent to stare in his direction. I'm guessing it's not just my empathy picking up Theo's emotional state.

Dominick walks off towards one of the tables near the dance floor with a laugh. When he's halfway there, he turns around looks directly at Theo and says, "Hope to have a taste soon, Rosabel."

No chance!

Theo turns back to me. His alpha energy has dulled but I can still feel his emotions through my empathy, and he isn't any calmer. He's obviously trying hard to push down his wolf. The noise in the bar picks up again as if nothing happened.

He downs his drink and slams his glass on the bar, the glass shattering in his hand. I notice he's trembling all over and after hearing a rumbling growl emanating from deep in his chest, I realise he's fighting the change.

Grabbing a bottle of Absinthe in one hand I jump over the bar and grab Theo's elbow with the other. I start dragging him, having no idea where to take him. As I look up, I catch Misty's eye; she mouths the word 'office,' pointing in its direction.

Why didn't I think of that?

I focus on getting him behind that locked door. When I feel that I'm no longer dragging him, he seems to be coming easily and the trembling is easing, too. I enter the code and push the door open and practically shove him inside, slamming it shut behind us.

Taking a deep breath, I remove the lid from the bottle and swallow down a huge swig. I need it. The adrenaline rush is making my wolf twitchy. Theo's energy is running over my skin, it almost feels like his fingers are stroking the fur of my wolf. I pass the bottle to Theo, who's perched his behind on the corner of Misty's desk. He takes an even bigger swig, and although the trembling seems to have dissipated, I can still feel the anger emanating from him.

He holds out the bottle for me to take again. "Absinthe?" He pulls a face, like he has just sucked on the sourest lemon ever grown.

"It was the closest thing to my hand when I jumped the bar. You would have turned furry and no doubt drawn Dominick's blood if I had wasted time looking for something more satisfying." We both laugh, passing the bottle back and forth after taking a swig.

Theo makes a show of eyeing up my height. I can guess what he is going to ask before he even says it, "You really jumped the bar?"

"Yeah," I say, with a shrug as I settle in next to him on Misty's desk.

"How did you manage that? You're only what five-foot? The bar comes up to your chest," he says, nudging me with his shoulder.

"I don't know. It must have been the adrenaline…or something!" We both laugh softly.

We sit in comfortable silence for a moment before Theo breaks it. "I'm sorry for putting you in danger with Dominick. I came over to try and protect you. I never would have told him you were a lone wolf if I didn't think they were part of our pact."

I place my hand on his forearm. "It's not your fault, Theo. Thanks for trying to protect me." His energy feels like electricity entering through the palm of my hand. I can't feel the anger anymore; this is more like the first time we touched. "How are you feeling now?"

He lifts his head and his eyes penetrate mine. "In control again. You stopped an ugly scene unfolding in there. Thanks."

I lose myself in his beautiful green eyes for a second. "I should get back behind the bar. It will be last call and I'm needed to help clean up. Do you think you can handle going back in there now?"

He pushes himself off the desk and makes a step for the door. "No problem."

I open the door and gesture for him to lead the way through to the bar. The propped open bar door gives us a clear view of the empty room.

Misty stops wiping the bar down and comes straight over to us as we walk through the doorway. "Theo, how ya doing?"

"Much better, thanks to Bel here." He passes her a handful of notes. "For the bottle," he explains.

I walk off, leaving them to their conversation and start clearing the tables. Once the tray is overflowing with dirty glasses, I head to the dishwasher behind the bar. Theo is still leaning against the bar watching me. Misty must be in her office and Lucy must have left while we were in the office. She usually leaves before last call because she has a baby sitter to relieve. It's just him and me in the empty bar.

"How are you getting home?" he asks, before taking another swig from the bottle of Absinthe.

"Oh. I-I'm getting a lift with Misty," I manage to stutter, shocked at the strength of the protection emotion I can feel coming off him.

"When you get home, will you be alone?"

"No. Misty has offered me a room at her place." He must be worried about Dominick following me home and attacking me. I quickly try to ease his mind. "The building is secure; no one can get in without a key. There's a guard on the door and in the elevator."

Theo watches me walk back to the dishwasher and fill it

with the last load of dirty glasses. "Good. I'll make sure you get in the car safe, before I leave."

I pause to watch Theo's reaction to my next question. I need to know how much danger I am in. "Do you really think Dominick will want to taste me? As he so nicely put it."

He grimaces. "Dominick doesn't say anything he doesn't mean. So, yes, he will taste you. It's just a matter of when. I'm going to do everything I can to delay the inevitable." He reaches in his pocket, pulls out a business card and hands it to me. It reads: Theodore Wilson, and has contact numbers with an email address TWilson@gymwolves.com. "If you need anything, don't hesitate to call."

I slip the card into the back pocket of my jeans. "Thanks."

4.

BLOODTHIRSTY WEREWOLVES

ROSABEL

Thankfully, the next few days pass with no sign of the bloodthirsty Dominick. Misty informs me that Dominick is the head vampire—although he likes to be called 'the King of New South Wales'—which is brilliant. I don't have just any vampire yearning for my blood, but the King Vampire of the state.

LOVELY.

I'd much rather have the local pack's alpha yearning for me. Come to think of it there has been no sign of Theo, either.

Misty has been begging me to go to the gym with her. Apparently, she needs a gym buddy because if she goes on her own she can't get in the zone. Me? I'm not a gym person.

A weekly run in the forest as a wolf is usually about it, but I haven't had the chance to find anywhere safe to run since arriving in Mount Roxby. Working from late afternoon until the early hours of the morning and then sleeping until lunch, doesn't give me many hours to explore the town.

I'm not complaining, I love Misty's. I meet lots of people; some of whom come in every night. I get to use my empathy on those troubled and in need. Misty sends me to some of her friends, or regulars, who need it, which benefits me too because the bar ends up feeling like a much happier place once I've helped people. I'd just like to be able to find somewhere that I can run freely.

I have caved and we are pulling into a large car park. There are only two other cars in the empty car park, but not many people will be insane enough to go to a gym at two o'clock in the morning. Did I mention it was a twenty-four hour gym? *Why did I say yes?*

I WANT MY BED.

After filling out the forms and handing the membership fee over to the woman behind the counter; whom I believe wants to be in bed just as much as I do, we walk through the door with a female figure on it. A room full of at least twenty private cubicles. The cubicles surround a large open area, with a few benches, for non-private changing.

We change in the open area, into the crop top and shorts the gym gave us. Even though the clothes were included in the membership, they are kinda cute. There's a little picture of a wolf weightlifting on the leg of the shorts and on the breast of the crop. The gym is called 'Gym Wolves,' so I guess the wolf is their icon. We pick our lockers on the far side wall and dump our stuff. I try not to think of whose sweaty neck it has already been around as I place the key on its dog tag chain around my neck.

I walk into the gym via a door next to the lockers. The equipment is all set up in sections like I imagine most gyms are. Treadmills together, weight machines all together and so on. We head straight for the treadmills with useless TVs on them, it's not like there would be anything on at this time of the night. We choose neighbouring machines and start them up. I put a music channel on my machines TV and crank up the sound so we can both hear it over the noise of the machines and our feet pounding them.

I put the speed up to eight, a gentle jog for me, to stretch. I don't jog for long because jogging just doesn't do anything for my energy level—neither does sprinting in human form—but it's the best I can get in a gym. I up the speed until I'm pushing the machine to find a sprint to satisfy my needs.

Misty is just slowing her treadmill down but I still feel the need to keep sprinting. I suddenly sense someone approaching. I don't bother trying to identify them. It's not like anyone I know will be insane enough to be in the gym at this time of night.

"Hi, Misty. Are you having a good work out?" I can only just make out the male voice over the sound of my blood pounding in my ears and my feet thudding on the treadmill, not to mention the music.

I didn't hear Misty's reply.

"Bel. Why didn't you just go to the bush and shift? It would be a hell of a lot more satisfying." The lovely gravelly voice I hear from right behind me is the last person I expected to encounter here. I'm so shocked, I totally lose rhythm of my sprint and start to stumble, tripping over my own feet.

Brilliant. I'm going to fall flat on my face.

Theo reaches his arms out to steady me, noticing my struggle. Unfortunately, his good intentions only make matters worse, before I can hit the stop button I'm hurtling backwards towards him. He doesn't have enough sense to get out my way and before I know it, I've knocked him off his feet and we're both on the floor, laughing.

Misty is standing next to the treadmill doubled over in laughter. After the laughter passes, Theo gets up and reaches down, offering me his hand. I take it gratefully.

I must have knocked my knee somewhere during the fall because it's bleeding and stinging like a bitch. I'm not too worried about it being hurt. Being a werewolf, small injuries like this heal quickly. It's the blood dripping down my leg and pooling on the carpet that bothers me. I start hobbling towards the locker room but all I manage to do is make more of a mess.

"Where are you going?" Theo asks in a slightly amused tone. "You'll heal in a minute or two."

I glare at the mess I'm making on the floor. "I know but I'm dripping blood on the carpet. I was trying to get to the locker room. At least the tiled floor in there will clean easily."

He reaches his hand over his head, grabs the back of his shirt and pulls it off before throwing it at me. "Here. Press this against your knee."

As I catch it, I get a whiff of his scent and I can't help but hold his shirt to my nose, taking in more of that delectable scent. Misty's giggle snaps me out of it and I realise what I'm doing. I glance around quickly to see Theo's reaction, but luckily he is nowhere in sight. I breathe a sigh of relief hoping he didn't witness that.

I pull the material away from my knee to check if the bleeding has stopped.

Misty gasps jumping back, just as I hear the growl from behind me. I turn around slowly; not wanting my back to the werewolf I can smell behind me, but also not wanting my movements to provoke an attack. I realise it's two nights from a full moon. Mix that with the smell of blood and the young were that's now facing me won't be able to stop the change.

He's on his hands and knees, thankfully still in human form. His growling is not very comfortable in this situation; not to mention that a wolf's growl looks and sounds wrong coming out of a human's mouth.

He's about a metre away from me, slowly crawling closer. Reaching me in no time, he starts sniffing at my knee, which has healed but is still covered in fresh blood. I glance at the bloody t-shirt in my hand. Deciding it's already ruined, I offer it to him, but he's not interested in that at all. Instead of taking the shirt like I hoped, he does something that I really don't like.

He straightens up and nuzzles his face against the bare flesh of my stomach.

Why did I pick a crop top from reception and not a t-shirt?

The stomach is the easiest place for a werewolf to rip you apart—no bones to get in the way. I start to panic. If I don't do something quickly, his teeth will pierce my skin and then it'll all be over. Before I come up with a plan I hear the scariest growl, almost a roar, that I have ever heard coming from behind me. Whatever creature belongs to that growl is going be a lot harsher killing me than this pup here.

He stops nuzzling to look around me at the creature. He's not moved away enough for me to escape, the only thing he moved was his head.

Misty is between that scary growl and me. She is only a human. She has no chance of fighting back. A number of options for what I can do run through my head when I hear a familiar commanding voice.

"Leave her alone, Paddy."

"She smells so good," the voice in front of me says, as a rumble comes from his chest. I try to stay as calm as possible, fear will only make him want to rip me up even more.

Theo's wolf's energy runs down my back as he steps up close behind me, making my wolf stand to attention. "Step back from her, Patrick."

Patrick takes a small step back and looks up towards Theo, who's leaning over my left shoulder with his chest pressing against my back. I would probably find it arousing, if we weren't staring down a hungry wolf. Patrick's eyes have no humanity in them. They are the wolf's eyes, not Patricks. He's so close to the change. It will only take a shudder and I'll be dead in a second.

Theo's hands come down on my shoulders making me jump. I feel a rumble coming from him. His energy is leaving him in a wave and going through me. Once it hits Patrick, his eyes are sea blue and so human it's unbelievable. He looks mortified as he realises what happened. "Paddy, you should go home now, mate," Theo orders.

Paddy looks me up and down until he gets to my stomach that has his bloody face print on it. "I'm so sorry."

Theo squeezes my shoulders, silently urging me to accept the apology.

"It's okay," is all I can manage to spit out as the shock kicks in. Hearing my words, Patrick turns and leaves without another word.

Nobody moves until the doors shut. Theo spins me round and leans back to look at my face, still holding my shoulders. I think if he let go, I'd crumple to the floor.

"Are you okay, Bel?" I just stare at him blankly visualising all the bad things that could have just happened.

As he pulls me into his chest and wraps his arms around me, I can vaguely hear talking. "She's in shock." But I can't seem to pull myself into the here and now. I start to come around a bit and realise it must be Misty who he was talking to.

God. Is she okay? She wasn't that far away from me or the almost wolf.

It's then that it dawns on me why I'm in such a serious state of shock, my empathy is feeding it. My own shock has made me lose a handle on my protection barrier causing me to channel Misty and Theo's shock. *Great.*

As I focus and put my barrier back up I notice that Theo is still holding me tightly against his chest. Oh my. His bare chest at that, and what a nice chest it is. Smooth and so toned, and wet? As I pull back wondering why his chest is wet, he wipes a tear from my cheeks. *Oh god, I've been crying. Have I not shown myself up enough in front of this guy, already!*

"How are you feeling now?" Theo murmurs as he rubs my arms with calming motions.

"Like an idiot. Your chest is soaking." I laugh nervously,

shaking my head in disbelief at how unlucky I seem to be around this guy.

"Don't worry about that," he soothes.

Misty appears next to us with a tray containing three cups of what smells like very sugary but strong coffee.

Theo uses his hold on my arms to direct me to sit on one of the weight benches, taking a coffee off the tray and handing it to me. He takes a seat next to me, whilst Misty sits facing us on the next one along.

Misty passes Theo a cup and takes the other for herself before leaning the tray against the leg of the weight bench. We all drink in silence. The energy zinging between mine and Theo's touching thighs distracts me from even thinking about making conversation.

"Sorry, I ran off, but Paddy wasn't the only one close to his wolf. I didn't think anyone else was here. If I'd stayed, I might not have been able to control myself because of the pull of the moon. I wouldn't have been as slow as Paddy, I would have ripped you both apart in no time," Theo says, as he breaks the almost uncomfortable silence. His tone of voice says he was ashamed to own up to it. Alphas are known for their control. If an alpha can't control his own wolf, there is no way he can control a pack.

"How come ya came back, if you were worried ya might change?" Misty asks in her cute British accent.

"I felt Paddy's change coming on; it kicked my wolf into gear. The need to protect Bel overpowered the need to feed the bloodlust *with* Bel," he says on an embarrassed chuckle, and shakes his head. "Sorry to talk about you like you're edible."

"That's all right, I'm getting used to it. I've only been in town six days and I've had three people wanting to take a bite out of me," I joke

His face suddenly turns deathly serious, "Have you had any more bother from the good King?"

"No. I haven't seen him since Friday night." I try to sound cheery, hoping to ease his mind.

"Good." He doesn't sound very convinced. But he had warned me it was only a matter of time before the King tries to get his taste. Apparently, when Dominick Drake sets his sight on something, he gets it.

I glance up at the clock and blanch at the time. "Misty, we better get going, it's nearly five." She looks half asleep. I'm just hoping she can manage the drive home.

We all slowly stand. Misty and I stroll back into the changing rooms to get our belongings out of the lockers. Theo goes into the male changing rooms, presumably to get his own belongings.

When we enter the foyer through the changing rooms, we find a shirtless Theo leaning against the wall waiting to walk us to the car. As we reach Misty's Beetle, she shoots by and jumps in the car to start it, leaving Theo and I alone in the empty car park.

"Thanks again for helping with Paddy. I didn't want a death on my conscience after only being in town for such a short time."

"It's my job as Alpha to keep my wolves in line. Paddy is going to be feeling so low for the next day or two. He was looking forward to meeting 'the new hottie.'" He rolls his eyes whist making air quotes. "Eddie's words. And he blew it by losing himself to his wolf's blood lust."

"He's young. He'll get over it. I'll have to remember to thank Eddie for the nice description," I reply with a laugh.

Theo reaches across me to open the car door. I slide into my seat and he closes the door for me before leaning into the open window. "Drive safely, Misty." He shifts his eyes from Misty to me. "Take care."

We manage to get home in one piece thanks to the chilly night air blowing through the open windows.

5.

PAIN OF THE PAST

THEO

*A*s I walk up to my front door I know I won't be having the quiet night I had planned. I can hear Eddie ribbing Paddy over his disaster first encounter with Bel.

"You wolfed out...That's just..." Eddie can't even finish his sentence through his fits of laughter.

"Fuck off. I didn't turn full wolf."

I walk into the lounge to find Eddie rolling around the sofa and an agitated Paddy sitting opposite.

"Is she okay?" Paddy questions as soon as I walk into the living area.

I sit down next to Eddie, slapping him across the back of the head with one hand, while swiping a beer off the coffee table with the other. "Bel's fine. She's just glad she didn't have to kill you. She didn't want a death on her conscience."

"It was the blood and the moon calling to me. I can't believe I lost control like that. If I wasn't trying to eat her, I would assume it was due to her being unmated and wanting to claim her."

"You want to claim her?" I barely contain my growl. She is my mate. No one but me will be claiming her.

Ours. My wolf is in total agreement with me.

"It doesn't matter if I did! I've blown it now. I've got no chance. Her wolf will think I'm weak, losing control like that," he says, nervously peeling the label off his stubby.

The growl I'd been holding starts to rumble out. Eddie throws an arm across my shoulders to hold me in place before I can pounce on Paddy. It's a suicidal move on Eddie's behalf because I immediately turn my anger on him. He pays me no attention as he speaks to Paddy. "You had no chance anyway. She's Theo's mate. His true mate." His words calm me. Someone, other than myself and my wolf, was acknowledging that she was mine. I relax back into the sofa and Ed removes his arm from my shoulder and leans forward to grab a fresh stubby, acting as though nothing had happened.

Paddy glances up from the bottle he'd been playing with and his shocked eyes land on mine. "Why haven't you claimed her? She's been in town long enough." Realising his mistake in questioning his alpha, he quickly apologises, drops his eyes to the floor and submissively bares his neck to me. "I'm sorry, I didn't mean any disrespect."

"It's fine, Paddy. I've been asking myself the same question since that first night I left her in Misty's. She's been brought up by a were-lion and his human wife. She hasn't learnt anything about us. I don't think she even understands what our connection, and the physical reactions we get, means." I swap my empty stubby for the last full one.

Ed gets up and grabs another six pack out of the fridge before sitting back down again. "She seems like a bright girl. Surely she would see that it's only you that causes these feelings and reactions. Her wolf would know even if the human doesn't."

"I'm the first Alpha she's met. She is probably putting it down to my alpha vibe."

"You're planning on claiming her though, right?" Ed pops the top off a stubby and passes it to Paddy, who takes it gratefully as he downs the last dregs in the one he'd been holding.

"Of course, I do. I just don't want to force her into it before she realises what it is. My last relationship was a disaster. You know that. It was nothing but lies and deceit. I want this one to go right."

Ed places a comforting hand on my forearm. "Theo. She is your true mate. It won't go the same way as things did with Selena."

"I know, but I thought I loved her. Not only did I lose her, I lost a brother too. It hurt. It still does. Even though I know it wasn't love, not like that of a mate."

"Cain was jealous when you took over the pack. He turned bitter." Ed wasn't around when I took over the pack but anyone could see that Cain was bitter and jealous about me being Alpha—even years after the fact.

"Cain didn't want the pack, though. He's the one who killed Dad. He should've been Alpha after that, but he handed it to me. That's why I don't understand his jealousy."

Wes, my Beta, walks into the room and joins the conversation. "That's not why he was jealous. He was jealous of the pack. The pack took your attention away from him. He was young and he idolised you. He slept with your wife to get back at you for abandoning him. He knew it would piss you off."

I hadn't even heard him enter the house. He must have been working in my office. That revelation floored me, but now that the thought was in my head it made complete sense.

"Why had I not connected the dots?" I mumble to myself, whilst shaking my head. The revelations would do no good. Cain is AWOL now. No one has seen or heard from him in a year.

I stand from the couch and start to strip off my clothes. "I need a run."

Talking about my ex and brother always gets me worked

up. A run is what I need to burn off the extra stress it's stirred up. I'd rather a run than hold it in and snap at the wrong person. By the time I make it to the back yard and shift into my wolf form, there's a trail of clothes leading outside and three other wolves standing next to me, waiting to follow my lead.

I lead. I run through the forest with my pack brothers following me. The day's stress runs off my fur as my paws pound into the dirt of the forest floor. The only thought that stays with me is that our mate still needs claiming.

6.

WITCHY PERKS

ROSABEL

No sooner had I fallen asleep than I was waking up again; time to get ready and go to work. Both Misty and I were so tired when we arrived home after the gym that we agreed to sleep all day, making sure to get up as late as possible, leaving just enough time to get something to eat before work.

Walking through to the kitchen and finding it empty, I pause to listen for any noise indicating that Misty was in the land of the living. I hear nothing other than the humming of the ducted air-con.

"Misty, wake your arse up!" I shout through the apartment. The rooms below could probably hear me but I couldn't care less. I have to listen to the couple in the apartment below my room constantly having sex so they can suck it up!

I start pulling food out the fridge to make us both a sandwich. I'm just plating up as Misty walks into the room blurry-eyed but dressed.

"Coffee. I need coffee."

I point to the steaming cup I placed next to her sandwich. She grabs the cup, mumbles something unintelligible then swiftly guzzles the full cup; slamming the cup on the side as she glances up at me. "Thanks, Bel."

"That was hot. I only just made it." How have her lips not blistered?

"Oh. I did a quick cooling enchantment," she states before tucking into her sandwich.

It's going to take a while getting used to living with a witch.

* * *

We spot a couple of customers standing outside the doors as we drive by and around the back. Misty pulls the handbrake and dives out the car. She starts chanting something as I follow her and the back door pops open without her even getting her keys out.

"Cool," I announce in awe.

"Oh, that's nothing, honey!" she replies, running to the bar.

She opens the front doors via chant again. That is one cool trick!

Over the next hour or two a steady stream of customers come and goes. A familiar face catches my eye and I make my way over to take his order. He's with another guy I haven't met yet. He's definitely werewolf, I can feel his power, and it's strong. He has to be high up in the ranks.

"Evening, Ed. What can I get you?"

"Hi, beautiful. You haven't met Wes yet, have you?" he queries pointing to the wolf next to him.

I shake my head and extend my hand to Wes. "No, I haven't. It's nice to meet you, Wes. I'm Bel."

He smirks as he takes my hand, "I've heard a lot about you. It's nice to finally meet you."

"All good stuff I hope. What can I get you guys to drink?" I let go of his hand and wipe the bar down with the cloth I keep tucked in my apron, trying to get rid of the nervous thought that people are talking about me.

"Just a Toohey's, thanks," Wes orders. "We're both on patrol, so we best steer clear of the hard stuff."

I grab their beers out of the fridge under the bar and pop the tops off before handing them over.

7.

HALF BLIND DATE

Waking up, I realise we made it through the night without any bother. The night was a blur of customers. Then again, we were both on autopilot so a tornado could have hit without either of us paying a blind bit of notice.

I head into the kitchen in need of a coffee fix. I need to function when I get up in the morning. Knowing Misty needs coffee more than I do, I'm not surprised to find her already there with two full cups. What does surprise me is the shit-eating grin she has on her face.

"Good Morning," she says over-enthusiastically. She's definitely up to something.

"Okay. What is it?" I ask, reaching for the cup she offers me.

"You're having tonight off," she practically sings as she leans against the breakfast bar.

I take a sip of coffee before reacting. "Should I ask why?"

"Don't bite my head off, but I've set you up on a blind date. I know you like Theo, but he's being an idiot by avoiding you. Anyone can see the chemistry between the two of you. Your wolves are dying to jump each other. He still hasn't shown you where you can run safely." She has a point. I might like him but he has been avoiding me, apparently before I started working at Misty's he was in there on a daily basis.

"Who is it?"

"One of my friends from the bar last night. He started asking about you so I suggested a blind date. He's going to take you to the cinema." She looks extremely hopeful.

I can't help but complain. "So it's not a blind date. He knows what I look like. It's just a half blind date. *Great!*"

I hate the idea of blind dates. Why would two people who know nothing about each other want to meet up and spend a torturous couple of hours together? Living with a were-lion pride meant there weren't many dating opportunities for me. I guess I dated Jared but our early dates consisted of training to fight so I could stay alive. It wasn't the usual get to know each other thing. I can feel her disappointment press against me when she thinks I'm going to say no.

I find myself agreeing to the half blind date before I really even consider it. Misty has been so good to me since I arrived in Mount Roxby, the least I can do is go on a measly half blind date. "How will I know it's him? When and where am I meeting him?"

"You'll go?" she asks suspiciously.

I nod my reply.

She pushes of the side and pulls me into a huge bear hug. "Thank you. Thank you."

She calms down enough to release me but she's still bouncing on the spot. "He's called Emmanuel. He's pretty hard to miss at six-foot-five and built like a wall. He'd make a great rugby player. He's South African. Dark skinned and believe it or not, bright blue eyes. He'll be waiting for you at six fifteen just in front of the ticket booth at the cinema opposite the bar. You can have a few drinks for Dutch courage before going across."

"Okay. I'm doing this for you," I say, giving her another hug just to try and hold her still. Her bouncing about is starting to make me feel queasy, or is that the nerves?

"Thanks. You won't regret it. He's a really nice guy," she assures me.

I believe her. I just can't help thinking about Theo and how I should be dating him and not this other guy. What am I thinking? Theo isn't interested. My wolf needs to get the idea of him out of her horny mind.

I don't do much for the rest of the day. I hunt for something to wear in my very limited selection of clothes. Misty offered for me to try some of her clothes, but she's a foot taller than me so it's all way too long. I finally decide on my little black dress that never fails me, and some black heels with silver sequins.

I email Benji to fill him in on the last couple of days. He replies immediately demanding a play by play of my date as soon as I get back tonight.

When we arrive at work, it feels strange being all dressed up and showing so much flesh. The uniform I normally wear is black cropped trousers and a tight black t-shirt that has a purple 'Misty's' logo embroidered on the breast and a cocktail list printed on the back.

The customers start coming in. I have to practically sit on my hands to stop myself from getting up and serving them. Every time I move, Misty glares at me and reminds me, "Night off!"

"What do you want to drink? It's on the house. It might chill you out. You are so fidgety it's driving me crazy," says Misty.

"A Johnnie Black Sazerac, please," I say with a laugh.

"Okay. Coming right up," she shouts over her shoulder, as she bounces off to mix it up.

"Make that two, Misty," says my favourite rumbly voice.

I turn to see Theo taking a seat on the stool next to me.

"Okay, Theo, two it is," she shouts back from the mixing counter, pouring the ingredients into a shaker.

Trust him to turn up when I've made plans with someone else.

I flash him my sexiest smile. "Hi, I didn't see you come in." Or feel him. Gee, I must be distracted not to have noticed him.

He returns my sexy smile tenfold. "Hi yourself. You're looking ravishing tonight."

I can feel my face blushing. I hate compliments. "Thanks."

"Aren't you supposed to be on the other side of the bar?" he asks, even though he can tell by the way I'm dressed I'm not meant to be on the other side of the bar tonight.

Misty comes over and places our drinks in front of us.

Theo slips off his stool and grabs his wallet out of his pocket. He's ready to hand some money over when she puts her hands up.

"On the house as a thank you for the other night."

"There's no need for that, but thanks." Theo places his wallet back in the rear pocket of those tight fitting jeans—the ones that hug his perfect butt just right.

"It's Bel's night off. She's going on a blind date with a friend of mine—to the cinema across the road."

For a split second his face drops and anger rolls off him in waves. A customer further down the bar calls out for Misty and she dashes off to serve him.

Theo turns to me. "Do you know his name? I might be able to tell you whether he's a nice guy or not, if I know him." I get the distinct feeling no matter whether he's a nice guy or not, Theo isn't going to be happy about it.

"Emmanuel," I say, shrugging and taking a large swig of my drink. "I'm only doing it to keep Misty happy. She's done a lot for me since I arrived. The least I can do is suffer through a date that I don't want to go on." I don't know why I'm explaining myself. I just feel the need to let him know. *Maybe it's an alpha thing.*

His body relaxes slightly and he takes a mouthful of his drink. "I know Emmanuel. He's not a bad guy, for a witch."

"She didn't tell me he was a witch. Not that it really makes a difference." I look at my watch and realise I'm already two minutes late. I still have to get across the road and traffic is usually a nightmare at this time. I quickly down what's left of my drink.

"I've got to go. I'm already late. Can you tell Misty I've gone and I'll see her later?" I jump off my chair and head for the door.

"No problem."

When I get outside I notice Theo is behind me. I look at him and frown.

He must be able to read the question on my face because before I even open my mouth to ask, he answers it. "I'm walking you across the road. It's dark and dangerous. A woman looking as good as you shouldn't be walking the streets on her own."

I glance at the cinema across the road. "I'm only going across the road. I'm a werewolf, I can handle it."

He grabs my hand, linking our fingers. "I don't care. Dominick has already shown his interest. I'm not taking that chance."

Every man and his dog are driving past leaving us no chance to get across the road. We walk down to the traffic lights on the next corner to cross safely.

"What will Emmanuel think when he sees you and me like this?" I lift our joined hands to get my point across.

"I don't care what he thinks as long as you're safe."

We get to the meeting point five minutes late and as Misty assured me, Emmanuel is un-missable. He's good looking but doesn't make my heart skip like a certain someone holding my hand does. Theo's energy is currently running up and down my arm. It's causing my wolf to pace. She wants to greet him; be it just her energy or full wolf form she isn't fussed.

Emmanuel spots me and waves. I can tell the exact second

he notices Theo holding my hand because his emotions have become erratic, and he can't seem to settle them. I have to fight to keep my barrier up.

"Hi Rosabel, Theodore." He nods in Theo's direction as he says his name

I quickly let go of Theo's hand and take a step away. "*Hi!*" I say, a little over-enthusiastically. This is such an awkward first meeting for a date.

Theo throws a concerned look at me before turning his attention to Emmanuel. "Good evening, Emmanuel. I was just escorting your date here safely."

I turn to stand next to Emmanuel and face Theo. "Thanks for the escort, Theo." Then without realising what I'm doing, I lean in and kiss him on the cheek.

"Anything for you, Bel," he says deliberately loud. He then turns and walks back towards the bar without another word.

I turn to Emmanuel, who's still looking at the spot where Theo had been standing. An angry emotion flows off him. *Time for distractions.* The last thing I need is an angry witch putting a hex on one of my only friends.

"So. What are we going to see?" I ask, nodding towards the movie list flashing on the LED on the wall.

He deliberates for a second before answering. "How about a comedy?"

Time passes quickly during the easy going movie. Before I know it the credits are rolling and the lights are slowly coming on. As I stand and stretch, I feel Emmanuel's eyes on me so I glance at him mid-stretch, only to find him staring at the hem of my dress as it exposes more of my skin. As I slowly lower my arms to cover myself, he snaps out of it.

"Sorry," he apologises, realising he's been caught ogling. I don't know how to feel about him watching me like that. I'm a woman and, come on, we all feel sexy when we are being admired, but part of me just doesn't feel right about it. He has my wolf's bristles up, whether it's because he isn't wolf or because he is a witch I don't know, but I won't write him off just yet. She might warm up to him.

I laugh at his embarrassment as he gets up and leads me to the foyer, with a hand against my lower back. Glancing at my watch I notice it's still fairly early and the company isn't that bad, so I decide to prolong the blind date that isn't turning out as bad as I expected.

"It's still early. Do you want to grab a coffee in there?" I offer pointing to the little cafe in the corner of the foyer. "I just need to dash to the bathroom first. That coke has gone right through me."

Emmanuel quickly agrees. "Sounds good. I'll get the drinks while you…freshen up." He struggles to find the appropriate word, but at least he didn't blurt out a pee reference. "What would you like?"

"A caramel latte would be great, thanks. I'll be right back." I dash off in the direction of the little girl's room before he sees me blush.

As I head down the corridor leading to the toilets I can feel someone behind me, and there is a malicious emotion coming off them. I need to try and find out who it is and whether the emotion is towards me or someone else. That's the problem with empathy. I can feel the emotions of strangers towards other people, and it can be so strong as I pass that it feels like it's aimed at me. Most of the time it isn't.

I take a deep breath to see if I can pick up a scent. I smell death—vampire and male. Before I can pick up on anything else, someone grabs my arm and pushes me out the emergency exit near the female toilets.

Once outside he spins me around to face him, pinning me to the wall. I recognise who it is.

Dominick!

He tilts his head and leans in to kiss my neck. I brace myself for the bite but it doesn't come. He stops just as his lips brush against my skin.

"I told you I would taste you soon," his warm breath whispers against my neck, sending shivers over my body. Before I can react or reply to his words, his fangs sink into my throat.

I push with all my strength, trying to move him off me, but he's far taller and weighs more than me so it's like trying to move a brick wall. I can feel myself weakening from the blood loss. It's pointless! I can feel him pulling at my vein, moaning as he swallows.

After what feels like forever, but is probably only seconds, he retracts his fangs, licking my neck with his tongue, sending another unwanted shiver throughout my body.

"Are you happy now you've had a taste?" I ask snidely, still plastered to the wall by his body.

The amazement is clear on his face. I guess he wasn't expecting that to come out of my mouth. Maybe he thought I'd fall all over myself for more.

"You would have enjoyed it more if I wanted you to, but I expect making you enjoy it would have pissed you off more. I actually like you and would like you to respect me, to a degree."

"Whether I enjoyed it or not, I still won't respect you. You lost any respect I had for you the moment you sank your fangs in me and took from me what I wasn't willing to give," I honestly inform him.

He seems to mull over my remark before responding. "I suppose not. To answer your question, I'm extremely happy. You taste even better than I expected. I don't think I've tasted anything as satisfying in my whole two thousand plus years."

"Wow." I could kick myself for letting my surprise at his age show.

Before he can react to my surprised remark, his phone starts to chime.

"Yes?" he says answering it.

He walks back in the door leaving it ajar for me to get back in, never even looking back in my direction. When I shut the door behind me, he's nowhere to be seen. Charming! He could have at least said goodbye or thanks, after what he just did. After all, I did just give him his feed for the night.

When I get back to the cafe, Emmanuel waves me over from a table next to the window. The last thing I want now is to carry on with this date so I force a friendly smile as I make my way over to him. He stands and pulls out a chair for me. I sit and try to make small talk. It isn't his fault that Dominick just fed from me. We talk about the usual first date things jobs, family, and the like. He tells me about his job as a swimming coach and I just can't help imagining him in his Speedos. The thought makes me wonder if the date might be salvageable after all.

"I'm really sorry to cut the date short, but I have the early shift at the pool tomorrow." He sounds genuinely upset to be leaving.

"That's fine. I've had a great night," I assure him, as we stand and make our way outside.

We swap numbers and as he leans forward to hand my phone back, he goes for the kiss. I have very quick reflexes and manage to turn so his lips make contact with my cheek. I counter with a quick kiss on his cheek. It's not that I wouldn't want to kiss his lips. They look very kissable, but I have had more than enough intimacy for one night.

"We'll have to do it again soon. I'll call you," he says, walking off into an alley down the side of the cinema.

I head towards the crossing. The road is still quite busy and I don't fancy playing chicken. I walk into the bar and find it heaving, which is unusual for a weekday. There must be about twenty customers. We're lucky if we get ten in at the same time on a weeknight.

I spot a couple of empty stools so I sit and wait to be served.

It only takes Misty thirty seconds to notice me and come running over. If I didn't know better, I'd think she had the senses of a were.

"I want all the details. How did it go? Are ya gonna do it again?" She's as excited as a kid on Christmas morning.

"Get me a drink first," I say distractedly, rooting through my purse for the ten dollar note I know is in there.

She immediately starts making me a Johnnie Black Sazerac. "Was it that bad? I thought ya'd like him." Her emotions tell me how disappointed she is.

"I like him. He's real sweet. We swapped numbers so we might do something again. It's just something that happened when Emmanuel was getting the coffees." I secretly hope she won't have time to ask me anymore questions. She's passing me my drink and taking my money when a regular named Tommy, answers my wishes by waving her over to be served. I wave her off promising to fill her in when we get home later.

I sit and drink in peace, ordering another off Lucy when my glass is empty.

8.

TESTY WOLVES

THEO

I've been sitting in the back corner of the bar for the longest three hours of my life, nursing the same beer and forcing myself not to get up and storm into the cinema complex across the road. I want to find Bel and tear her away from Emmanuel, whether she's having a good time or not.

When the very woman I can't stop thinking about finally walks in the door, my wolf relaxes. He's been pacing for the last three hours so it's a welcome relief.

The other pack members who are also enjoying a drink in the bar glance around; trying to see what has calmed me down. At the beginning of the night they all kept coming over, trying to offer comfort and calm me. But when I almost bit a chunk out of Smithy's throat, they all decided it was better to keep a safe distance.

Those who know about Rosabel, quickly get back to minding their own business. Those who don't, keep watching, searching for any clue as to what might be calming me. I don't care what the pack think. I can't take my eyes off Bel, whether I want to or not.

The little black dress she's wearing hugs her curves and

shows off her sexy legs. I want those sexy legs. No—need those sexy legs—preferably wrapped around my waist.

I can see other guys, especially my pack brothers, watching her too, which is understandable. She's an unclaimed fellow wolf. My wolf doesn't like it. Bel is ours but he knows that if any of these guys even try to make a move, we can take them out. They have no chance. Bel isn't leaving my sight for the rest of the night. I will be escorting her home, or following her if need be. My wolf won't accept anything less.

I manage to allow her to finish her first drink. I watch the tension drop off her with every mouthful she takes. Although she's seated, she starts torturing me and every other male in the bar by dancing in her seat. She has no idea how sensually she can move. I can tell by the slight tension still clinging to her shoulders that something must've upset her on her date.

I try to leave her as long as possible, knowing she probably needs the time to herself, but I just can't take the distance between us anymore. I have to touch her. My wolf needs to comfort her. It's his job as alpha and mate.

As I place my hand on her shoulder from behind, I can feel how distracted she is. Her wolf isn't even greeting me by running her energy along my skin, which is unusual. That's one of the reasons I've been trying to stay away from her. My wolf wants to claim her every time she does it, and until she knows what those feelings mean, he can't.

My hand barely touches her shoulder when she spins around and clocks me right on the nose with a mean right hook. I don't even have time to stop her or step out of her reach before I feel my nose crack and the warm blood pour down my face.

I feel the pack members throughout the room bristle, ready to come to my aid. I quickly and silently send out an order with a wave of energy to calm them down, reminding them that I am alpha and I can handle the she-wolf myself.

"Oh. My. God. I'm so sorry. I didn't realise it was you," Bel quickly apologises as she reaches over the bar. She grabs a towel and pulls it over the bar.

"That's a good right hook you've got there. Was your date that bad?" I joke, reaching out and taking the towel from her as I straighten my nose. It clicks back in place and the bleeding pretty much stops. I start healing immediately and if it wasn't for the fresh blood that I could still feel smeared on my face, no one would know she'd hit me.

"No, Emmanuel was nice. It was something that happened when I dashed to the bathroom that has put me on edge. I'm sorry."

Misty takes the bloody towel off me and leans over the bar wiping my face with a wet towel. "There all gone. Have this on the house," she says, passing me a drink that smells like straight whiskey.

I take a large swig of my drink and I lean towards Bel, pulling her into a hug. "Don't worry about it," I say, trying to calm her. As I speak, I take a deep breath and immediately regret leaving her in Emmanuel's care. I can smell Dominick on her and not just his scent. I can smell his saliva. Trust me; saliva has its own scent. If you don't believe me next time you drool in your sleep, smell your pillow. I pull away quickly and spot the bite marks on her neck. Cradling her neck with my hands, I stroke the bite gently with my thumb.

"What happened with Dominick?" I can't help but demand an answer. The alpha in me needs to know. Her mate needs to protect her.

She stares at me blankly for a second. I ready myself to hear her deny it. Surely she knows I can smell him. I see her brain catch up and she explains about him feeding on her in the alley. The whole time I stroke her neck, I'm sending my energy into her wound forcing it to heal quicker. I don't want that blood sucker's mark on her.

As it starts to fade, I know for certain that she is my true mate. I wouldn't be able to use my energy to heal her if she wasn't. I can't help the satisfied rumble that leaves my chest. She is mine, and as much as I want to explain this to her, I can't.

I need to get the problem of Dominick out of the way first.

"Do you know what this means?" I ask, knowing that she most probably won't have a clue. She wouldn't have had any contact with vampires in Quilpie. Grigori Dorfman runs a tight town. There wouldn't be any vampires stepping foot on his land.

Her frown tells me I'm right before she even opens her mouth. "What? He tasted me. You said he would."

The satisfied feeling I had totally disappears. An angry growl leaves my lips and my energy flares. I'm not surprised one bit when Wesley approaches us.

"Boss. Is everything okay?" he asks, knowing from my energy that it's not.

"No, Wesley." I don't look at him as I answer, I can't. I can't take my eyes off the place where Dominick's fang marks had marred Bel's neck. "Pack meeting in an hour. Do you think you can organise that?"

"Yeah, no problem, boss. What's it about?"

I turn a glare on him. "You'll find out when you get there!" I practically scream in his face.

Wesley leaves without saying another word. He knows full well that he should never question his alpha while I'm in this state.

It takes a few minutes to calm down and address Bel. I can't help but feel sad as I look into her beautiful chocolate brown eyes. "Dominick didn't just taste you, he formed a tie."

When her eyes fill with tears, I realise she must be channelling my sadness.

"What does that mean, a tie?"

"If a vampire drinks from you without draining you or turning you, a tie is formed. Its effects are different with each vampire. It could be that he can read your thoughts, or sense where you are, or even control you to make you do anything he wishes. With Dominick being so old and King, he might be able to do a lot more. Can you see why I'm so upset now?" I can't control the anger in my voice.

"I can see why I should be upset, but why are you upset?" she snaps back.

How do I explain this? Dammit I should have claimed her days ago. Then we wouldn't be having this problem.

"Because he forced you into this, and it complicates things."

"What things?" she asks warily.

I wrack my brain to come up with some reasonable complication that won't make me sound like a crazy, possessive stalker.

"I'm supposed to be helping him find out who's kidnapping his vamps, but the more pissed off I get with him, the less I want to do it." As the lie comes out my mouth I know she's able to pick it up, but I can't do anything to cover it. I just hope my emotions tell her that I'm not completely lying.

"How can someone kidnap a vampire?" she asks, calmly sitting back on her stool. "They're too strong." I can see she's trying to calm me by taking my thoughts away from Dominick.

I want to kiss her for not calling me out over my lie. I refrain and answer her question as best I can. "That's why he's asked for my help. He was convinced it was a vamp, but after interrogating every vamp in the state and coming up blank, he's moving onto the next thing. And the next thing strong enough is a were. He wants me to question the pack."

"Couldn't they have lied to him?" she asks, toying with her empty glass.

I sit down on the stool next to her. "No. You can't lie to Dominick. He's been here two thousand years. He knows a lie when he hears one. When you have extra senses you can pick up on lies when you know what to look for. Raised heartbeat, perspiration, changes in breathing just to name a few."

I catch Misty's eye as she yells out last call and push both our glasses forward to indicate that we want refills.

When she comes over with our drinks, Bel jumps in and pays her while pushing one of the glasses towards me. "An apology drink."

I can't help but laugh as I accept the drink and the apology.

While we finish our drinks, Misty and Lucy close up. It's not long before Misty comes over with her bag and the keys in her hand.

"Ya ready to go?" she says to Bel.

"Yep," Bel answers, jumping off the stool.

I don't know whether to let her leave with Misty or bring her with me to the pack meeting. By the time I decide I need to bring her, they're both in the car and saying bye.

Before I can say anything Bel's window opens. "You okay, Theo?"

I decide to go with my initial thoughts when I ordered Wesley to organise a pack meeting. I need to fix this and that is what I am going to do. "No. It doesn't feel right leaving you. Will you come with me, please?" I answer honestly.

They both chuckle and Misty shouts through the car. "Are you trying to get in Bel's knickers, Theo?"

Her comment throws me for a loop and it takes a moment to register what made her think along those lines. Not wanting either of them to think I would ever try to get her home just to get in her underwear, I quickly clarify my intentions. "No. I didn't mean it like that that! Not at all." I look directly at Bel. "I need you at the pack meeting, as evidence."

Her face drops and her wolf throws a wave of anger at me. "Fine."

She gets out of the car and slams the door. She drops her

head into the open window. "Drive safe, Misty. I'll see you at home in a little while."

Misty drives off without a word.

A very pissed off Bel turns to me and grumbles, "Lead the way."

What the hell have I done?

9.

DECLARATIONS

ROSABEL

As he leads me in silence to a very snazzy black car, I realise I may be out of order for being so upset. It's not as if he has ever really made me think he would ever try to 'get into my knickers,' as Misty put it. As much as I want to stay mad at him, I feel like I should apologise. Curiously, my wolf won't let me do it. She's spitting mad at Theo for something.

I try to break the silence. "This car is gorgeous. What is it?"

His face changes from hurt and confused to the sexiest smile as he appraises his car. He gently strokes the bonnet. "It's an Aston Martin, Vanquish. She's my baby."

He unlocks the car with a beep of the remote. It's just as beautiful on the inside—all leather and a new car smell that wraps around me along with Theo's scent.

I'm glad I chose to put my belt on. He isn't exactly sticking to the speed limit as he zooms through the streets of Mount Roxby. I grip the edge of the seat for dear life, trying my hardest not to rip the leather with my claws, which appear as my fear sets in.

"It's okay. I won't crash," he says with a laugh.

"How the hell do you know that? You're driving like a

maniac. Do you know how easy it is to crash a car?" I really shouldn't be so demanding towards an alpha, but I can't help it.

He's scaring the shit out of me.

"I'm a werewolf, remember? You know very well we have lots of extra senses and extremely quick reflexes that humans don't."

My claws retract with that reminder, but my grip on the seat doesn't ease much. "Oh, yeah. I didn't think of that. I would still prefer it if you slowed down a little."

He finally slows down, taking a right turn onto a long winding dirt track. It leads into a large opening that holds a magnificent mansion-style house, surrounded by forest. We pull up alongside a dozen cars parked in front of the house.

Theo exits the car and I sit admiring the building and the steps that lead up to it. There are only about eight steps but the way the front entry is designed it is majestic. My door opening pulls me out of my trance.

Theo offers his hand to help me out the car. *Such a gentleman.*

He grips my hand gently in his strong, warm fingers as he leads me into the house and through to the lounge room, which is full of werewolves. Okay. I should clarify that they're werewolves in human form. But they are Pack and I'm an outsider. The full moon is tomorrow night and I can feel the tension in the room as they all turn to watch us enter.

I don't belong here.

Theo addresses everyone as we walk through them, still holding my hand. "Thank you for coming at such late notice and hour."

Everyone nods in unison. It's an extremely unsettling thing to watch.

Once we reach the far side of the room, we stop in front of three chairs that are facing the pack members. Theo stops before the empty middle seat.

An extremely large, scary looking guy, who's dressed in leathers, occupies the seat to his left. He looks like he belongs to a biker gang, not a werewolf pack.

In the chair on Theo's right, is Wes. I had thought he must be high up in the ranks. I can tell by the seating arrangement that he's Theo's second. That makes Biker Guy his third.

Theo directs me to Wes' chair.

Wes stands from his seat and stands behind it without a word. Theo sits me down in the now vacant seat. It's against all my natural instincts to have a were standing that close behind me, but unfortunately I have no choice but to endure it.

Theo releases my hand before turning to the pack. "Please be seated."

The pack drops to the floor.

Once everybody settles into their seated positions, he addresses the room. "First things first. This is Rosabel McGuiness. As you can smell, she's werewolf. Unclaimed and unattached to a pack. She's new to town after travelling from Quilpie; home to a large were-lion pride. Rosabel's been living with this pride since she was a child. She is now trying to find a pack to call home."

"Do I need to put her in the census?" Wes asks from behind me.

"I've already seen to it personally. As you all know Dominick Drake is trying to pin the vampire kidnappings on one of us." A murmur runs through the room.

"I know none of you are guilty, but none of his vampires are either and no matter how hard we try we can't seem to come up with a viable lead. We have been working together to solve this mystery but now Dominick has taken something without permission. It belonged to me and was under my protection."

I look across to Theo in surprise. *Surely he isn't talking about me and the bite. I'm not his.*

"What did he take?" a guy with a buzz cut seated near the front asks.

Theo explains and when he finishes, the guy still isn't satisfied.

"But she isn't pack. She doesn't belong to anyone. The pact we have with the vampires only protects the pack, not lone wolves. I don't understand how this affects us, or why it bothers you."

Theo's gaze penetrates my eyes with concern flowing deeply from his emerald green eyes. Through my empathy I feel a wave of guilt coming off him. "I'm bothered because she is everything to do with me. She is *mine*." He ends his statement on a possessive growl.

My wolf instantly stands to attention. *Finally!* Happy to hear him talk about me in a possessive way. *Ours.* My wolf sends the word through my mind.

The tension in the room doubles. Ninety percent of the wolves in front of me are extremely irate.

"She's your true mate? Why haven't you claimed her? True mates are always claimed at that first meeting between them; from both sides. I'm sorry but Ms. McGuiness looks just as surprised on hearing this information, as the rest of us here," suggests a beefy looking guy in the back.

Theo slips from his chair and kneels in front of me. He leans in and presses his body between my legs. My heart is pounding in my chest. I want this badly, but I am terrified. His left hand squeezes my thigh as his right hand slides up to the back of neck. He pulls my mouth towards him. I feel his hot breath against my lips right before he presses his mouth hungrily to mine; devouring my lips, tongue, and breath in a deep, 'owns me, my wolf and my soul,' kiss.

My eyes close and my hands roam around his strong neck, through his soft hair, gripping the back of his neck. He groans against my mouth. We break apart, panting. I have been owned, in front of his pack. I open my eyes, once again seeing the room full of werewolves before me.

"Yes. That is exactly what I am saying. I will spell it out just in case some of you still don't quite understand. Rosabel McGuiness is my true mate, and I am claiming her."

His wolf's energy brushes against me, covering me in his spicy scent.

That's when I feel my wolf's energy reciprocate by releasing her sweeter scent and brushing it along his body. I close my eyes and concentrate, feeling every inch of him as she touches him. It feels just as it would if I was touching him with my own fingers. He feels divine. Audience or not, with the feel of him under my wolf's energy and his wolf touching every inch of me, I'm just about ready to pounce and take him right here.

I think it's safe to say he feels the same. If the bulge I see him trying to hide as he stands has anything to do with it.

As he steps away and turns to the furious pack, I can smell our scents have combined making the most amazing fragrance.

I have so many questions going through my head.

Are we mates?

Does this happen to all mates or is it just a typical werewolf thing, between two wolves?

An angry scream pulls me away from my questions.

"That is ridiculous! She hasn't even been in town two minutes. You have plenty of females in the pack to choose from. You can't choose her." A brunette female is standing in the middle of the crowd demanding everyone's attention.

"I AM ALPHA!" Theo shouts. His Alpha power spreads throughout the room making his point. I can feel it prickling against my skin and I'm not even part of the pack. I dread to think how bad it hurts those he is forcing it onto.

"Bel is my true mate and I have claimed her." There's a deadly calmness to his voice. It sounds scarier than his previous statement.

A beautiful long-legged blonde parts the crowd. She stops in front of him, reaches out and trails her hands down his chest. It's the same Barbie that was coming onto him in the bar a few nights ago.

"You haven't finalised the claim. We all saw she was willing to do it in front of us all, but you didn't." She's referring to my reaction during our kiss. Her hands go lower towards his waistband.

"I can satisfy you—now and always," she whispers, before planting a huge kiss on Theo whilst her quick and nimble fingers work on his belt.

I release a ferocious growl, as I pounce towards her. I rip her hand from his belt and launch her across the room.

She hits the wall with a loud thump and drops to the floor, moaning—right before a large piece of plaster falls, lands on her head and knocks her unconscious.

I turn away from the crumpled Barbie to find everyone watching in stunned silence. It's then I realise what I've done. I have attacked a pack member in front of her whole pack—one night before the full moon.

To top it off, I was unprovoked.

I'm a dead wolf.

I turn to Theo in a panic, "Oh god, Theo. What have I done? I—"

Before I can finish my sentence, Theo cuts me off with a monstrous laugh. Everyone gasps as he throws his arms around me and sighs into my hair. "Oh, Bel."

Once Theo's laughter settles and silence fills the room, Wesley speaks up. "Now that that's all cleared up. What are we going to do?"

Theo releases me. "I have been thinking about that."

He sits me in his chair and starts to pace the floor. "The only way to break a tie with a vampire is through said vampire's death. That's going to be tricky. We're talking about Dominick after all."

Wesley nervously clears his throat. "No. I mean, what are we going to do about the elusive vampire kidnapper?"

"Oh, yeah, that. Well your guess is as good as mine. What I do know is we have to find them, if only to clear the pack," he says, still pacing the floor.

"The Pack isn't responsible, and according to Dominick, neither are the Vamps. Could there be a rogue were doing this? One we're not aware of?" Biker Guy suggests.

"It's a possibility, Billy. There have been reports of a rogue vampire, but for now we should all keep our eyes, ears, and noses open for any evidence of a rogue of any kind. We'll discuss this more at Saturday's meeting. Stay safe tomorrow. Make sure you're all at your designated places. Good night."

Without a word they all stand and start to file out the front doors.

"Can someone get Chloe out of my house on the way out?" Theo asks, pointing to the still unconscious leggy blonde laying in a heap on the floor.

A young guy, who was just about to go out the door turns, walks to Chloe and effortlessly hauls her over his shoulder, "Do you know where she lives?" he asks as he turns to look at Theo for an answer. It's then I recognise him as Paddy from the gym the other night.

Billy 'Biker Guy,' whom I have decided must be Theo's third, pats his pockets before pulling out a pen, a crumpled scrap of paper and jotting down what must be her address.

Paddy glances at it as he takes it from Billy's hand. "Cheers, Billy," he says, heading out the door with Chloe bouncing over his shoulder.

The room emptied, leaving Theo, Wesley, Billy, and me. I watch from my seat on the chair as Theo leaves the room through another door, Billy and Wesley both follow. Not knowing what to do, I rest my head back against the chair and close my eyes. *I could really do with getting to bed soon.*

"It's much comfier in the other room, you know." Theo's gravelly voice makes me jump.

"I didn't know if you were discussing pack business. I thought I'd just close my eyes until someone told me different," I confess.

He slides his fingers around my wrist and pulls me to my feet, leading me towards the doors to the room he had been in. It must be a dining room. I can now see a beautifully restored antique twelve-seat table pushed against one of the walls. It matches the three chairs Theo, Wes, and Billy were using in the meeting.

Billy and Wesley are now sitting on a red L-shaped sofa when we walk into the lounge room.

Theo pats the seat next to him, suggesting I sit there. When I sit down, Theo throws an arm around my shoulders and pulls me against his chest, and puts his feet up on the solid oak coffee table.

Once everyone is comfortable, the brain storming starts.

The three men go over ideas on how to find the rogue vampire. I lose interest pretty quickly and close my eyes, listening to the strong heartbeat under my ear, and it's beating in time with my own. I can feel his voice vibrating through his body and in no time I feel myself drifting off to sleep. Try as I might, I just can't stop myself.

---

*A*n incessant twitch in my thigh wakes me from a deep sleep.

I try to move my arm so I can slap the offending body part, only to find it tangled with an arm that doesn't belong to me. I only have to use my nose to work out who it belongs to. I can feel Theo's energy pulsing off his body, and his scent is everywhere.

"If you don't stop that phone from buzzing, I won't be held accountable when I break it," Theo grumbles as he burrows his head under the pillow.

With that, I realise it isn't my thigh twitching; it's my phone vibrating in the pocket of my dress. I take note of the time, quarter past five in the morning, and the caller ID, Misty, before hitting answer.

"Misty, I am so sorry for not calling," I apologise, thinking she must have been worried that I hadn't made it home yet.

"Theo called to let me know ya'd fallen asleep and he wasn't waking ya."

Theo places his arm over my middle and pulls me towards his body. His energy running along my skin comforts me and I relax into him.

"I'm not calling about that. Ya've got a visitor. I can't get out of him who he is. He's in a bit of a state."

I sit up immediately.

Jared has found me. I bet he's drunk. I hope he doesn't get aggressive with Misty. He isn't usually violent unless he needs to be. He isn't a bad guy.

"I'll be right there, Misty. If he gets violent you lock yourself in another room, you hear me?"

"He doesn't seem like he'll hurt me but I'll keep that in mind," she says before disconnecting the call.

I grab my shoes from the floor alongside the bed and pull them on. The bed moves as Theo gets up. My mind is running away with me imagining all the damage Jared could cause while I'm on my way.

God. I hope he stays human.

Theo appears in my line of sight, crouching before me. He rubs my forearms with his warm hands. "Everything is going to be okay. Let's go and see what's happening."

Instead of going through the front entrance like I expect, he leads me through a door that brings us into a garage. I hear the click of a car unlocking and look around the array of cars. It isn't the black car from last night that flashes its indicators; it's a 4x4 of some kind. I'm not much of a car junkie. The badge tells me it's a Mitsubishi and that's about it. It's white, if that helps.

It doesn't take us long to get to Misty's. Theo pulls up outside her apartment block and starts to exit the car. I lean over and grab his arm to stop him. "Theo, wait."

He closes the door and sits back in his seat.

I release my hold, allowing my hand to relax against his arm. "You can't come up. If it's who I think it is, all hell will break loose if you do."

He gives me a worried look. "If there's a threat I don't want you going up there without me."

"He isn't a threat to me. He'd never hurt me. But he will be a threat if he sees you. Please Theo," I plead. I need him to let me go up alone. I don't know if Jared will recognise my change in scent, but if Theo goes up too he'll flip. He'll attack Theo and I can't have that on my conscience.

"Okay. But I will wait down here, until I hear that you're safe. If I hear anything that sounds violent I won't be able to stop myself from coming up there."

Knowing it's the best I'm going to get, especially from an alpha; I grab his face and give him a quick kiss before exiting the car.

"Thank you," I call over my shoulder as I dash into the building.

I walk into the apartment, expecting the worst. A fight with Jared or worse yet, a bloody Misty if he'd lost it, in my absence. My brain takes a minute to catch up to what my eyes are seeing. My cousin Benji is sitting on the sofa. A suitcase is by his feet and tears are streaming down his bruised and battered face.

"Oh, Benji," I whisper, dashing to crouch before him.

"I'm sorry…he made me…made me tell him," he says between sobs, as I pull him into a hug.

Misty comes into the lounge from the kitchen with a tray loaded with coffee and cookies. She gives me a worried smile as she catches my eye.

"Don't cry, Benj. Did he do this to you?" I ask pointing to his face. Neither of us needs to say the name, we both know who we're referring to. Jared.

Taking a few deep breaths he calms down and reaches for a coffee and a cookie. "Yeah, I tried not to tell him. He didn't want to hurt me, I could tell. But he wanted to know where you were and he knew I could find out. I pinged the GPS on your new phone. I'm sorry."

I'd bought the new phone a few days before leaving so Jared couldn't get a hold of me or ping my GPS. Looks like my purchase was pointless.

"It was all pointless. I should have just stayed; he wouldn't have done this to you then." I reach out and stroke his bruised face as I try pushing away the feelings of guilt.

Benji smiles at me but it's sad. "No. You needed to leave. You don't belong there. You need a pack. You always have."

My phone starts vibrating in my pocket. When I look at the ID and see Theo's name I jump up from my seat and pace to the window.

"Oh shit," I say to no one in particular before hitting answer.

10.
HUNT

THEO

I barely hold back from storming into the building. I'm an Alpha, the leader, the protector. Allowing my mate to go upstairs alone to face an unknown danger goes against all my natural instincts. I last five minutes before I can't take it any longer.

I reach into my pocket and manage to pull out my phone without crushing it in my hand.

Bel answers fairly quickly. "Theo."

The relief of hearing her voice causes me to lose control, leaving my phone a crumbled mess in my hand.

"Dammit!" I yell, throwing the useless pieces of phone across the cab.

I try not to slam the door as I get out. I don't need a busted truck to go with the busted phone.

Once in the apartment block, I take one look at the elevator and know I won't be able to handle waiting. I storm straight for the stairs, taking them two at a time.

I hear the security guy calling me.

"Sir, you can't go up there. You need to be signed in. Sir!" It doesn't sound like he's following me up the stairs. His lazy arse probably took one look at the stairs and decided to leave me to it.

I barge into Misty's apartment, only calming down when I see Bel standing unharmed in front of me.

"Theo? The call's not going through," she says, waving the phone in her hand about.

"Yeah. Technical glitch with my phone. I thought I better just come up." I look around the room and find Misty on the sofa.

"Sorry for just barging in Misty. I wanted to make sure you were all safe." That's when I notice the visitor next to Misty. His face is battered and bruised and he looks like he's been crying too. Bel and Misty might be okay but this guy isn't. The Alpha in me wants to jump in and help.

"Everything is fine, Theo. This is my cousin, Benji." She gestures towards the black and blue stranger on the sofa. "He's been in a spot of bother but he's safe now."

I watch her saunter towards me. The sexy sway of her hips makes things stir beneath my jeans.

"Thanks for checking on us." She leans up on her tiptoes and kisses me on the cheek. If that isn't a dismissal, I don't know what is.

"Always," I reply before taking her mouth with mine. I'm not leaving without tasting her. "See you tonight at the hunt?"

"Oh, no. I won't be hunting."

"Not hunting. Why?" It's unheard of for a wolf not to join in a hunt on the full moon. Even a lone wolf will hunt alone. We feel closer to our wolves on a full moon because she sings to us, begging us to change. Nothing but pregnancy will stop us from changing on a full moon and sometimes even that doesn't stop us. That's why miscarriage rates in werewolves are so high. Sometimes the wolf just takes over and the change is too violent for a foetus to survive.

"I've never hunted. The pride would never allow me to hunt

with them and they made sure to run their hunts in time with the full moon, no doubt out of spite. I'll just shift here. I'll be fine." She reaches around my neck and pulls me down to whisper in my ear. "I don't feel comfortable leaving Benji in this state. We've only just stopped him crying."

I hold her waist as she drops back down on her feet. "I'm not happy about it. A wolf in my town should be able to hunt. But I understand your reasons. How about I take you on a special hunt on Monday—just the two of us? I'll pick you up about noon."

She smiles gratefully and steps out of my arms. "Yes, that would be great. Monday at noon it is."

I nod and say goodbye to both Benji and Misty as I head for the door. I can feel Bel following behind me, her energy brushing against my skin. I turn to find her standing in the doorway.

As I reach to pull her into my arms again, the lift dings and the doors open behind me. Glancing over my shoulder I see a security guard with a face like thunder barge out.

"Sir, you need to leave. You can't just storm into the building like that. We have a security system to keep the residents safe." He dismisses me and turns his attention to Bel. "Ms. McGuiness, I'm sorry about this blip in our security. I will escort this man out and personally make sure nothing like this happens again."

"It's fine, Bob. He's a good guy." Bel starts to back away out of my reach. "Thanks again, Theo. I best get back in and see to Benji." She reaches for the door and closes it without even a goodbye kiss.

The lift behind me dings. The security guard must have already called it back.

"You need to leave now, sir."

Holding my growl in, I turn to the security guard. My wolf is unhappy with being ordered around by this man. He's just a human. He doesn't realise the dangers of giving me orders. I keep telling myself that I can't attack a defenceless human as he glares at me.

I place my hand on the doors and wave him in—my wolf can only take so much. He might not consider the guy a threat, but that doesn't mean he will give him our back.

It doesn't take the lift long to make it down to the ground floor, making me think he must have stopped to check all the lower floors before getting to Misty and Bel's floor.

I head straight for the front door, ignoring the guard behind the desk whom had decided to take it on himself to give me a lecture about signing in and calling up to the residents before going up. I close the door behind me while he's still mid-rant.

I walk around the house when I arrive and head to the back yard. I can hear the pack members fooling around.

Wes is flipping burgers on the barbie. Alyssa, his mate, is lounging on the grass with a couple of other females; Rachel, Chloe, and Delly. Eddie and Matthew are throwing a football around. The only member missing is Paddy.

The rest of the pack are all in groups at other locations. It's too dangerous for us to hunt together. We can be noisy on a hunt. Humans would notice large groups of us, making our existence harder to keep from them.

There are already dangerous groups of humans who grow up knowing that fairy tales and monsters are real. They like to call themselves 'the Cleaners.'

Their mission is to cleanse the human race of all supernatural beings. They're trained generation after generation to destroy us. If we hunted in one large group, we would be giving them the opportunity to wipe out a whole pack at once.

We rotate locations and members so we all get a chance to hunt together. It's safe and it works, so we stick to it.

I reach out for the footy, grabbing it as it soars straight towards my head. "Nice try Eddie but you know I'm too quick for you. I don't know why you bother."

My comment doesn't stop me from throwing the footy back in Eddie's direction at full pelt, aiming for his arse.

He easily catches it with a laugh and carries on his throwing game with Matthew. It's virtually impossible to catch a wolf off guard. Our reflexes are just too quick.

"Is Paddy on his way?" I ask no one in particular.

Everyone looks at me but not one of them offers a reply.

I turn my attention to Ed and head for Wes at the grill. "Ed. You two are pretty good mates. Why isn't he here? He's usually one of the first to arrive, he loves the hunt."

"I haven't heard from him today. I just figured you'd sent him to track for the rogue vamp or whoever is kidnapping the vamps. He often goes silent when he's tracking." Ed makes his way towards me, digging his phone out of his pocket. He taps the screen and holds it out. We can all hear it without even putting it on speakerphone. The seven of us crowd around as we listen to it ringing out before Paddy's voicemail finally kicks in.

"You've reached Paddy. I'm either ignoring you or I can't answer the phone right now. Depending on which category you fall in, leave your number and I might call you back."

I speak up knowing he'll call back immediately on hearing my voice. "Paddy, call me."

Ed wanders off, redialling his number.

I close my eyes and feel for him through the pack bonds. I find him in no time, agitated and scared. I open my eyes.

"Something's…not right. He's scared. We need to find him,

retrace his footsteps." I think back to the last time I saw or heard from him. The pack meeting. He left last night with Chloe over his shoulder.

I focus my sights on Chloe. "What happened when he dropped you off last night?"

"I'd come around by the time we arrived at my house. I thanked him with a peck on the cheek and left him in his car. He didn't drive away until I closed the door behind me. Was I the last person to see him?" she asks, sounding devastated at the thought.

"Fuck! He's still not answering. When I got home and he wasn't there I thought he'd gotten lucky with Chloe. I should have fucking called him. Some mate I am," Ed says, pacing around the yard with his wolf riding him. I can feel the energy flowing around him.

Delly steps up to him, placing a comforting hand on his arm. "Don't beat yourself up, Ed. You won't be any help to him if you turn wolf now. You know turning so close to the full moon means you won't shift back until morning. We have a few hours before we have no choice but to shift so let's make the most of it."

He nods his agreement and they all look to me for direction. The problem? I have no fucking clue how to find him. He was in a car; meaning there's no scent trail to follow.

"Wes. Can you call the rest of the pack and make sure no one else saw him after he dropped Chloe off?" Wes wanders off with his phone in hand.

"What if the person taking the vampire's has him? Are we safe? Could it be the Cleaners?" Alyssa asks, with a trembling lip.

I pull her petite frame into my arms. "He's alive, sweetheart. It's not the Cleaners. We all know they wouldn't keep him alive. Whoever has him, we'll get him back. To make sure everyone is safe tonight, we'll bring everyone here for the hunt. It will just have to be a quiet one."

"What about the Cleaners?" Alyssa gasps as she steps out of my arms. We all know the dangers of hunting in the full pack.

"It's a last minute decision. Even if they find out about it they don't have the time to organise an ambush. We'll just have to be extra alert. Do you think you could organise getting everyone here?" Giving her a job will take her mind off worrying about Paddy and the pack's safety. Alyssa doesn't need to worry about those things. That is my job as Alpha.

"Sure." She nods and runs into the house, probably to use the phone in my office.

"We'll get some food together for when the pack arrives," Delly offers, taking Chloe—whose sole attention is on Ed and his phone calls—by the arm and heading into the kitchen.

Matthew and Ed are the only two left in the yard.

"We'll go see if we can pick up anything at Chloe's. It's the last place we know he was so it's our best option."

I look closely at Eddie. "Do you feel like you can handle coming with us? Your wolf was riding you pretty hard a minute ago; we can't have you shifting in the middle of Chloe's street."

He takes a solid minute to weigh up his wolf and whether he will be calm enough to allow him to join us. "I'm all right now, boss. He's settled down."

Taking him at his word, I turn and head for the truck, hoping for everyone's sake we find Paddy and this is all some silly mistake.

If someone has taken him, all hell is going to break loose.

11.
CONS OF A TIE

ROSABEL

When Theo left, the three of us spent the day catching up. Because it's a full moon, I need, the night off to change so Misty heads off to work alone, leaving Benji and me to have a movie night.

"What do you fancy watching, Bel?" Benji asks, flicking through Misty's DVD collection.

I make my way to the bedroom to shift.

"Surprise me," I shout, before shutting the bedroom door behind me. I can normally wait until later in the evening before shifting, but I haven't had the chance to shift since moving here, and my wolf is antsy and ready to come to the surface.

Hoping to ease the shift, I remove my clothes and drop down to all fours. Shifting is not a nice feeling. Essentially your bones are all breaking, realigning again within seconds. The whole process is over in a matter of minutes but it's painful. If you haven't changed in a while, it hurts more than normal. Once I release my wolf she practically pounces out of my skin. I can't help the grunts of pain coming out of my mouth. The grunts soon turn to a howl. I shake out the last tingles of pain just as the door opens.

"That sounded painful." Benji winces at the thought as he

holds the door open for me to exit, making sure to stay clear. After a painful shift, your skin stays sensitive for a while.

I trot to the lounge, curl up on the floor in front of the sofa. I'm not sure where Misty stands on the animals on the sofa front, so I feel more comfortable sticking to the floor. My eyesight has changed with the shift but I can still see the TV; it's just colourless. I can smell the sage Misty has been burning. She's always burning something. This morning it was sage for protection against Jared apparently.

Benji follows behind me, plonking his butt down on the floor next to me. He grabs the popcorn off the coffee table and presses play.

Benji chose the movie Rent, which is one of our favourites. We like to sing through the whole thing. It's not something I can do in wolf form but I won't enjoy it any less.

Halfway through the movie my wolf starts getting agitated. I get up and pace through the apartment, finding myself stopping and staring at the front door every time I pass. She wants out. She wants to join Theo. She feels she should be hunting with them because she has some insane idea about Theo being *ours*.

"Bel. You aren't normally like this. I don't know what to do for you. If you don't stop whining, someone might come up to see what's happening."

Whining? I didn't even realise I'd been whining.

"We don't want them to find you. They might not believe you're a dog and you know I can't lie for shit," Benji says, crouching down between me and the front door. He smooths his hand over my head and down the fur on my back. It does the trick and calms me enough to stop my whining.

Benji stands and heads back to the lounge and the TV. "Come on, let's go put another movie on. I'll even let you drool over Brad Pitt in World War Z."

*T*he day after the full moon I find myself walking into work carrying Benji in my arms. He can't pass Misty's ward because he's human. He keeps wanting to turn and run away, even after she mutes it enough for him to go through without dying.

When we open the front doors to the bar, Tommy is waiting. He's like a piece of furniture. The bar wouldn't feel right if he wasn't propping it up.

As the night goes on I notice it's nowhere near as busy as it usually is. We actually find ourselves standing around between serving customers.

I wipe the already clean bar down for what feels like the fiftieth time. "It's so quiet tonight."

"It always is after a full moon. The werewolves are all recovering from their wild night." Misty's voice sounds muffled as she answers while cleaning out one of the fridges behind the bar.

The only customers we have are Tommy, Vera, and Mike; all witches. I give them all fresh drinks.

Misty moves on to the last fridge. "Why don't you and Benji pick a few songs on the jukebox and have a boogie. It's not as if we're rushed off our feet."

We choose a few silly songs to dance to. The first one that starts to play is 'Stop' by The Spice Girls. We both know the dance off by heart so we're pretty entertaining.

Misty, Tommy, Vera, and Mike are all whooping and cheering until from out of thin air Dominick appears beside me.

My protective instincts kick in, but not before I jump.

"Here. Get a drink. Stay at the bar. I'll be there in a minute," I say, pushing some money into Benji's hand. He practically runs to the bar without argument.

"Rosabel. Your little friend is safe with me. I'm not interested in his blood after tasting yours."

"What do you want, Dominick?" I grumble. I am pretty sure this isn't going to end nicely, especially if past encounters are anything to go by.

He grins, reaches out and trails his fingers down my neck. "Isn't that obvious? You. I want you to become my feeder; my servant."

"Not a chance, Dominick. I will never be yours. I want you to remove this damn tie, too," I growl, stepping back from his touch. My wolf may want to find a pack to join. When you join a pack you are connected to each and every member. You can feel them. It's comforting. It's not that I can feel a connection to him but even the idea of being connected to a vampire is just all kinds of wrong.

"Oh. You know about the tie?" He sounds disappointed, until he speaks again. "The tie can't be removed. I'm sorry."

I glare at him, hearing the lie in his apology. "You're not sorry, and a friend informed me it can be removed with *your* death."

He laughs. "Is that a threat, Rosabel?"

I try to be as serious and intimidating as possible, when I open my mouth next. "If that's the only way to break it, yes." Being intimidating to a King Vampire, who is two thousand years old, is virtually impossible, at least I thought it was but Dominick's face is telling me something else. Maybe I did manage to intimidate the good king a little.

"You meant every word of that. You would kill me. I can feel it." He looks puzzled for a moment.

"Are you an empath?" I ask. It would be the only way he could feel my emotions like that.

"No. But you are," he says in surprise. "It seems the tie has given me two gifts that I know of. One, I can materialise wherever you are by just thinking your name. And two, I can use your empathy against you." His words make me want to punch him. How dare he!

He smirks, stepping towards me again. "Now, now. Don't get angry."

"STOP THAT!"

Laughing sinisterly, he leans in and kisses me on the cheek and before I can get a punch in, he leans away licking his lips.

Cocky bastard.

"The friend that told you how to break the tie wouldn't happen to be Theo, would it?"

"It was your intention for him to find out. That's the main reason you did it." The taste of a werewolf may be enticing for him, but he wanted to get at Theo and biting a werewolf because of a loophole was always going to rub the alpha the wrong way. Dominick seems to get off on it. Even I can see that and I haven't been in town long.

"Of course, it was. Has he worked that out already? He's smarter than I gave him credit for." He leans forward, inhaling my scent. "You've mated."

I nod as I lean away. "He chose me in front of his pack."

"And you chose him in return, I can smell the scent. But you're worried about it, why." It was a statement not a question, "You haven't sealed it yet. That is why it's not so dominant, and I can't let you seal it." He's worried. He might be able to use my empathy against me, but I could still use it against him too. *Why would he be worried about us sealing our mating?*

I glance over to see Misty and Benji huddled together in deep conversation at the bar. "You can't stop us, Dominick." When I don't hear a reply, I turn back to find that Dominick's nowhere in sight.

When I get back to the bar, Misty pushes a glass of what looks and smells like my usual towards me. "Looks like ya need it. What did he want?"

"Just to rub it in about the tie. I hate him," I mutter before taking a nice large mouthful of my drink.

Misty gasps and drops the glass she'd been drying. It smashes at our feet. "Don't say things like that, it will get you killed."

We both bend down and I start picking the big bits of glass up. "If that's the case, my name will already be on the execution list. I told him I'd kill him if that's the only way to break the tie. He knows I meant it too. He could feel it through my empathy. And thanks to the tie, he can now use it against me."

Misty grabs the dustpan and brush, sweeping up the smaller shards as she speaks. "You have to tell Theo. He is the only person that could protect you against Dominick."

Our three customers leave during our clean up so Misty decides that since we've only had the three customers all night, we may as well close up early.

I wake up Monday morning grateful for our early close the night before. It meant I could actually wake up on the first alarm at eleven o'clock, instead of hitting snooze three times.

I quickly get ready as my nerves start to kick in. I'm excited to be going for a run with Theo but I'm nervous of how he will be with me. I don't really know where we stand with the whole mating thing. *Was it just an act or was it real?*

When the clock reads three o'clock, I accept that I've been stood up.

Relief washes over me when the phone rings half an hour later.

I can hear Benji answer it in the lounge room. "Hello." I'm not close enough to hear the person on the other end. If I was in the same room as him I would hear them no problem, but I'd been sulking in my room.

I dash through the apartment.

"Yes. You've got the right number. I'll just get her for you." He holds the phone out towards me, mouthing the name. 'Emmanuel.' I can't help feeling disappointed.

I take the phone and try not to sound as disappointed as I feel. "Hi Emmanuel. How are you?"

"Good thanks, Rosabel. I just wondered if you wanted to go out again. Misty told me it's your night off."

Another date? Part of me doesn't want to. I can't stop thinking about Theo. I should accept that Theo doesn't want me and see where things go with Emmanuel? "Yeah, that sounds good. Do you mind if we just go to Misty's though? It wasn't busy last night and I feel like I had a night off. I'd like to be there to help if things get busy."

"That's fine. I was going to suggest Misty's anyway. Seven thirty sound okay?"

"Perfect, I'll see you later."

"Bye," he says before disconnecting the call.

I place the phone back in its cradle on the sideboard.

"Ooh, a second date," Benji teases, taking a seat on the sofa.

Misty walks in from the kitchen, practically jumping up and down. Obviously she's been earwigging on the phone call. "I'll entertain Benji at the bar. I might even let him help me out behind it."

"Sorry, Benji, but Misty you might not want to do that. Benji has two left hands. They just don't seem to coordinate," I warn her, deadly serious.

12.
SECOND DATES

ROSABEL

I have to carry Benji into the bar again. I think we might have to figure out how to get him in without the wards affecting him at all.

I offered to work until seven o'clock. That gives me half an hour to get some Dutch courage.

Seven o'clock comes around fast.

Benji takes my place behind the bar as I take a seat on his vacated stool. He experiments on me with his first drink. It tastes just right. It's a shame he smashed three glasses in the process. I get the feeling that poor Misty won't have any left by the end of the night.

Emmanuel walks in the door at half past seven on the dot, catching me off guard with a kiss on my cheek. He orders a drink from Benji, who manages to make it without breaking a single glass.

We sit at one of the smaller circular tables to chat for a while. I start to think it could be great if something comes out of this between us. He's sweet and attractive but then I remember he isn't what I want.

Emmanuel jumps. "How did you do that?"

"Do what?" My questioning frown disappears the second I hear the unwanted voice behind me.

"He's talking to me, my delicious, Rosabel. Not you."

I turn to face Dominick. Trying out my intimidating expression again. "Unless you have come to remove the tie, you might as well just disappear again."

"Rosabel. You know Mr. Drake?" Emmanuel asks.

"She knows me intimately."

I feel rage coming off Emmanuel in waves and wonder why he's so mad. This is only our second date and we haven't even come close to discussing exclusivity.

"Tell him the truth, Dominick," I order. "Tell him that on our last date, you trapped me in that alley behind the cinema and drank from me without my consent."

"Oh. You do spoil my fun," he whines. "Do you really want me to leave you with this witch? He's not worthy of you. You deserve so much better. I thought you're mated with Theo, anyway? If you're not, you might like to try dating me."

I feel resentment coming from Emmanuel. Which quickly changes to happiness. *Odd. Out of Dominick's last sentence, what would make him happy?*

"My private affairs are none of your concern, Dominick." I grab my drink and take a sip as I try to calm my wolf down. She wants nothing more than to take control of my body and rip Dominick to shreds.

"Well. I came here to do you a favour but if you don't want me to give you the warning, I'll just let you find out by yourself." He turns, making a show of leaving.

I stand and grab his arm, forcing him to look me in the eye.

"Are you threatening me?" Funny how Dominick asked me the same question only yesterday and yet they sound so different. He'd been amused. I am far from it.

"No. I would never threaten you. I had a were-lion come to

me requesting a living order today. He was asking for your address."

"Jared." I sigh, slumping out of my threatening position.

"Yes. I believe that was his name. Should I have withheld your address?" He actually sounds concerned.

"If you hadn't, it would have only been a matter of time before he followed my scent. Thank you for the warning. I appreciate it." I sit back in my seat and down what's left of my drink.

Dominick grins. "See. I'm not as bad as you think."

I beg to differ.

Dominick leans in and presses his lips against my neck, forcing me to lean away until the table presses into my ribs.

My heart starts to race, knowing that his fangs will sink into the skin any second now. I feel the short sharp scratch as they break the skin. I'm surprised when they don't sink deeper and he dematerialises into thin air. I touch my neck and see the blood on my fingers before turning back to Emmanuel.

"You're bleeding. Did he—"

I cut him off. "No. He was just showing me he can feed off me if he so desires. Can we just forget about it?" I am really getting sick of Dominick and his controlling ways.

Emmanuel grants my wish. Changing the subject, as he reaches for his own drink on the table. "So. Jared has found you."

"How do you know? Misty. Is there anything she doesn't tell you?" I joke, playing with my empty glass.

"Don't blame her. I was digging for information."

"I'm not going to have to worry about you stalking me as well, am I? Dominick and Jared are too many stalkers as it is. I don't need another one." Even though I say it with a laugh, I'm serious.

We both laugh and enjoy some more easy conversation over a couple more drinks.

As the last call is announced, he offers to walk me home. It's a nice fifteen minute walk. Misty and I usually use the car as it's the safe option. Two women walking the streets at two or three in the morning is a little dangerous. Walking with Emmanuel, I am pretty sure nobody will bother us.

Our conversation still flows well on the way home.

Emmanuel pulls me to a stop outside the apartment building, "I had a really good night."

"Me too," I reply honestly.

Before I know it. He quickly takes my mouth with his.

I won't deny him anymore. I like him. This might actually lead to something if I can stop my wolf thinking about Theo. I fist my hands in the front of his shirt as I deepen the kiss.

He lets out a moan and pulls away.

Wow. What a kiss.

"I was thinking the same thing," he says, with a laugh.

Oh good god. Did I say that out loud? What is it with men and me making a fool out of myself in front of them?

He brushes his thumb over my lips. "I better leave before I kiss you again."

We say our goodbyes and he leaves without any more kisses.

I enter the apartment building in a happy daze, still thinking about that kiss.

My happy mood disappears when I step out of the lift; thanks to the sight of Jared sitting on the floor against our apartment door. He looks like he's been there a while. God only knows how he got past the security guards. *Am I ever going to catch a break?*

Looking dishevelled, he jumps up as soon as he sees me. His usually well-styled blonde hair is a mess; no doubt from running his hand through it every two seconds, exactly like he is doing as he stares at me.

"Bel." He sighs, leaping towards me, trying to take me in his arms.

I manage to push him off before he gets a hold. "Jared, don't. I've had a week full of annoying, pushy men and I'm not in the mood to deal with another. I shifted on the full moon but I haven't run since arriving in Mount Roxby. I don't want to have a forced shift."

"I just want to talk, baby. I've missed you so much."

I let him have his moment. I really don't have the energy to argue about it. I open my mouth to reply, and close it again, having no idea what to say.

The lift pings and Misty and Benji step out from it. *Saved by the bell. Thank you, angels.*

"Look, Jared, it's late. If you really want to talk, meet me at work tomorrow. My shift starts at five o'clock. It's a bar called Misty's down Main Street. Have you seen it?" A big public place is the best place to meet him. Misty's is perfect.

"Yes. I saw it earlier. I'll be there. Thank you."

I step around him to unlock the door and gesture for Misty and Benji to enter before me. I daren't look back at Jared. I might just break my resolve and fall into his arms. I have missed him. I love him. Of course, I have missed him; I just know we shouldn't be together. We're not right for each other.

I need a pack, and he needs his pride.

"He's a bit intimidating—alpha level intimidating," Misty mutters as we make our way through to the kitchen. She opens a cupboard and takes out three glasses.

I run the cold tap and fill the glasses one by one, we all like to take a glass to bed with us. "Yeah. He'll be taking over as Pride Leader when his father steps down. I hope you don't mind me telling him to meet me at work, I just figured it would be better meeting him in a public place."

"Not at all. It's safer that way. You'll be able stick to your guns about not being together easier in public."

13.
WOLFING OUT

*W*aking up the next day my wolf is practically crawling out of my skin. I really wish Theo had turned up to show me where to run. I am desperate for a good run, but because I don't know anywhere safe to go, the gym will have to suffice.

The gym looks busier than the last time. I head straight through to the lockers and dump my stuff; taking a towel and bottle of water with me and placing the locker key around my neck.

Just as I place my bottle in the holder on the treadmill, Wesley stops beside me.

"Rosabel, hi. Theo isn't here today."

"Hi." I frown. "Why would I think Theo was here?"

"He owns the place, I thought you knew," Wes says.

I remember the card I memorised, the one Theo gave me with his number on it. His email did have the gym's name in it. *Why hadn't I put two and two together?*

"I didn't realise. I'm just here for a workout. I don't know anywhere safe to run so this treadmill will have to do." I step on and crank the speed up. I really shouldn't take my anger out on Wes but I can't hold it back.

As I start to run I expect Wes to leave, so I am surprised when the next question comes out of his mouth.

"You haven't seen Paddy have you? The guy who almost wolfed out on you?"

"I know who Paddy is." I laugh, remembering how embarrassed the poor guy was. "No. I haven't seen him since he left Theo's after the meeting. Why?" I step off the treadmill so I can give Wes my full attention.

"He hasn't been seen or heard from since he dropped Chloe home after the meeting. It looks like the kidnapper has moved on from vamps to werewolves."

"Oh, no." I didn't know what else to say. What can you say to someone whose pack brother is missing?

"I know."

Looks like I am not the only one who's short for words. His phone rings and he digs it out of his shorts pocket. He glances at the screen before speaking again. "I have to get this. Enjoy your workout, Rosabel," he says as he walks away to answer the phone.

I work out for an hour before deciding it's pointless. My mind is too busy thinking about poor Paddy—not to mention the equipment just isn't doing anything for me. My wolf wants out, to run and nothing less will suffice. She feels more on edge than before I started.

When I arrive home Misty and Benji have already left. I quickly change into my uniform, having showered at the gym.

I arrive at work at the front entrance just as Misty opens up.

"Hi, Tommy. Looks like ya have company today," Misty says, laughing at her own joke.

Tommy walks through the doors heading straight for his stool. "Sure do, Misty."

"Sorry I'm late. The gym was a waste of time. I don't know

why I even bothered," I grumble, following Misty through the bar.

"I bumped into Wesley. One of the pack members has gone missing. They think it's the vamp-napper moving on to were-wolves." I go into the office and offload my bag before joining Misty behind the bar.

"Who's missing?"

"Paddy. The one that nearly turned wolf on me last week."

"Poor thing, he's a nice guy. I hope they find the kidnapper before anyone else goes missing." Misty starts making Tommy his usual.

Benji's sitting in his usual seat with a drink in front of him. He's starting to become like Tommy. "How did you get in here today?" I can't see Misty carrying him in, not with the way he thrashes about trying to get away.

"I walked right in. Misty made me a bracelet that negates the ward for me." He holds his wrist up showing me the bracelet. The ordinary looking piece of leather cord suits his bony wrist. I reach out to touch it hoping to feel the magic, but I can't feel anything. It just feels as ordinary as it looks.

A group of seven witches come in together, and just as I hand the last one his drink Emmanuel walks in. He heads straight to my side of the bar and sits next to Benji.

"Sorry, but I couldn't stay away from you," he says with a grin.

Oh what the hell! I lean over the bar and give him a peck on the lips. Only, when our lips connect, I get a lot more than a peck.

I hear a growl coming from the door and I pull away, expecting to see Jared. When I get far enough away from Emmanuel's scent I catch the spicy scent from the other night and I realise too late that the growl belongs to Theo. I don't need to be an empath to know that he's sad and angry, when I catch sight of his beautiful face. The mix of emotions coming from him is so overwhelming; I can't even pinpoint one of them confidently.

He takes slow, sure strides towards me. "Bel, we need to talk." He glances at Emmanuel before adding, "In private."

"Use the office," Misty says, sidling up beside me. The last thing she wants is the alpha to go wolf in her bar.

I head to the office without saying a word. I have no idea what to say to him. Part of me feels guilty about being with Emmanuel, yet another part keeps reminding me that he stood me up.

He follows me to the office in silence. He closes the door and rests his forehead against it.

I can feel his energy pushing at my skin. "What's going on, Theo? I've already told Wesley I haven't seen Paddy."

"It's got nothing to do with Paddy." That spicy scent coming from him is getting stronger by the second. He takes a deep breath and spins around to face me. "There is a were-lion asking about you. He wants to reside here. I sent him to Dominick so I would have time to warn you." I could tell that isn't what he wanted to say.

"You're too late. He turned up last night, not long after Dominick warned me he'd passed on my address. But that isn't what you really wanted to say though, is it?"

"Yes, that's it. I guess I could have told you in the bar after all," he lies.

"Theo. I'm an empath and a werewolf. If I couldn't feel your emotions through my empathy, I'd still know you are lying. My wolf can tell. What do you really want to talk about?" I slam my hand on Misty's desk to emphasise my impatience. I really don't want to be pissed, but he's blatantly lying and I can't stand it.

"An empath," he repeats, stunned. That's not exactly a good sign. Maybe I should have told him before. "Why were you kissing the witch? We're mated."

"Theo." I sigh. "You haven't said two words to me since leaving Misty's on Saturday morning. You promised to show me where it was safe to run on Monday but stood me up. I assumed everything said at the meeting, must have been bullshit, or at least the full moon causing you to do it. So when Emmanuel asked me out again, I said yes."

Theo finally steps away from the door, coming to a stop when I'm within reach. He reaches out and brushes my hair behind my ear. He doesn't crowd me. He can probably tell that I'm angry and fighting my wolf for the change. I may not be part of his Pack but he is an alpha. He'll be able to sense my wolf and how much she wants to get out.

He takes a deep breath. "I'm sorry. Paddy going missing hit the pack hard. I've not had two seconds to even think since then. I know it's no excuse. I came here tonight to beg for your forgiveness and to see if you would go on a date with me, since we pretty much skipped that step."

My anger dissipates with his words. How can I be angry with him when he has so much on his plate? "Theo. I forgive you."

Before I can say more, he grabs my face between his hands, and takes my mouth with his. As he runs his tongue along the seam of my lips, begging for entry, I pull away.

"Wait. What about Emmanuel? He's a nice guy; I can't just trade him in."

He's looking at me with such adoration that I can feel his love wrapping around me.

I'm kissing him again before I even realise that I've moved. My hands are around his neck, fisting his hair. Our scents mix and Theo lifts me by the hips and places me on the desk, knocking papers to the floor. As his hands roam my body, mine take a journey over his muscular chest and down his abs. As I reach his belt and start to undo it, his nimble fingers work at my zipper.

"I can't let you do this," Dominick says from behind me.

Theo jumps away from me startled. "Where the fuck did you come from?"

"Didn't Rosabel tell you? One of the gifts I received from the tie gives me the ability to materialise wherever she is at just the thought of her name." He smirks as I get off the desk and face him.

"Why the fuck are you here, Dominick?" I ask him pointedly.

"I told you the other day. I can't let you seal your mating," he tells me.

"What does our mating have to do with you?"

Theo and Dominick answer my question at the same time.

"Death isn't the only way to break the tie."

"Sealing our mating breaks the tie," Theo adds with a smirk.

I glance between them both, not knowing who to address. I focus on Dominick. "Is that true? When Theo and I seal our mating, the tie between the two of us will be broken?"

"I believe so, yes," Dominick states as the door opens and Misty comes in.

"Sorry to disturb ya but I need ya out there." She hooks a thumb over her shoulder indicating the bar. "Jared and Emmanuel are both getting anxious. I can't serve and keep them calm." She glances at Dominick as he dematerialises. "What the hell?"

I dismiss the empty space with a wave of my hand. "He arrived the same way. He's a pain in my arse. Sorry about leaving for so long. I'll be right out."

Misty closes the door again leaving the two of us alone.

"I need to go. Neither of us wants Jared losing control. He'll cause a lot of damage and probably take a number of people out before anyone can subdue him."

Just as I reach the door to the bar, Theo spins me by the shoulder and pins me against it. His mouth descends on mine without warning. I kiss him with everything I have. How could I not? We were about to do a hell of a lot more in that office before Dominick dropped in. Theo pulls away from my lips resting his forehead against mine.

"It might be a while before I get to do that again. It sounds like you're going to be busy. I love you." I stand there taking in his words as he pushes the door behind me open, giving me no option but to exit.

I work my way back to the bar, without reacting to his words.

I love you.

Did he even realise he said that? I walk behind the bar in a daze, watching Theo join Wesley and a beautiful, petite redhead at Lucy's side of the bar.

I shake myself out of my stupor and make my way to Emmanuel. "Sorry about that. We had some crossed wires we needed to sort out." I'm not going to dump him in the middle of a packed bar.

He grabs my hand and presses his lips against it. I smell the spicy scent and turn to see Theo watching. I give him a smile to let him know everything is fine as I pull my hand from Emmanuel's grasp.

I hear the beginnings of a roar, a rumble coming from the back of a throat. It's coming from beside Emmanuel. I glance over to spot Jared.

Here comes World War Three.

I tap Misty on the shoulder as she pushes the drawer back in on the cash register. "I'm sorry I've been a pain in the arse tonight, but do you mind if I take Jared to one of the booths so I can get this chat over with?"

"Don't worry, ya can't help it. As long as war doesn't break out in my bar, I won't dock ya wages," she says with a grin, before heading off to serve another customer.

After hearing my conversation with Misty, Jared gets up and walks towards the tables.

I follow him to an empty booth, ignoring half a dozen eyes I can feel watching our every move. Not only are Emmanuel and Theo watching, but so are the pack members who are scattered throughout the bar.

"Okay. Jared, you wanted to talk, so talk!" I say before my butt even hits the seat. Once I'm sitting and my eyes connect with his. I can see the heartbreak in his eyes. Who am I kidding? I feel it too. Jared was the first person not related to me that actually loved me. He stood up for me when everyone else wanted me dead. He put his life on the line for me.

"Why did you follow me Jared? You know we can't be together. Your pride wants me dead. They won't let you lead if we are together. You were born to lead. I can't be the reason you don't."

He reaches across and wipes a tear from my cheek before grasping my hand on the table. "I love you, Bel. I needed to make sure you were safe. We're meant to be together. I would've left with you."

My wolf starts to pace inside me, agitated. She doesn't want him. She's always liked Jared. He protected us. I don't understand her change in heart.

I knew Jared would act like this. Putting his life on hold to protect me is what he does. "As you can see, I'm safe." I let go of his hand and lift my arms to gesture at my unharmed appearance. "You need to go home, Jared, back to your pride."

"Bel, we have been through this a million times. It's my father's Pride, not mine." His voice rises and everyone in the bar looks our way. The werewolves are no longer pretending not to be listening.

Seeing red, I stand up. *"Dammit Jared!"* Before I can even finish berating him, my wolf takes my temper and uses it to come through. I'm suddenly no longer a human but a wolf. I hadn't even felt the usual pain.

Growling at Jared, my front paws on the table and my snout in his face; I can see he's trembling, no doubt fighting his own change. But that doesn't stop me snarling.

Theo's calming energy alerts me of his presence.

"Rosabel. You're not going to rip Jared's throat out, are you?" I can feel his alpha energy pushing at me to obey. As much as I don't like the thought of him being able to make me obey an order, it pushes my wolf back enough for my human half to realise the mistake I'm making. I don't want to rip Jared's throat out, especially not in Misty's bar.

I look into his concerned emerald eyes and rub my head against his hip. I jump down off the bench seat and lay down on the floor next to the table.

Theo sits in my vacated seat and begins talking to Jared in a hushed voice. I can feel the tension throughout the room—even though everyone has returned to their own conversations. Emmanuel is blatantly staring in our direction but not making a move to approach.

"Jared. I understand that you have protected Bel for a long time."

I growl, insulted at the fact that Theo is insinuating I needed protecting.

Theo ruffles my fur to calm me down. "We know she doesn't need protecting, but I'd like to thank you for keeping my true mate alive."

Jared's anger dissipates within seconds. I look at him to see defeat in the slump of his shoulders.

A whine leaves my throat as I rub my snout against his shin.

"Your true mate?"

Theo nods his head as he rests his chin on his steepled fingers. "If you choose to pursue her, I will have to take it as a challenge."

"If you really are her true mate, I have no right to challenge you. I love Bel. I wouldn't hurt her by challenging her true mate." Jared glances over his shoulder towards the bar before leaning further across the table towards Theo. "Why was she all cosy with the witch?"

Theo laughs. "Let's just say things have become a little complicated."

14.

STALKER STATUS

THEO

Things sure did get complicated.

My plans for tonight involved making it up to Bel for not being around since Paddy's disappearance, and relaxing with my mate.

As I sit opposite Bel's ex, I thank my lucky stars he's deciding to back off. It's not that I don't think I could handle taking him out in a duel but seeing us fight would be hard for Bel.

"I won't pursue, Bel, but I'm taking a break from the pride for a while. Both me and my father believe I need to see more of the world before I take over as leader so I'd like to stay in town if you'll allow it?"

He'd kept Bel alive for years. I owe him. I give permission with a nod.

Without a word, he stands and starts to leave. As he moves, I catch Paddy's scent in the air.

Within seconds I am up and have Jared pinned to the wall with my arm across his chest. Bel is growling beside me but I don't have time to deal with her. I need to find out why Jared has Paddy's scent on him.

"What the fuck?" Jared spits, looking at Bel; who is growling and baring her teeth to him. She would have caught Paddy's scent too.

I reach into my pocket and pull out one of the missing person flyers Alyssa had been pasting everywhere.

"Where did you see this guy?" I ask, shoving the flyer into his chest. I quickly release him, needing to stay calm. I can feel the pack crowding in around us and I don't need them ripping into him before we get answers.

I watch with bated breath as Jared looks at the flyer closely before answering. "I've never seen this guy."

"You have his scent on you. Can you explain that?"

"I swear. I have never seen this guy. Maybe he brushed past me in the street. I've been knocked by so many people today, maybe it was transferred from someone else." I can sense the truth in his words.

I step back allowing him to exit.

"If you do see him, I'd appreciate it if you could let me or one of my wolves know."

"Of course." Jared exits the bar without glancing back at any of us.

After watching him leave, I crouch down and take Bel's head in my hands, making sure to scratch behind her ears. "As much as my wolf wants to come out and play with you, you really need to change back. You're putting the pack on edge." Her tongue darts out to lick my cheek. I stand and she stretches out but doesn't shift.

"You might want to take her somewhere private. She isn't keen on a public naked parade," Dominick announces from behind me. God. This guy is pissing me off; I shouldn't need a fucking vampire to tell me what my mate needs. If he hadn't stopped us earlier I would know what she needs and what she is thinking.

As I look apologetically at Bel, ready to lead her through to the office she silently shifts before my eyes.

I can't contain the growl leaving my throat. I didn't think this through. I don't want all these people seeing my mate naked, pack members or not. We may be used to nudity and don't always look at it sexually but I don't care.

I don't want them seeing her.

Billy must have read my mind because before her change is complete he hands me his full-length leather trench coat, which I cover her up with.

"Thanks," Bel says with a grin, as she pulls the coat around her.

I silently fasten the buttons and tie the belt saving her sensitive fingers the job.

Ed approaches, his eyes on the door Jared had just exited. "Should I follow him, Boss?"

I step back from Bel and turn towards Ed as I answer. "He was telling the truth. There's no need to follow him." Seeing the sadness in Eddie's eyes is tearing me apart. I reach out and pull him into a hug to comfort him. "He's alive, Ed. We can all feel him. I promise you we will get him back."

Emmanuel pushes past us and throws his arm over Bel's shoulder and pulls her in close to his side.

I release Ed and don't hide the fact that I'm listening to what Emmanuel has to say.

"Misty told me to take you home. Before you complain about leaving her in the lurch, Benji is going to work the rest of your shift."

Bel steps out from under Emmanuel's arm and wraps her arms around my waist. "Theo thanks for stopping me from losing it with Jared. He would never have let me live it down if I'd drawn blood."

"I'm Alpha; it's what I'm here for."

Standing on her tiptoes she stretches until her mouth is to my ear. "It was something a mate would do, too." Brushing her lips against my earlobe she lets me go, she leaves the bar without another word. Emmanuel follows closely behind her.

My wolf growls at the sight. She's my mate. Why am I standing here watching her leave with another guy in tow?

Fuck it. I'm not.

I leave Misty's in a rush, not caring what anyone thinks about my rude departure. Once outside, I follow Bel's scent, sticking to the cover of the shadows from the buildings I pass. I feel like a stalker following them home but it's all I can do to keep my wolf calm. I'm not far behind them when I pick up their conversation.

"What is it like to shift?" Emmanuel asks.

"It varies. Depending on the situation. If you choose to do it, it can be great, therapeutic even. It's always painful to a degree, but again it varies depending on how much you need to change. Tonight for instance, I didn't feel a thing. My wolf was riding me too hard. Changing back can be embarrassing if you are in front of a crowd. It's not so bad if they are all weres. We see naked people all the time. We hardly ever notice it. But tonight I was in a bar full of witches and vampires too."

"How did Dominick know what you wanted?"

His mother fucking tie, that's how. Thankfully, I didn't say that out loud. My stalker status would be revealed if I had. I really don't need that getting out.

"When he drank from me, we formed a tie that gave him certain abilities. Materialising wherever I am is one, feeling my emotions is another. I am pretty sure that isn't all he has up his sleeve."

It's a quiet night out tonight and we seem to have the street to ourselves. I watch in the darkened doorway of the building next to Misty's apartment as Emmanuel kisses Bel. It isn't a lingering kiss but, nevertheless, my wolf doesn't like it.

Emmanuel waits, looking at the door expectantly.

Bel, you better not invite him up.

My wolf will not allow him to cross that threshold. My stalker status would well and truly be blown. Bel will already know I'm here. She'll be able to feel my energy. If the wind is blowing in the right direction she could probably catch my scent too, but Emmanuel will have no clue he's being watched.

"It's really not safe for you to come up tonight. My wolf is still on edge, she could easily take over at the slightest provocation."

More like I would kill the bastard.

"It's okay. I can control you."

I'm not at a good enough angle to see his face so I don't know what context he's saying it in, but regardless, I don't like the thought of him controlling my mate in any way, shape, or form. I force myself to stay still and calm.

"What do you mean? How can you control me?" Bel sounds wary.

Emmanuel looks around taking in his surroundings. He looks edgy. I don't know what he senses. I'm not picking anything out of the ordinary up. He's not happy about it—whatever it may be. "Forget I said anything." He glances at his watch before adding, "I've got to go now but can we meet for lunch tomorrow?" He's already retreating.

"Sure. Text me the details," Bel shouts after him.

I watch Bel walk into the building before pulling my new phone out and hitting the buttons to dial her number.

"Hello," she answers breathlessly. She must've run up the stairs.

"I thought he'd never leave."

"Same here, until something spooked him, that is."

"You caught that too?" I ask intrigued.

"I couldn't sense anything. Could you?"

I reach out once again, feeling for anything unusual that could have spooked him. Once again, I feel nothing.

"Not a damn thing," I reply as I start to pace on the pavement. No longer having the need to hide. My wolf is torn between needing to claim his mate and protecting her against whatever dangers lurk in the dark of the night.

"He's lucky you didn't invite him up. He wouldn't be breathing right now if you did. In fact, if I go solve that breathing problem, you could go out to lunch with me instead of him." If I am being honest that isn't a joke. I'd willingly kill him just so I could be with my mate.

"Be good. I need to go out with him to let him down gently. But if you come into Misty's tomorrow night you might get a repeat of our earlier kiss. A treat for being so good." The giggle I hear through the phone makes blood flow to what's beneath my zipper.

"Oh, well, that's me sold. I'll behave. That means I have to get off the phone though, because if I don't, I can't guarantee I'll deserve that kiss tomorrow." I know full well she can hear the arousal in my voice.

"Night then," her voice sounds all breathy before she cuts the connection.

I place my phone back in my pocket and force my feet to walk away from her building and back towards the bar.

I have a pack member to find.

15.

FRIENDS

ROSABEL

After waking up and getting dressed, I am ready to face the day. I walk through the apartment to the kitchen in the hope of finding some coffee. I can't believe I shifted in a bar full of customers. I'd taken Jared to the booth to save the customers from the dangers of anyone shifting, but I never thought I would be the danger. I'm usually calm and in control. It must be Theo and this mating thing that has my wolf in a tizzy.

I stop in my tracks when I see Benji on the couch. His bags are packed by his feet; his eyes are red and swollen indicating he's been crying for some time.

"Benji. What's wrong?" I dread his answer.

"Oh, Bel." He jumps off the couch and dives into my arms. I give him the hug I can see he needs—until he pulls away—all while wondering what the hell has him in this state. He sits back on the sofa as if he'd never moved.

I take a seat next to him before he speaks.

"Mum rang during the night. The Cleaners ambushed the pride during the hunt. Dad was injured. He's out of danger now but Mum needs me. She wants me back in the protection of the pride. I have to go home."

I can't stop the tears running down my cheeks. Uncle Jack has always treated me like his own. If it wasn't for him teaching me how to fight once he took me in, I would never have survived my first fight. Jared may have helped keep me alive by fighting for me, but Uncle Jack is the original hero.

"When do we leave?" It's not a question of whether I go. Aunt Lillian and Uncle Jack need me. I might not be pride, but my family is, and they need all the help they can get.

"*We* don't. I do. You have too much here. You have to stay. You've found your home with Theo and his pack. Claim it. If the Cleaners are still hanging round the pride, it's too dangerous for you to return. You know the pride would trade you in for their safety in a heartbeat."

Knowing he's right, I won't argue. "I'm going to miss you. Sorry we haven't been able to do much while you've been here. I promise, when you come back I'll show you everything this town has to offer. You are coming back aren't you?"

"I'll come and visit again, but it was never going to be permanent. I love you, but you need to find out who you are—what it means to be a wolf. I don't belong in that life," he says sadly.

"I love you, too, Benj." I can't say anything else without bursting into tears, but I don't need to add more. He knows everything I'm unable to say.

We walk down to the street and find a taxi already waiting for him. I give him one last hug as the driver puts his bags in the boot.

"Thank Misty for me. I'll ring you when I arrive," he says, turning his back to me and getting in the car.

"Of course. Give Aunt Lil and Uncle Jack a hug from me," I say, closing the door on him.

I glance at my watch and wave to the car as it drives into the distance, noticing that I only have ten minutes before I'm supposed to be at the cafe Emmanuel text me last night. I dash upstairs to grab my purse, phone, and shoes.

Finding the apartment quiet and seeing no sign of Misty, I decide to leave her a quick note explaining about Benji, telling her where I am going and that I will see her at work, if not sooner. There are people going missing left, right, and centre. You don't need to be a brain surgeon to realise it's best to have someone know where you are heading and when you should be back.

I close the cafe door behind me and look around the greasy spoon cafe for Emmanuel. There are fifteen booths on either side of a narrow aisle and it doesn't take me long to notice him sitting at the furthest booth on the right. I recognise the Motown music playing quietly. Uncle Jack is a huge Motown fan. Being lunchtime, there are only a couple of free tables.

Probably thinking I haven't seen him, Emmanuel waves. It's pretty hard to miss his big frame, but I guess he might forget that.

I take a deep breath to ground myself, preparing for what I need to do. As I start to make my way towards him I get a strong whiff of Paddy's scent. I glance around. One of the customers must have been in contact with Paddy recently. One of them could be the kidnapper. There must be twenty people in here plus staff. There is no way I can pinpoint the culprit without an interrogation.

Taking another deep breath, I focus on my empathy to I see if I can pick up any suspicious emotions. I don't hold much hope because unless they are focused on the kidnapping at this very minute they are probably feeling happy about their food, which means I won't be able pick up on the bad stuff.

As expected, I find nothing.

Thinking the scent could be cross-contamination, I decide to focus on one thing at a time and get this thing between me and Emmanuel finished.

Ever the gentleman, Emmanuel stands as I reach the table. He leans over and kisses my cheek and we take seats opposite each other.

"Rosabel. Is everything okay? I can't help but notice you looked a little distracted."

"Benji left this morning. There has been an attack on the pride. That's playing on my mind," I say, plastering a reassuring smile on my face. It's only partly a lie.

The waitress comes to a stop at our table, halting our conversation. Her pen poised on her pad ready to take our orders. "Whatchahaving?" she asks, mashing her words together. Next time someone complains about Misty's accent I'll remember to send them here to Trudy.

I quickly look at the menu that Emmanuel pushes across to me.

"I'll have a hamburger and tea, please," he says.

I order the first thing I see. "Chicken salad and a coffee for me, please." Coffee is no-brainer since I didn't get one this morning.

Once the waitress leaves, Emmanuel reaches over the table and grabs a hold of my hand. "You should've told me you were being bothered by your ex. I could have warned him off."

I don't want to make him feel insignificant by reminding him that Jared is a were-lion and wouldn't take a blind bit of notice of a witch. I decide to brush it off. "It's sorted now. Don't worry about it."

"Yes. He won't be bothering you anymore," Emmanuel says, grinning up at me. Anyone looking at him would think he chased Jared off, not Theo.

My mobile starts vibrating in my pocket. I pull it out of my pocket and look at the screen to see a number I don't recognise. I glance at Emmanuel apologetically. His sort of smile and barely nod don't deter me from answering it anyway. It could be someone from the pride about Uncle Jack.

"Hello?" I answer warily

"Is that Rosabel?" If it wasn't for the pure fear I could hear in the person's voice, I would suspect it was a stupid telesales call.

"Yes. Who is this?"

"Wesley. Have you seen her?" He's so anxious, my empathy doesn't work over the phone but it's pretty easy to pick up from his tone. I have no idea who he is talking about.

I put as much authority into my voice as I can muster. "Wesley. You need to calm down and explain what is going on, slowly and clearly."

I can hear him take a deep breath and then the line is silent.

I give him a full minute of silence before speaking again. "Welsey. Are you still there?"

"Yes," he says, sounding unbelievably calm. It's like he's a different person to the one who called. "It's Alyssa, my mate. She's gone missing. Have you seen her?"

"I don't think so. What does she look like? I don't think I know who she is."

"MY MATE!" His yell is loud enough that even Emmanuel hears him. He reaches for my phone but I swat his hand and lean away. I can handle being yelled at by a distraught werewolf.

"Shouting at me won't help, Wes."

I can hear Theo in the background. "Who are you shouting at now, Wesley? I was sure you had scared everyone in the pack as it is."

"Wesley, put Theo on the phone. He'll be able to explain the situation better."

I hear a few noises as if the phone is changing hands, along with Wesley's muttering to himself. "My fucking mate is missing. That's the goddamn situation."

"Hello." I would recognise that gravelly voice any day.

"Hi, Theo. What does Alyssa look like and how did she go missing?" Wes doesn't seem like the type to let his mate out of his sight if he didn't think it was safe.

"Bel." He sounds surprised to hear my voice. "I told him you wouldn't know who she was, let alone what might have happened to her. She was at Misty's last night. She's about your height with long, red curly hair. Sometime during your time as being a wolf, she went to the ladies room and never came back."

"Sorry. The only time I saw her was when we came back from the office. She was at the bar with Wesley. I didn't see anything on the way home."

"I know. I followed you remember? I didn't see anything and told him as much. There was no need for him to bother you." I can hear the anger in his voice.

"It's okay, he's just worried. Do you think it could be the person that took the vamps and Paddy?" I smile apologetically at Emmanuel, assuming he must be pissed that I'm on the phone on our date. He doesn't even acknowledge my smile. He's too engrossed in my side of the conversation to notice.

"Unfortunately, it's looking that way. She wouldn't just leave and not be in touch with anyone by now. Even when they argue and she storms out she always tells him where she is going." Theo's voice is full of concern.

The waitress arrives with our food and drinks. Emmanuel tucks straight into his burger.

"God. I hope you find her." If it is the same person that took the others someone needs to do something about them. They can't be invisible. Someone has got to have seen something. I would hate to be Theo right now. As alpha, it all lands on his shoulders.

"We will find them all. I won't have it any other way! In the meantime, will you make me a promise? Ring me every hour to check in. I need to know you're safe. I couldn't bear you being taken," he says, with a voice full of honesty.

"They won't be interested in me, I'm not pack." I stab a piece of lettuce with my fork and slide it in my mouth as I listen to his reply.

"You are my mate and that makes you pack. If anyone is trying to get to me that makes you on the top of their list. The tie to Dominick could make them interested too. They've taken two of his vamps so they could be trying to get to him too. I don't like the thought of that. Maybe I should put a guard on you." The last sentence was said more to himself.

I agree quickly. "I promise. I will check in every hour."

I don't want a guard on me.

"WESLEY!" he shouts away from the phone. "Bel, I've got to go, Wesley is picking a fight, with Chloe, of all people."

"Bye," I say to the dial tone. I place my phone on the table and have a large swig of coffee.

"I'm guessing another pack member has gone missing," Emmanuel states.

I chew a mouthful of chicken before answering. "Yeah, last night. I don't know what Theo is going to do but it isn't going to be good for whoever is taking them—not when he finds them."

He turns the conversation to mindless banter as I finish the rest of my meal. The waitress collects our empty plates. "Can I get you anything else?"

I need to end this with Emmanuel—whatever *this* is.

"Another coffee, please?" I reply, with a nod.

She looks at Emanuel for his order. "Nothing for me, thanks."

I wait until the waitress places my coffee in front of me and leaves again before talking. "Look, Emmanuel. I don't know how to say this, or where to start, so I am just going to be blunt and honest, okay?"

"O-k-a-y?" He sounds wary.

"I think it would be better if we are just friends. You know about me and Theo being true mates? Well—"

He cuts me off before I can finish my sentence. "That's just your wolves. They're only a part of you. Not all of you."

"That's not how mates work, Emmanuel. We are meant for each other on all levels. We are the missing piece of each other. I didn't know any of this until yesterday. I just can't feel anything other than friendship towards you and you deserve more than that from a relationship."

He stares at me dumbfounded.

I don't know what else to say so I offer him my hand in a handshake over the table. "So…friends?"

He glances down at my hand. I can feel anger emanating from him but he takes it with a false smile. "Friends."

This is, no doubt, going to bite me on the arse later but for now, I'll take it as a win.

16.
ALLIES ATTACK

ROSABEL

As we open up at work I fill Misty in on Benji leaving, and my decision about Emmanuel. I was worried about how she'd react because he is her friend, but thankfully, she agreed that I'd done the right thing by him.

I was just going out the back door with my arms full of rubbish bags when I get hit by a wall of anger. I can't see over the bag so I use my other sense, smell. Taking a deep breath, I pick up three scents; Dominick's, Paddy's, and a female werewolf I don't recognise.

Letting the bags down as quietly as possible, I slowly creep out deeper into the alleyway. It takes me a moment to comprehend what exactly I'm seeing. Paddy and Alyssa have both jumped Dominick. Alyssa is on his back and Paddy is attacking him from the front.

Dominick grunts as Alyssa claws at his neck with her nails. He flings her off and she hits a bin with a thud. He then turns his focus on Paddy, pushing him away. I can see he's trying not to hurt them. He could easily kill them if he wasn't holding back. He isn't the King of the New South Wales vampires for nothing.

Within seconds, there are no longer three people in the

alley before me. There are two great big wolves and Dominick. They both pounce at him again, but he's still not fighting back. I watch as they both start tearing chunks out of his limbs.

I can't just stand and watch this.

I quickly remove my clothes, not wanting them destroyed as I shift. If I get through this fight in one piece I don't really want to have to walk into Misty's naked. Once my wolf comes forward, she takes me through the shift fairly quickly. I don't have time to get hung up on the pain. I need to help Dominick.

I run at Alyssa and sink my teeth into the fur on her back. I manage to pull her off Dominick, flinging her a good three feet away. I take a second to hope Dominick can handle Paddy on his own before readying myself in a crouch to pounce at her.

I watch as she mirrors my crouch. Her back legs brace to pounce only she doesn't. She freezes and just stares at me. I reach out for her emotions hoping to get some clue as to why she hasn't followed through the attack, only to feel nothing. She isn't feeling one single emotion. As I'm staring her down trying to decide what to do, she turns and sprints away.

I watch her run until she is out of sight. I don't want her changing her mind and coming back for a surprise attack while my back is turned. Happy that she isn't returning, I turn to help Dominick against Paddy, only to find Dominick in a heap on the floor and Paddy tearing at his body as if it was a delicious deer. Surely vampires don't taste *that* good. Their stink makes me gag enough I don't want to attempt tasting them.

I growl to get Paddy's attention as I stalk towards him. He'll probably think I am after his meal and defend it, taking his attention away from what's left of Dominick and focusing solely on me. We are very territorial over our food. Only once he sees me, he chooses to leave his meal and retreat in the same direction Alyssa had.

I trot over to Dominick and nudge his face with my muzzle.

"I'll be okay once I feed," Dominick mumbles.

I lick one of the wounds on his arm and regret it instantly, *bloody animal instincts*. I was correct, vampires taste as bad as they smell. I feel a grip of steel around my left flank. I turn and get a glimpse of another vampire before I am soaring through the air.

"*No!*" yells Dominick.

There is nothing I can do to stop the momentum. I hit the side of a building with a thud and a loud crack sounds in my ears as I'm propelled into darkness.

I slowly start to come around. I can hear a mumbling but can't make out what exactly is being said. I concentrate trying to recognise the voice. Dominick.

"She saved me you idiot! I'd be dead if not for her, and what do you do? Thank her by throwing her at a brick wall." I feel hands roam my body, looking for injuries.

"Sorry, boss. Look. She's waking up," says a voice I don't recognise.

"Rosabel. Can you hear me? It's Dominick." The hands on my body stop roaming to gently cradle my face.

I slowly open my eyes and find Dominick centimetres away from my face. All I can see is the deep endless pools of black that are his eyes. I know you're not meant to look a vampire in the eyes because they can take over your mind and enslave you, but I can't seem to tear my eyes away. His eyes are just so beautiful.

"You need to change back to your human form so we can see what injuries you have," Dominick says with surprising concern.

I close my eyes and try to ignore the pain in my head. I concentrate with everything I have to push my wolf back and return to my human form. Thankfully she doesn't fight and the change is fairly painless. I open my eyes and can no longer see my furry snout.

Dominick is standing with his trench coat spread out

around me. I stay tightly curled to try and hide my nakedness. He nudges a pile of clothes towards me with the toe of his shiny dress shoes.

"Here. I got your clothes. Get dressed. No one can see." I look at him with a frown, "Okay. No one except me, but I've seen it now so there is no point in turning around."

I guess he has a point.

I slowly sit up, which is not a good idea. Everything starts to spin and the nausea hits. I *need* to get dressed. I try to ignore the spinning and nausea, but have you ever tried to get dressed when the world is spinning? It is such a hard task to get your limbs into the right holes in your clothing when they won't stay still. Somehow, I finally manage to get fully dressed.

Dominick drops his arms and secures his coat once again. I see the vampire that threw me at the wall standing behind Dominick. He's tall, lanky, and wearing a neon yellow t-shirt under a black leather waistcoat with black leather trousers that leave nothing to the imagination. I'm surprised the lack of circulation doesn't cause permanent damage. His short bleached blonde hair and blue eyes remind me of Spike from the TV show Buffy. The more I stare at him, the more I realise he is attractive in his own way.

"I'm sorry about that." He shrugs, pointing to the wall that's now decorated with a nice crack in the mortar. "I thought you were attacking, Dominick."

I suddenly remember the state Dominick was in before I hit the wall. I glance at him, now standing tall and looking as strong as ever. If I hadn't just witnessed the fight and seen the state he was in, not to mention the tears in his clothing, I wouldn't believe he'd been in a fight.

"How do you look so good? You looked like death warmed up a minute ago." Realising who and what I am talking to I quickly add, "Well, you know what I mean."

Dominick looks over to where he had been in a heap on the

floor. My gaze follows his and falls upon a woman who seems to be staring at Dominick, smiling as though she is getting high just looking at him. The sight of her is quite disturbing.

I quickly look back at Dominick. "Where did she come from?"

"When Chomp saw the state I was in, he extracted her from the street." I'm guessing Lanky Leathers is Chomp. Interesting name choice.

I can't stop myself from glancing back at the woman. "Will she be okay? She looks a little…high." I couldn't think of a better word, maybe star-struck would have been more fitting.

"She's fine. It's the compulsion. I didn't have time to let her go; I needed to check on you. Chomp, you may release her now."

Chomp follows his order immediately, kneeling down in front of the woman. I watch as he turns her face from looking at Dominick, when their eyes meet she gazes at him for no longer than thirty seconds before becoming a normal person. She takes Chomp's hand, politely thanks him and walks away without a glance in our direction.

Dominick's hand appears in front of me and I reluctantly take it. I don't think I would manage to get up otherwise.

My head pounds. I put my free hand to my head hoping I can't feel my brain falling out. Satisfied it all feels normal, I pull my hand away to see it covered in blood. That means I'm not going to be able to go straight back to work. At the very least, I need a shower and change of clothes first.

The three of us walk in the back door of Misty's. Dominick is practically holding me up, my jelly legs aren't much use. Not only is Misty going to kill me for having to go home for a shower and change, but she's going to dance on my grave for bringing customers through the back door.

As we walk through the door leading into the bar, Misty catches sight of me and gasps.

"Bloody hell! What happened to you?" she asks.

The whole bar suddenly falls silent and I know without looking around, that every eye in the bar is on me. I must look as bad as I feel.

Theo comes running over from the far end of the bar.

"LET HER GO!" he yells. "What the hell did you do to her?"

"If I let go of her, she will probably fall down and I didn't do anything to her. You need to speak to some of your wolves. She wouldn't be injured if they hadn't attacked me." I hear the smugness in his voice. No doubt his face looks just as smug.

Theo gently pulls me away from Dominick and into his own embrace. "What the hell are you talking about?"

"Theo, he's right. I was there." Turning in his arms, I tell him everything that happened in the alley.

While Theo takes it all in we move to a booth, and Dominick gives us his theory. "It looks to me like your wolves have gone rogue, oh mighty alpha."

"Dammit Drake. Now is not the time for jokes," Theo chastises. "Alyssa wouldn't be able to go rogue. She's mated to Wesley. When you're mated you have that other wolf's energy connected to your own. The only way a mated wolf could go rogue is if both of them go rogue."

As if summoned by the mention of his name, Wesley charges into the bar, aiming straight for our table.

"ALYSSA! What's happened to Alyssa? Her scent is all over the two of you," he growls accusingly.

"Wesley. You're lucky they didn't do anything to her. She attacked them." Theo's voice is full of authority, making it hard to argue with.

"No. She wouldn't do that," Wes says unbelievingly, yet defeated, his Alpha wouldn't lie to him.

"Whether she would or she wouldn't, she did. We need to find out why? Go see if you can track her scent out the back. That's where it all happened. Billy, go with him," Theo orders.

Billy appears out of nowhere, but more-than-likely he was somewhere else in the bar, listening in to the conversation, like all the other wolves were.

As they exit through the back of the bar, a grief-stricken Emmanuel enters through the front doors. He glances around looking for someone. His eyes land on me, widening in horror. He barges through the pack members surrounding the table all while muttering, "I'm sorry."

Please don't let him be here to beg for us to try again. I really don't need that while my head is pounding, especially not in front of the bar full of the pack.

He crouches down beside me and reaches for my face, gently caressing my head wound.

"I just heard. You shouldn't be hurt." Turning his attention to Theo, who is still holding me against his warm body. "What good are you as her mate if you can't protect her? Let alone from your own wolves."

"Emmanuel!" I jump to Theo's defence.

"No, Bel. He's right. You should never have come to harm and from my own pack members. Forgive me," Theo says, placing a kiss on the uninjured side of my head.

"There is nothing to forgive," I say, giving him a peck on the lips and not caring who sees. "Paddy and Alyssa didn't hurt me. I can't say the same for Dominick though."

"But your head, and all the blood?" Emmanuel asks, drawing my attention back to him.

"That's my fault," Chomp admits, stepping up to the table beside Dominick. "She's lucky the new law came in saying only Dominick or Theodore can kill another supernatural being because I would have killed her otherwise."

Theo's hand, resting on my waist, gently squeezes. "I'm taking you home; you need to get cleaned up."

I look towards Misty who is still serving behind the bar. She is just hanging the phone back on the wall bracket. "I'll be real quick, Misty."

"Don't even try it. You can't work with a concussion. You're not coming back in tonight. Lucy is on her way." I return the smile she is giving me and Theo gently lifts me into his arms.

"I can walk," I complain, not sounding too convincing. I quite like being held in my mates strong arms.

"Don't argue!" he demands, making his way through the bar doors and towards his gorgeous car. He opens the car door while holding me with one arm. That's werewolf strength for you. We can bench press a car. He's not going to have trouble holding me in one arm. He places me in the passenger seat and buckles me in. I don't complain, knowing his wolf will need the reassurance.

Just as he indicates to pull away from the curb, the Bad Boys theme song starts playing. He turns the indicator off and puts the car back in neutral before reaching into his jeans pocket and taking his phone out. He answers it without looking at the screen. "Hello."

I stare straight ahead out the windscreen, trying my hardest to give him privacy and not listen in on the conversation. With my hearing I can hear the other side of the conversation, no matter how hard I try, and he knows it. His hearing is just the same.

"Theo. I'm scared. I think someone is outside." The sexy female voice on the other end of the phone makes me forget all about not listening. If he wanted a private conversation, he would end the call and ring back after he has dropped me off at home.

"Chloe. I've told you that place has the best security system invented, so even if someone is outside, they won't be getting in."

"Oh, okay. How long are you staying out? I'll feel safer once I'm not alone."

He sighs and glances at me. I don't know what he is trying to read in my face but it makes me feel uncomfortable.

I quickly turn away and look out my window.

"I'm just taking Rosabel home. I won't be long."

"Thank you. I'll see you soon," she sings through the phone.

Theo hangs up with no goodbye, putting his phone back in his pocket. Expecting him to put the car in gear and pull away from the curb I get a shock when he just sits there, rubbing a hand over his face. I feel a wave of sadness coming off him.

"Sorry about that. Some of the pack members are worried about the kidnapper. Chloe lives on her own. My home is the pack's home. They're all welcome to come and go as they please. She's staying until things become safer."

I start to feel a bit jealous, I don't like the fact that Chloe, of all people, is staying at Theo's, especially since she's the one that said she should be his mate. I hear Theo chuckle and realise the car is full of my mating scent.

Great. Could that have not been kept a secret?

"Don't worry, she's got no chance. I'm yours, remember?" He says as he leans across the console and gives me a chaste kiss. I can smell his arousal and realise he's aroused by my jealousy. His body starts releasing his mating scent too.

We both laugh because it looks like we are both as bad as each other.

17.
POTENT STEAM

THEO

I can't help but be aroused by her jealousy. When Emmanuel made the comment about me being no good because I can't protect her from my own pack members, I didn't think her wolf would forgive me. I know she said she did, but to know that she's jealous makes me believe it that much more.

This beautiful woman sitting next to me in my car is actually my mate.

Mine!

I pull back from the kiss, not too far. I might want to take her lips again in a more passionate kiss. "Tell you what, why don't you come back to mine? You can shower there and I am sure I can find some clothes for you to wear," I suggest, grinning.

"Will I need clothes?" she asks with a cheeky smile, knowing exactly what her words are doing to me.

"Be careful. I might hold you to that," I warn, unable to hold the rasp in my voice back.

It doesn't take me long to drive us home.

We walk in the door to be greeted by Chloe in a lacy number that doesn't leave much to the imagination. How dare she prance around my house wearing that? I have a mate. What does she think will come of her meeting me at the door wearing something like that?

I smell Bel's mating scent and can't contain my anger.

"PUT SOME CLOTHES ON!" I shout.

Bel squeezes the hand she is holding and rubs her thumb over the back of my hand in a calming gesture.

I quieten my voice. "I don't appreciate you walking around my home half-naked, Chloe."

She turns and storms upstairs without another word, but not before giving Bel a deathly glare.

"Well. I give her a ten for trying," Bel jokes. If she can joke about it I can calm down.

I remind myself that this is the first time Bel and I have had some time together. With people going missing left, right, and centre, we need to make the most of it. It will only be a matter of time before something comes up. Hopefully one of my guys will get a lead on the damn kidnapper because my wolf sure does want someone to pay.

I lead Bel into the one room I know we won't get disturbed in—unless it's an emergency. Let me tell you, if someone does disturb us, someone better be dying. I lead her to my bedroom. I am not wild in my paint taste. It's just a good ol' cream. I like the bed being a focal point. That's what a bedroom is all about, after all. Glancing at the bed I am grateful for the clean black satin sheets I put on this morning but I'm starting to regret bringing her in here. My wolf wants to claim her. He always wants to claim her but seeing the bed is making him ride me harder.

I close the door behind us and show her straight to the bathroom trying to ignore the bed and my impatient wolf.

"Wow. That is some spa bath," Bel says, looking at my extra-large spa bath. It takes up most of the left hand side of the room.

I shrug at her comment. "I'm a large guy and I like a big bath."

I walk over to the two-headed shower and turn it on. I renovated this bathroom after my ex left, always keeping the idea of a mate in mind. What good is a shower if you can't fit two people in it?

"I'll just get you some clothes while that warms up," I say, heading back into the room to go through my chest of drawers and find a t-shirt and some boxers that will be suitable.

I can feel Bel's eyes on me, as she watches me while leaning against the doorjamb.

Once back in the bathroom, I grab a towel from under the sink and place the items on the bench next to the sink. Steam is filling the room and my wolf is getting antsy thinking about her being naked in the shower. I can smell her arousal so I know she is thinking along the same lines as me. I need to get out of here before I pin her in the shower. I try to remind myself she has had a knock to the head. It's not the right time to be pinning her anywhere.

"I'll be just outside. If you need anything, give me a shout," I say, quickly escaping the steam and the smell of her arousal.

I pace the room, having way too much energy to sit still. I chant to myself. "You will *not* go in there."

She deserves more than a claiming in a shower.

She deserves romance and sweet gentle love making.

"You will *not* go in there."

Bel's mating scent comes out from the crack under the bathroom door.

Oh fuck it!

I can't hold back anymore.

It's time to claim my mate.

18.
VANISHING ACT

I look in the mirror and see what a mess I am. I remove my clothes, wondering why Theo wasn't aroused by Chloe when we came in. She is gorgeous, and as much as I hate her, I can't deny it.

The room fills with my mating scent. It mixes with the steam of the shower, making it even headier. I step under the shower head and close my eyes, enjoying the feel of the water running over my face and body.

I feel a slight draft and open my eyes to find I am no longer alone. My eyes hungrily take in a very naked Theo before me.

"Do you mind if I join you? I thought I could scrub your back." He reaches around me for the soap with the cheekiest smirk on his face, knowing full well from my scent there is no way I'm going to say no. I am even more turned on now by his naked body pressing against me.

I pull the bottle of shampoo from behind my back and wiggle it in front of him. "You better start from the top and work your way down."

"Of course," he remarks, as he takes the bottle and pours some into his hand.

He carefully works the shampoo into my hair so he doesn't

hurt my injured head. The shift helped it heal a little and with every minute that passes it is healing more. It will be fully healed by morning. The water turns a rusty colour as it runs down my body and into the drain.

He lathers his hands with the soap. Knowing he's going to be rubbing them over my body makes it look erotic. I bite my lip in anticipation. I don't have to wait long. His hands start at my shoulders and work their way to my chest. He bends his head and latches onto a nipple. A growl comes from deep within me. My wolf's energy pounces out of me and latches onto Theo's wolf.

Theo straightens and I follow my wolf, pouncing at him. He catches me and I wrap my legs around his waist as my hands go to his hair. The feel of his hard arousal pressing against the exact spot I want him sets me on fire. He takes my mouth with his not caring about finesse, biting my lip to gain entry.

I can't help grinding myself against him. I can't believe I am acting like a hussy, but I need him. He's my mate and I need to claim him. He spins us around and presses me against the shower screen.

Everything starts to spin and I feel dizzy. The room passes by in a blur of colours, which start to change slightly as the spinning starts to slow, until it's normal again.

Only it isn't normal, because I am no longer in Theo's arms.

As I look around the strange room I find myself in, I start to panic. The arousal I had in the shower is long gone. It's obvious by the grand heavy wood desk in the middle of the room and leather chair behind it that it's someone's office. Someone with very expensive tastes, if the magnificent wall tapestries hanging to cover the stone walls are anything to go by.

As I get closer to the desk I can see what looks like a robe with a note on top. Reading the exquisite handwriting and seeing my name I pick up the note and read the rest.

———————————

My Saviour Rosabel,

I thought you would appreciate the robe, so you could be covered before I enter.

Forever in your debt.

— DOMINICK FILIOUS DRACONIS

Of course, Dominick would be at the root of this.

Just as I am tying the robe closed the door behind me opens and Dominick barely enters the room before I start demanding answers.

"How the hell did I get here and what have you done with Theo?" I shout as I poke him in the chest.

"Calm down, my saviour. I have done nothing to your lover. He remains where you left him. All be it, he may be slightly concerned about your whereabouts." He pauses and I open my mouth to yell some more, but he carries on, "You teleported here because I called you here. I wanted to tell you that I will allow you to claim your lover, even though it will break the tie between us. Think of it as a gift for saving me tonight."

"You pompous ass! Why didn't you just leave us to it?"

"I wanted you to know it was a gift. I thought you would prefer me to do it before rather than during the afterglow," he says, with a smirk that I would love to slap off his face.

I pace away from him trying to rein in my anger. The pacing helps me think.

"You wouldn't have been able to do it after because the tie would be broken. That's why you did it now."

"Oh, Bel. It isn't the tie that enabled me to call you here. You have turned out to be a very interesting creature indeed. You see, Chomp has a very specific taste in blood. He loves a Druid and you have druid blood in your veins. As a druid you can teleport and be called upon, once you learn how to control it you will be able to choose whether or not to go when called."

"Bullshit! I don't know any druids. My parents were both werewolves." I storm back towards him.

"I know nothing of your kin, but I trust Chomp's word and to have druid blood you must have one somewhere in your ancestry."

"Fine. I'm a druid werewolf. You have informed my about the gift. Send me the fuck back. NOW!" I scream.

Dominick steps around me and casually takes a seat behind his desk. "I can't send you back, only you can do that. I *can* talk you through it though."

"Let me get this straight. You brought me here knowing I knew nothing about these druid abilities and how to harness them?" I ask in disbelief.

"You are forgetting I can teleport myself, too. It may be from a different source but essentially it is the same ability. You just have to visualise where you want to be. See every detail, smell every scent, and will yourself to be there."

I take him at his word and do as he says. Closing my eyes I try to visualise Theo's room but I'm so angry, the only thing I can manage to picture is me slogging Dominick with a good left hook.

Taking a deep breath and clearing my mind, I try again and again with no luck. My mind is now too blank.

I can do this.

I once again close my eyes and picture the steamy bathroom —the two man shower along one wall and the huge Jacuzzi in the corner. I smell Theo's scent filling the room and mingling with my own. I feel the steam in the air caressing my skin, and finally I will myself to be there.

I know I am there before I even open my eyes. I can feel the smooth slate tiles under my feet and I can actually smell Theo's scent. I can't believe it, there was no spinning this time around.

Excited to be back it takes me a moment to notice that the shower is no longer running and I'm the only person in the room.

I run through his empty bedroom and down the stairs, in a panic, screaming his name.

"THEO? THEO!"

I come to a halt as I enter the dining room, which happens to be jam packed with Theo's pack. Every head in the room turns to face me as Theo barges through the crowd wearing nothing but sweatpants. He doesn't give me long to take in the sight. He reaches me in a heartbeat and pulls me into his bare chest.

"Bel. Am I ever glad to see you. One minute you were in my arms, the next you were just…gone. I thought…" he didn't need to finish, I can imagine what he thought. *The kidnapper.* He squeezes me harder. I breathe in his scent. It feels good to be back in his arms. My wolf wants to dig her way under his skin. She wants to become part of him.

"What happened? Where did you go?" His fear fading with me in his arms, I can now hear and feel the anger behind it. So much anger, not knowing who is to blame must be hard for him. He is an alpha. He's meant to protect his people. Someone just ripped me out of his arms and he needs to punish them.

I pull back a little to look in his eyes. "Can I speak to you in private?"

I let my eyes roam the room full of pack members to get my point across. I don't really want to tell him everything I have just learned in front of the whole pack. I'm back where I started in Quilpie with Jared. I'm the odd one out again, not worthy of him. The minute they find out, they will push me out. I won't be good enough for their alpha. Some of them already think that due to my upbringing with the pride, essentially Chloe. Chloe is going to love this bit of news.

He leads me back to his room with a hand on my lower back.

Once in his room I gesture towards his bed. "You might want to be sitting for this."

He follows my suggestion without argument and I recall everything that occurred since I left his arms in the shower. I wait for him to take it all in. I start to fiddle with the hem of the robe. He's taking too long to answer. I'm going to have to walk past the pack, humiliated.

Just as I am about to go and get the clothes he was lending me from the bathroom, he speaks.

"A druid werewolf? Okay." It sounds more like a statement to himself but I answer him anyway.

"Yes. If you just give me a minute to get dressed, I'll leave." I head towards the bathroom willing to wear my blood stained clothes, as long as I can just get away quickly. I only manage two steps before he grabs my shoulder and spins me to face him once again.

"Why do you want to leave?" I can feel the worry coming off him in waves. It matches what I see in his eyes.

"I don't want to leave but I understand you will want me to. I'm part druid, I'm not werewolf enough for you," I say, as I try to pull away from his hold.

"There is nothing I want more than to throw you on that bed and make love to you. You are my mate, my other half. I always thought that was a corny thing men said to women to keep them happy, but the second I met you I just knew. It doesn't matter what you are. You were made for me. It means you are more than enough for me."

He cups my face and presses his lips against mine. My wolf pounces on that kiss, her energy pressing for more. I kiss him like it's the last kiss I will ever have. His hands move down my body to my waist. He picks me up and throws me on the bed. I bounce once before he lands over me.

Are we finally going to do this? *With the Pack downstairs.*

"But the Pack?" I say, unsure about whether we should be keeping them waiting.

He gives the tie on my robe a tug and I can feel the cool air caress my skin as I become exposed. He grins down at me. "The Pack can wait."

19.

LOYALTY

ROSABEL

*L*ying next to my mate—my well and truly claimed mate —I could easily get used to being curled into his side, stroking his chest hairs as he plays with strands of my hair. I don't think my wolf has ever felt this calm or content.

Theo's energy suddenly changes from the blissful energy that was just flowing through the both of us to something that feels like fear. Before I can break the silence to ask him about it, he clears his throat.

"I was terrified earlier. I thought the kidnapper was behind your disappearance. I ran around the house like a lunatic. When you were nowhere to be found I thought I had lost you before I'd even really had you. I have never felt like that before. I have never been that terrified. Not in battle facing death myself. Not when my father was killed, not even when I became alpha. Never." He holds me tighter against him and I squeeze back hoping to comfort him and decide to get my thoughts about the kidnapper off my chest.

We could be looking at the wrong suspect.

"I've been thinking. Why are you so sure the kidnapper is a vampire or werewolf? Couldn't it be any supernatural creature, maybe a druid or a witch?" I ask, leaning up to look at him.

"It could be a druid but we haven't had any around town for a long time. I still can't see how a witch could overpower them if they are controlling them in some way? I don't know of a spell that could do that. They would have to be channelling something dark to be able to strip people of free will. It's not a white witch power like most of the witches in town practise."

Discussing the kidnapper and the pack reminds me that they all remain downstairs. "Do you want to go and deal with your pack? We've kept them waiting a while." I giggle, picking my words carefully so as not to sound like an order. No one gives orders to the alpha.

"*Our* Pack. We are true mates. You are the Alpha female. And you're right, they have waited long enough. We should go put them out of their misery," he says, patting me on the butt.

I shift, allowing him to get out of the bed.

He pulls on the sweatpants he removed earlier and grabs a t-shirt out of a drawer. He throws another at me along with a pair of shorts. They hit me in the face and I hear Theo laugh as I breathe in the scent on his shirt.

We both pad down the stairs barefoot, hands entwined. The bond from our mating is like nothing I could ever have imagined. I can feel him deep within me, like a comfortable blanket wrapped around my soul. I'm aware of his feelings, his contentment somewhat like my own, but it's nothing like my empathy; it's more internal than that. The pack are there, too. I can't pick out any specific members but I can feel them as a whole.

We walk through the lounge with the L-shaped sofas and I glance at them longingly. Theo must notice because he stops, questioning me by just the look on his face.

"Maybe I could just stay here while you talk to the pack?"

He shakes his head and smiles. "No. You *are* Pack remember. You have to face them eventually."

"Oh, fine," I concede.

I tug his hand for him to lead me into the dining room where the pack await us. Before opening the door, he pulls me into his arms and kisses my forehead, giving me time to take a calming breath. The deep breath I take is filled with his scent; calming me even more. I love how he can read me now and know exactly what I need.

"Thank you," I say, pecking him on the lips. I reach around him and open the door.

In our absence, the pack has gathered in groups to chat. Some sit, some stand, and some lean against the furniture that is in the middle of the room. Theo stops and stands in the doorway.

Everyone turns to look in his direction, curiosity written all over their faces. We had been gone for at least an hour. I can understand their curiosity.

"Thank you for coming tonight. I apologise for the late notice and the delay," he says, addressing the pack. "The reason I called you here no longer remains. As you all can see, my beautiful mate is no longer missing."

The pack immediately starts clapping, startling me into taking a step back and banging my back against the door frame.

Wesley steps forward. "I'd like to say, on behalf of the pack, congratulations. It's an honour to have true mates as our alpha pair." He kneels before the pair of us and bows his head. "Loyalty to my pack, loyalty to my alpha pair, for as long as I may live."

Theo steps forward bringing me with him and places my hand on Wes' shoulder and places his on the other. "Loyalty to my true mate. Loyalty to *our* pack for as long as I may live," he says, giving me a nod as he glances in my direction.

I stare at him blankly. I know I should say something but I'm not really sure what. My wolf pushes to the forefront of my mind, and with her she brings the knowledge and natural instinct. The words just flow out.

"Loyalty to my true mate and *our* pack for as long as I may live."

With that, the whole room drops to their knees. "Loyalty to my pack, loyalty to my alpha pair for as long as I may live."

The feel of the pack inside me starts to pulse, and with a snap I feel it solidify. I can feel every member. I can distinguish every member even the ones I have never been introduced to. I know who is mated and who isn't.

I am pack; there is no doubt about that now.

"Rise," Theo commands. Once every member has risen he proceeds, "Now that we have dealt with the formalities it's time to get our pack members back."

The room erupts with a chorus of agreement.

"As most of you know, Paddy and Alyssa attacked Dominick Drake earlier tonight. If Rosabel hadn't discovered the attack in time Dominick would have been killed; which would have resulted in an instant war. Rosabel brought up a valid point just a short while ago. She brought it to my attention that we may be looking at too narrow a suspect pool—that a druid or witch may be kidnapping and stripping them of their free will. The fact that neither of them would attack Dominick of their own accord makes me believe that Bel just may be right.

I think the best way to find this person is to start patrols. Alyssa went missing at Misty's and this most recent attack was there too, making me believe the suspect may be connected to that area. I suggest we start there and work our way out. Since he has two wolves, I want you in groups of three. Billy, I'd like you to take the first patrol tomorrow night. Who would you like to take with you?"

Billy, the biker, steps forward in his leather trousers, a black muscle tank and heavy boots. No jacket.

Shit his jacket is still on the sofa at home.

"I'll take Phil and Darren if that is okay with you, boss?"

"Yeah. I'm happy with your choice. Phil. That okay with you?" He nods to a guy in front of us who wouldn't be my first choice.

He's tall and so thin that if a gust of wind hit him he'd snap in half. He has a dark crew cut but it's his fashion sense that makes him stand out the most. His red and blue check shirt matched with beige trousers look great, until you look at his Jesus sandals with socks.

"That's cool."

"Darren. How about you?"

"I'm all yours," says a gruff voice. Now this guy I would choose. He's freaking huge in all directions. Honestly, he must have come through the front door sideways. It looks like it is all muscle, too. His shaved head has a nice shine to it. He's wearing a navy wife-beater with white-washed jeans and what look like steel-toe capped safety boots.

"Good. I suggest all three of you meet around the back of Misty's at half past five. I'm going to speak to Dominick and see if he will send some of his guys on patrols, too. Every man helps. I'll meet the three of you when Misty's shuts. If you see anything unusual before then call it in." All three guys nod and Theo looks around taking in the rest of the pack.

"You may all leave now, but be sure to stay safe and stick in groups. Thanks again."

I step away from the door as everyone moves to file out, many stopping to say a few words to Theo on their way. A few of them even greet me with a smile and welcome me to the pack.

Theo is so attentive to his members. I smile as I watch him deal with them all. This wonderful and gorgeous guy is my mate. When I left Quilpie to find a Pack never, in my wildest dreams did I imagine finding my true mate. A guy I can actually love. It hits me like a sledge hammer as I watch him follow

Wesley and Billy out of the room whilst chatting. I have only known him a short time but I do…I love him.

I am just about to follow him when I sense someone behind me. I quickly spin around uncomfortable with a stranger at my back. I find Chloe in skinny white jeans and a fitted fuchsia pink singlet with her long blonde hair straightened to perfection, to match the perfect heavy make-up. I try not to think about what I must look like after my hair had been left to dry wild and that all my make-up washed off from my shower. I don't think any woman could help but feel slightly inferior when standing next to the beautiful Chloe.

"Looks like it's just you and me now, Rosabel. They could be a while in there chatting pack business. Maybe we should take the time to get to know each other a little?"

I know, without a doubt, I am allowed in there with Theo and the others, and as much as I feel bad to think about leaving Chloe to her own devices, I haven't forgotten how she feels about Theo and I mating. She made it perfectly clear with the outburst at the last Pack meeting—not to mention the way she greeted Theo earlier this evening.

"There you are?" Theo says, popping his head around the doorway. "I was starting to worry you might have vanished again," he adds, jokingly.

"I'm coming," I say, as I turn towards the door.

A wave of jealousy from Chloe almost bowls me over. It's so strong I actually stumble. I was right to remember where she stands in regards to me and Theo. There is no way she is going to just move aside and accept this.

Glancing back at her I decide I need to keep my enemy close. "Sorry Chloe. Maybe we can get to know each other another time. Grab a coffee and have a manicure or something?"

She looks at me, the shock is written all over her face. "S-sure that sounds good," she stutters, as I leave the room.

I find Theo and Wesley in the lounge, sitting in the same place they had been last time. It's the first time I have really looked at Wesley tonight. He looks miserable. His sadness pouring off him and filling the room.

As I sit next to him, he looks at me with a puzzled look, probably wondering why I'm sitting next to him and not Theo. I ignore his look and put my arm through his, stroking his forearm in a comforting gesture.

"We'll bring Alyssa home. She looked well tonight. She didn't have any injuries. I promise we'll get her back." I give him a reassuring smile, which he surprisingly returns.

"I know we will. Thanks, Rosabel. You really are going to be a great addition to the pack."

I stand up and kiss him on the top of his head.

Shit! Maybe I shouldn't have done that in front of Theo.

I glance up at Theo, dreading seeing the look on his face, but he's giving me a heart-warming smile.

As I sit next to him he leans into my hair and whispers in my ear, "Thank you. That's the first smile I've seen on his face since Alyssa went missing."

Billy suddenly appears with five mugs on a tray. He hands us all a coffee and places a tea on the table for himself. We all give the fifth mug a curious glance,

"I thought Chloe might be joining us. What with her staying here and all. Shall I take it up to her or just leave it here, boss?"

Theo grabs the phone out of its cradle on the coffee table and dials a number.

"Hello," Chloe answers.

"Hey, there's a coffee here for you if you want to join us?" He hangs up without giving Chloe a chance to reply.

Chloe arrives in the room so quickly she must have been in the other room still. She sits on the floor leaning next to Theo's legs.

"Thank you," she says, taking a mouthful of her drink. She

really is grateful for us letting her join us. Her emotions are so strong.

We all enjoy our coffees in silence.

Looking at Billy reminds me that I still have his jacket. "Billy. I forgot your jacket. It's still on the sofa at Misty's apartment."

"No worries, Rosabel. It's not like I really feel the cold anyway. Just leave it at the bar tomorrow and I'll pick it up."

I could try my newfound trick. I suppose now is as good a time as any. "It's okay; I'll get it for you now."

As Theo and Billy both go to protest I put my hand up to silence them. I shuffle my bum in the seat to get more comfortable making all four of them look at me with puzzled expressions.

This will be so much more fun if I don't tell them what I'm going to do.

I close my eyes, take a deep breath and concentrate on breathing in and out. When I feel totally relaxed, I picture Misty's huge lounge, the cream leather sofa in the middle of the room with Billy's jacket on the back, the wooden sideboard with the telephone and answering machine on top, the three tall floor lamps; the one next to the sofa, the one next to the sideboard and the one in the far corner by the brown suede beanbag. I feel the thick, luxurious cream carpet under my feet and smell the lavender scented candle that Misty always burns before bed.

I open my eyes and see all that I just pictured behind my eyelids. I can't believe it worked first time. I grab Billy's jacket, pulling it on. I quickly pull a pen and paper out of the sideboard drawer to write Misty a note, too.

Misty,

I'll be staying at Theo's tonight. I promise I will fill you in on everything tomorrow.

— BEL

<hr>

Leaving the note on the sideboard for her to see, I place the pen back in the drawer and step into the middle of the room. Again, I take a few deep breaths as I close my eyes. I picture Theo's two red suede L-shape sofas; one opposite the other with the solid oak coffee table between them. I feel the cold slate floor under my feet. I smell Theo's lovely scent—Billy's, Wesley's, and Chloe's, too. I open my eyes to find myself standing behind the sofa.

Billy and Wesley are both staring at me stunned.

I walk around the sofa to Billy, while sliding the jacket off and pass it to him.

"There you go, one jacket. Thanks for the loan!" I turn and sit down next to Theo. Both he and Chloe are equally stunned.

"Wow. That really was something—minus the fear," Theo says proudly, sliding his arm around me and pulling me against his side.

"I figured I might as well try my new trick out," I say, with a shrug.

Billy finally remembers how to speak. "How the hell did you do that?"

Wesley and Chloe still seem to be struggling to pick their jaws off the floor.

I suddenly realise the consequences of my actions. *I'm going to have to tell them about the druid in me.* I hope this doesn't change how Billy and Wesley feel about me. They seem to have accepted me. It can't really change the way Chloe feels. She already hates me. I look at Theo and he seems to understand the inner debate I'm having. His reassuring smile gives me the courage to bite the bullet.

"When I disappeared earlier, Dominick called me to him. I thought he was able to do it due to our tie. He informed me that I actually have druid blood in me, giving me the ability to teleport just now and earlier when Theo called the meeting, although it was Dominick controlling my dematerialising earlier, not me."

No one speaks; they just stare at me like I have two heads. I am squirming. Theo can probably tell I want to bolt.

He stares at me intently. "Don't even think about leaving!"

It's an order. I stare into his beautiful eyes. My vision blurs as my eyes fill with tears.

He gently strokes my cheek with the back of his knuckles. "Okay. Now that you're staying put, you're going to listen to me."

I can only manage to nod, being too choked up with tears to speak.

"First things first. The pack has no decision in the matter of who I choose as a mate, they will respect you whether they like you or not. Secondly I love you, druid or not." He leans forward and kisses me on the forehead, pulling me in to hug him.

Once I get my tears under control I make a move to pull away, only to feel Wes and Billy both join in on a group hug. "You are our alpha's true mate, making you our alpha female. We all stated our loyalty earlier. We have accepted you just like Theo said, druid or not," Wesley says, making his feelings clear as we all take our seats once again.

"What is wrong with you three? Are you insane? She's a druid werewolf? She can materialise wherever she wants! What else can she do? She's playing you all. Druids are dark and evil. Well, I'm not falling for whatever spell she's put you all under. I do not trust her," Chloe hollers, as she stands.

The sofa vibrates with the growl coming from deep in Theo's chest. I grab for Theo's hand to try and calm him, but before I can get a hold on it he snatches it away.

Billy speaks first—probably trying to give Theo time to calm down before he bites Chloe's head off—and I mean literally bites it off. His eyes have already gone the deep black of his wolf's. The anger filling the room is stinging against my skin.

"Chloe, not all druids are bad. There are some that focus on the dark magic but not all. Some are healers. Before you ask, no we don't know which Rosabel is but I can sense and so can you that there is nothing evil about her. You're just jealous that Theo doesn't want you as a mate. If you accept that, you might notice there are plenty of others in this pack that actually would take you as a mate and be worthy of it, too. But you are too blind to see that."

"But—" she starts to argue before Theo cuts her off.

"No buts, Chloe. You need to apologise to Rosabel and you will respect and accept her. Do you understand?" His eyes are back to his human emerald green but if she doesn't agree they won't stay like that for long. His anger is still stinging against my skin. It hasn't even gone down a notch.

"Yes, I understand. I'm sorry, Rosabel," she says, bowing her head in submission. Her tone makes it blatantly obvious that she is anything but sorry.

"Get out of my sight. I don't want to see you again until you apologise and mean it," Theo demands.

Chloe turns on her heel and short of stomping her foot like a child, storms off.

"I'm sorry." The disappointment is clear in his voice.

"You don't need to be sorry. Like Billy said, Chloe wants you and no matter what or who I am, I don't think she will ever like me."

"Theo, I'm going to head off, if that's okay?" Wesley stands, looking at his feet.

"Goodnight," Theo snaps. *I think someone is still grouchy.*

Wesley walks out of the room and we hear the front door open and close.

I quickly jump up, realising that if I was in his shoes, there is no way I would want to go to an empty home with Alyssa missing.

Just as I rush past Theo I sense his concern. "I'll be back in a minute," I shout, running out the front door, hopeful of putting his mind at rest.

"Wesley. Where are you planning on going?" I ask, just as Wesley is unlocking his car door.

"I don't know. Our house is going to be so quiet and empty without Alyssa." He stares off into the distance with glazed-over eyes.

He isn't going anywhere.

"Lock your car! You're staying in one of Theo's spare rooms. If he can let Chloe stay, even after he got so mad at her, I'm sure he won't mind you staying! Come on. Let's go find you a room."

He locks the car and takes the hand I offer him as we head back into the house. I lead him up the stairs that are off to the left of the front door. They lead to the wing that Chloe is staying in. *At least I think they do.*

We reach the top of the stairs that lead into a narrow corridor. The walls are white with no photos, paintings or windows, just doors spread about seven metres apart on the left, and three doors right next to each other on the right wall. The first door on the left has some very strong anger seeping out so I think it's safe to assume that's the room Chloe is staying in. The three doors to the right must be some sort of storage; I'm guessing linen cupboard, since they're right near the spare rooms.

Once we reach the next door on the left, I open it door and find a larger room than I expected. It's been painted in a lovely lemon colour, which makes me smile. It's a happy colour. There is a king-size brass bed opposite the door with a window on either side of the headboard. It's neatly made with white satin sheets and has a lemon knitted blanket folded at the foot. There is a white painted chest of drawers against the left wall and hanging above that is a beautiful painting of a view of a sunset off the top of a mountain. *I will have to ask Theo where that was painted. That is a place I would love to visit.*

I check the bathroom for towels, toilet paper, and soap. "Is this room okay for you, Wes? Chloe is in the room next door. You don't want move further down the hall do you?" I say, knowing he can hear me from where he is sitting on the bed.

"No. This room is fine. I can ignore her," he replies. I can hear the smile in his voice.

Not finding any towels in the bathroom I head back out to what I hope is a linen cupboard in the hall. If I am wrong, I might have to ask Chloe where the spare towels are. *I really don't want to talk to her, if I don't have to.* Thankfully my guess is correct. I take a couple towels back to the room and place them on the end of the bed.

"There's a couple towels; if you need more there is plenty in the cupboard out in the hall." He probably already knows all of this, no doubt having stayed over before.

"Thanks, Rosabel, for everything. You are going to make a great alpha female," he praises.

"You're welcome. I am sure Theo would have offered you the room himself if he wasn't so worked up about Chloe. Now. You get some sleep so we can find Alyssa tomorrow."

20.

HEART TO HEART

THEO

Having heard Bel enter the house again a few minutes ago, I decide to go track her down. I know Chloe is down at the front of the house. I don't want her to be causing any trouble while I'm not there. I know Bel would be able to handle herself against Chloe. She has lived through numerous duels after all, but Bel doesn't need the hassle or guilt if she injures Chloe.

I head towards the front of the house with Billy following behind. It doesn't take me long to realise that I made the right decision. I can clearly hear Chloe and Bel at each other's throats.

"Are you threatening me?" Chloe demands. I have no doubt that she probably threatened Bel first.

"I hope there aren't any threats being thrown around in my house," I command from the bottom of the stairs. Neither of them could have heard me approach because I watch helplessly as they both stumble around at the top of the stairs, grabbing opposite walls to steady themselves.

"Theo you surprised us both so much we nearly toppled down the stairs one after the other. You might have had two dead women to deal with." Bel chuckles nervously. The fear I can feel in her makes me think she very nearly did do just that. I should have been more careful. They were in a heated discussion. Of course, they wouldn't have heard me.

"Sorry," I grumble, still thinking about what I could have caused.

"There are no threats here, are there Chloe?" Bel asks as she glares at Chloe. She can no doubt sense that I can't handle much more tonight before my wolf comes out to play.

"No," she replies, before going into her room and slamming the door.

Bel jogs down the stairs to join us by the front door.

"Night, Rosabel. I'm going now! I'll probably see you tomorrow at Misty's," says Billy.

"I have the night off, so maybe not. Then again, I can't seem to keep away from that place so you're probably right," she says, with a laugh.

I open the door and my laugh falls flat when I spot Wes' car. "I thought Wes left. Why is his car still here?" I give Bel a questioning look.

"Oh, yeah. Erm...you were mad, but I didn't think you'd mind. He's in the lemon room. He didn't want to go home without Alyssa. He wouldn't have been able to handle the emptiness. I'm sorry," Bel rambles, with her head bowed in submission. She is my mate. She doesn't need to show me submission like that.

I tilt her chin up with my hand until her worried eyes meet my stare. "Thank you." I pause, not hiding how mortified I am. "I can't believe I didn't think of that. What kind of an alpha does that make me?"

I shouldn't be allowed to call myself Alpha if I can't even care for my pack members like I should.

"Come on, boss. You have a helluva a lot on your mind at the minute. You were furious when Wes left. You had Chloe's shit in your head and fighting your wolf wasn't helping you with being considerate and compassionate," Billy says.

I catch the worried expression he throws Bel's way. I know what that expression means. The last thing the pack needs is the alpha to be feeling weak. It will cause the whole pack to weaken. The pack is weak enough at the moment. I need to find them. We can't go on without clues much longer.

Bel's voice brings me out of my internal musing. "Billy is right, Theo. I only thought of it because of my empathic ability. I could feel Wesley's emotions. I couldn't let him leave feeling like that."

Billy looks at Bel, clearly astonished. "You're an empathetic, druid-blooded werewolf?"

We all laugh.

"Let's just say I'm unique!"

I gaze at her admiringly. "You certainly are, but in a good way."

"Right. I'm off before Little Miss Unique Wolfy here decides I'm not fit to leave and sends me to the pink room," Billy jokes as he steps out the door.

I laugh. "Have no fear; Chloe is in the pink room."

We both stand and watch as Billy walks to his bike, straddles the saddle as he turns it over and speeds off down the drive.

As I lead Bel back to the lounge I can feel her energy changing by the second. She is worried about something, no longer laughing and joking. I can't leave her to worry like that. We are mates now. She has me to talk things through with.

"What are you thinking about? You feel sad and worried." I sit on the sofa opposite her. She seems to be staring into space and my question jolts her back to the here and now. She looks around the room as if she doesn't even remember getting here. She stands up and picks up the tray with the mugs from earlier on it.

"Do you mind if I make another coffee?" she asks. Not exactly what I was hoping for, maybe the coffee will relax her enough to talk to me.

"Go ahead. Help yourself." I watch as she goes into the kitchen to make her coffee.

I have a bad feeling that she is trying to delay something and, from what her feelings through our bond is telling me, I'm not going to like where this conversation is going.

She walks back to the sofa with two mugs, placing one in front of me and then sitting down opposite me again. "I don't know how you take it or even if you wanted one. I hope it's okay."

"I'm not fussy. It'll be fine," I say absentmindedly, as I reach through our bond hoping for some insight into her thoughts.

"You regret what happened between us earlier?" I ask. "Upstairs?" I quickly clarify. I can't stop the sadness escaping me. The bond might not be telling me what exactly she is thinking, but her regret and sadness are coming through loud and clear.

She takes a calming breath before speaking. "Yes, in a way I regret it, but not because I didn't enjoy it, or want it, or because I don't think we are true mates. We are, I *know* that. I love you, Theo. I want to be able to do what we just did every night. I want to be able to wrap my arms around you and fall asleep cuddling you like my personal teddy bear." She stops to catch her breath and I take the opportunity to ask the most important question.

"But we can do that, every day. So why regret it? I can feel it's the truth you speak, but I can feel your regret too. I don't understand why you regret it?"

"Please. Let me finish. It might take a while but when I'm finished you'll understand, I promise." Her begging does me in. I nod for her to carry on, imitating zipping my mouth locking it with a key. I lean over the table to pass her the imaginary key.

Her laugh is magic to my ears. It wipes the sadness from the room, if only for a second. "Thank you," she says, just before the sadness creeps back in. "Okay, the reason I regret it is because it has complicated things. It's made this conversation and decision so much more painful." Her eyes fill with tears but she doesn't break down. She steels herself and carries on. "When I started seeing Jared, we were eighteen and totally besotted with each other." She chuckles and I can't help but frown wondering what her past with Jared has to do with now.

"His pride wouldn't accept me. Jared wasn't leader, but he would be. One day his father would step down and he would takeover. The pride loved him. He had a happy life. When I came along it all changed. I'm not a lion. I'm a wolf—a predator. That makes me a threat. I came here to find people like me and I really thought I had found that in you and your pack. But I'm not just a wolf like you. I'm druid as well and that makes me a threat again. Chloe, and no doubt some others of your pack will feel that way."

I open my mouth to speak but remember my promise to allow her to finish, so I close it without speaking.

"We were together for six years and not a week went by without one of us being challenged. As besotted as we were, he would only end up resenting me for turning his happy life into a constant battle. You know his feelings haven't changed; he is still as besotted as that first day we met. Having to fight day after day made us miserable, we couldn't enjoy each other. I finished with him in the end because he deserved better; to find a mate that the pride accepts. At first I thought they would give in and accept me, but I was kidding myself. I got over him. I guess knowing now that I have a true mate made it easier. I loved him but maybe I was never really in love with him, especially not as much as he was with me. I knew he would never accept us not being together, that is why I left Quilpie. I thought once he knew it was over and that I had left with no trace for him to follow, he'd move on. But we both know I was wrong."

"I still love him but in a sibling capacity, like I love Benji. You met Benji, didn't you?" she asks, looking at me with her sad eyes.

I nod, but again, I don't speak. I need her to get to her point.

"I can't live like that again, Theo. Challenge after challenge. I'm not going to be the cause of your pack's destruction. I'm not destroying your life, Theo—not yours. You deserve so much more. You deserve love and if we end this before it starts now, you'll get that. There are plenty of people in this town that would jump at a date with you. One of them is upstairs in the pink room." She stops talking as the tears stream down her face.

I can't hold my tongue anymore, whether she has finished or not.

"But what about you, Rosabel? Don't you deserve the love you want—the love that wants you?" I make my way to her, kneeling before her and holding her shoulders in each hand. "It won't be like that with us. I am alpha, it *will* be different." I give her a pleading look, hoping she can feel the hope I am sending through our bond.

I see it in her face as she rides my hope but within a second it's gone and the tears come thicker and faster. "Chloe has already challenged me, Theo. We've been together properly, what, a couple of hours? And the challenges have already started. That's the first of many. I could feel the hatred towards me in that meeting and it wasn't all coming from Chloe. Once news of my druid blood comes out there, will be more that won't accept me."

The hope I had disappears instantly. If this is what she really wants I need to accept defeat. I'm her mate and I can't even make her happy.

"You're right, but they won't all challenge you. Only a few of the more dominant will. The submissives will accept defeat and welcome you. Don't forget some of the most dominant already accept you, like Wes and Billy. You said Chloe has already challenged you. What did she say exactly?" Even I can hear the hope creep back into my voice.

"She said you might have mated with me but she'll make sure you change your mind and I'll get thrown out. And when that happens, killing me will be right at the top of her to-do list." Threatening death is a challenge no matter when you plan on doing the deed. Chloe has challenged her. There is no getting away from that unless Chloe revokes the challenge.

"Chloe is strong," I say, pulling her close as my concern gets the better of me. Earlier I had thought Bel could handle Chloe without a problem, but that doesn't mean she won't get hurt in the process. Chloe is one of the most dominant females in our pack.

Bel pulls away with a laugh. "You think she'll beat me!" she says, sounding astonished.

"Like I said, she's strong. She's on par with Billy and she often likes to bring it up. I'm not sure who would win between the two of them. It would be close."

She grins from ear to ear. "If she really is as dominant as you think, we could make this work." Having no idea what she is getting at I frown.

"You and me, a couple," she adds. I feel my smile mirror hers.

"What are you planning?" I ask a little dubiously.

"We will have to take it slow. Don't force me on the pack like you have been. No more meetings. I know they've already officially accepted with the words but they need to feel it, too. I can feel through the pack bonds they don't all feel what they said. They need to get to know me as just Bel, fellow pack member, not alpha female."

"But what about Chloe and her challenge?"

"She said she will kill me. I have to take it as a challenge. But that might help us if she is as dominant as you say. If I win, others won't be willing to challenge me. So we fight." She shrugs nonchalantly.

"Yes, that will work." I cringe at the excitement I can hear in my voice. I sound like a kid on Christmas Day.

I move my hands to cradle her face and lean in to kiss her. My mouth brushes against hers as my tongue licks at the seam of her lips. She grants me entrance by parting her lips slowly. Her hands grip the hair at the back of my neck before she pulls away, leaving us both gasping for air. Our arousal is thick in the air. I stroke her cheek with my thumb, unable to keep my thoughts away from sadness and worry.

"What are you thinking about? You look sad and you shouldn't—not after that kiss," Bel queries.

I drop my eyes to the floor. "That I am in love with you, Rosabel, I have only just found you and I don't want to lose you to Chloe."

She mirrors my movements from earlier, tilting my chin so my eyes meet hers, stroking my cheek with her thumb. "I am dominant and I am strong. I have duelled and beaten stronger than Chloe. If I went up against Wesley I wouldn't be able to bet on a winner, but Chloe I can handle."

I struggle to keep the shock off my face. "Really?"

"Yes! I'll beat Chloe, trust me," she says confidently.

21.

TAKEN

ROSABEL

We both pull away to look at our watches when the doorbell rings. *It's four in the morning, who would be at the door at this time?* I glance up at Theo who looks just as uncertain as I feel.

We both walk to the door. Before opening it, we both close our eyes, trying to sense who it is on the other side.

"I can't smell any scent through the door. It's too thick. They don't feel like Pack, familiar but not Pack." Theo confirms my own thoughts.

"Whoever it is they're scared, hurt, and female—young too," I say, using my empathy.

Unlocking the door, he opens it cautiously.

A girl that looks about sixteen, give or take a year, pounces at Theo shouting, "Ted." between sobs. She throws her arms around him and hangs off his neck. She is just a bit shorter than me—although Theo isn't tall, she is hanging a good ten inches off the floor. Theo is hugging her in return so I relax, assuming he must know her.

As I take her in, I see a similarity in her. Her long ringlets down to her waist are the same colour as his and her eyes are the same shape only more sage green not emerald. I can see a nasty looking bruise on her right cheekbone.

"Rubes, what's happened? Why are you here?"

She lifts her head and looks up at him giving him full view of the bruise.

The anger leaves him in such a strong wave that it actually knocks my feet from under me, leaving me sprawled on the floor like an idiot.

"That bastard!"

She buries her face into his chest and sobs even more.

"Theo, she needs some ice on her cheek. Have you got any?" I get up and shut the door, hoping to calm him by making him realise he needs to care for her, not get angry at someone who isn't even here.

He pulls her against his side, leading her to the kitchen.

I can feel Wesley following behind me. "You okay, boss?" He sees the girl then, "Ruby? Hi."

She turns to look at him, but before she replies he sees her bruise.

"Oh shit! Are you okay, sweetie?" He strides over to them. By the feel of his anger, I'm guessing the whole pack would be willing to rip someone to shreds for Ruby.

Ruby sits on the counter top in silence with the ice pack pressed to her cheek and the two men hovering in front of her like bodyguards.

I walk over to Theo and touch the small of his back with my fingers. He must have been somewhere else with his thoughts because the touch catches him by surprise. He spins around on his heels and the anger in his eyes terrifies me so much I take an involuntary step back.

Never back down too easily from a werewolf.

They find it fun and will probably tear you apart!

"I'm sorry. I didn't mean to surprise you," I practically whisper.

He shakes his head like trying to shake a vision from his sight.

"I'm going to head home. You're busy and we have sorted our problem. It's my night off tomorrow but you know what I'm like. I'll be at the bar anyway just on the other side of it for a change." I stand on my tiptoes and kiss his soft lips with a gentle brush of mine. He returns my kiss and I pull away smiling. "I know you are going to be busy so I'll understand if you can't make it to the bar. Don't worry."

He nods and turns to Wesley. "Wes. Can you give Bel a lift home?"

"I'll go 'teleport' in the other room," I remind them both with a grin before Wes can reply.

I walk into the dining room and close the door behind me. Closing my eyes, I picture my room at Misty's and open them to find I am there. *This teleportation is getting easier with each attempt.*

The room feels empty and lonely without Theo. He's my mate I should be with him. I'm missing a vital piece of myself when he isn't around. At least I know where he is. I don't know how Wes is managing with Alyssa missing.

I go to the bathroom but decide to skip changing into my pyjamas. I climb into bed in Theo's shorts and t-shirt so I can fall asleep feeling safe and secure as I breathe in his scent.

A startled cry wakes me up. I instantly dive off the bed into an attacking stance before even opening an eye.

"I'm sorry. I got ya note. I thought ya'd be at Theo's? I've just done some washing, I was going to put these clean clothes on ya bed. Ya scared the crap outta me," Misty says, clutching at her chest with an armful of folded clothes.

I quickly straighten up and sit back on the bed. "I forgot

about the note. I only got back just after four, I should have left you a new note."

I look at the little alarm clock on the table next to the bed, it's one o'clock in the afternoon. I can't believe I slept eight hours straight, I usually get up at least once to use the bathroom through the night.

"Thanks for the washing," I add, as she places the pile on the end of the bed.

"I've just made a fresh pot of coffee. Do ya want me to bring you a mug?" she asks, turning to leave the room.

I stand up and head for the bathroom. "No, thanks. I'll be out in a second. I'll just get changed and join you." I really don't want to change out of Theo's clothes. They're a comfort to my wolf, but I need to act like a normal human being and not be hung up on someone's scent, mate or not.

It doesn't take me long to get washed and changed, and find myself walking into the kitchen.

Misty greets me with a steaming mug of coffee, and a bacon and egg sandwich.

"Thanks, Misty. Do you realise you'll never get rid of me if you keep spoiling me like this?" I joke.

"That's my point. I don't want ya to leave. I love your company. Now tell me everything." Misty loves gossip.

Who am I to keep of it from her? I fill her in on everything that happened after I left work last night.

"Wow. Nothing is boring when you're around, is it?" We both burst into laughter at how true her statement is. I've been here only a short time, yet so much has happened. I'm turning into quite the drama magnet.

"Do ya think he'll meet ya at the bar later?"

"I'm only guessing that Ruby is his sister, but the state she was in when I left, I don't think he'll leave her home alone to come and see me," I reply. If I was in his shoes I wouldn't leave her.

"Ya said Chloe was staying at his. She might be happy to keep Ruby company for an hour or two."

I laugh at that comment. "Did you hear me when I mentioned that Chloe challenged me because she wants Theo for herself? There is no way she would make my life that easy."

Before we know it, it's time to get ready for work. Even though I'm not working I decide to go in with Misty and help her open up.

As soon as the customers enter she demands that I get on their side of the bar. I'll comply for now but if it gets too busy I'll be jumping over to help out.

Emmanuel comes in and sits on the stool to my left. As awkward as I feel, it's a small town and we need to be civilised with each other.

"Hi. How has the last twenty-four hours treated you?" Emmanuel asks, breaking the silence. *Was it really only in twenty-four hours? It feels like days.*

"Hectic. How about you?" I ask.

"Yeah. It's been pretty busy for me too."

I feel a hand on my right shoulder. "How's our Little Miss Wolfy doing?" I didn't need to look to see who the voice belonged to. The scent and accent, along with the pack bond, told me it was Billy.

Evidently Emmanuel did have to look and he gives Billy such a glare that I think if looks could kill a were, Billy could possibly be dead right now.

"I'm fine thanks, Billy, but I thought I was Little Miss *Unique* Wolfy? Am I not unique anymore?" I pout.

"Don't be silly." He chuckles. "You'll always be unique. It was too much of a tongue twister for me."

"So. Are you here to tell me that Theo is standing me up?"

Panic crosses his face. "No, no. He's just running late. He's outside talking with Dominick, trying to persuade him to send some of his men to help us out. He's not too keen but I don't blame him. They are the ones that keep getting attacked, we are just the ones that get kidnapped and controlled." He rolls his eyes.

Realising I have just made it sound like Theo is my new boyfriend in front of Emmanuel, I turn to make sure I haven't upset him, only the stool is empty. I look around the bar but he is nowhere in sight.

Billy looks at the stool too and shrugs before sitting on it himself. "Weird guy!"

Misty comes to a stop in front of us. "What do you two want to drink?"

"I'll just have a bottle of something low-strength, thanks Misty. I'm patrolling and Theo won't be happy if I do it drunk. What do you want, Wolfy?" He looks at me with such a serious face.

I burst out laughing. "Little Miss too much for you now?" I shake my head at his laziness, "I'll have a Cosmopolitan, thanks."

"Coming right up." Misty turns to the mixing area to make my drink.

"How come you have a night off anyway? You only worked half a night last night?" Billy asks.

"I know. I'm such an unreliable employee. Misty has a heart of gold. She still thinks I deserve a night off." Misty places our drinks in front of us.

"Keep the change," Billy says, handing Misty some notes.

Misty gives him a flirtatious smile, which he returns. *I think I may have a cupid-style job coming up in the future.*

Billy finishes the bottle in two swigs. "I better get off. It's time to meet my men." He gets up and kisses me on my cheek before turning and walking towards the door.

I suddenly get a bad, gut feeling deep within me. I don't know what it is that unsettles me but I don't think tonight is going to be without violence. "Billy?"

He spins around to look as he pushes the exit door open. "Angel?"

"Be careful." I give him a smile, which he returns with a confident one.

"I will...*Shit!*" I watch his face change from confident to pure fear.

"What's wrong?" I shout. I can feel it deep inside the pack bonds. Something is seriously wrong.

"Trouble," he says, running out the door. He moves so fast I don't even see him leave, not even a blur. His voice just comes from the empty air.

I only sit there for a second wondering what to do before deciding to follow. I'm a werewolf and I have a pack now. That pack is in danger and I need to do anything I can to help.

I don't make it two steps before Dominick falls in the door. "Rosabel they took Theo and killed Chomp," is all he manages to spit out before collapsing in a heap on the floor.

A female vampire rushes in after him shouting. "Someone needs to feed him! He'll die without the blood." Not one person in the bar steps forward to offer their blood. They all just stare at Dominick's lifeless body in silence.

"Misty, ring Wesley. Tell him they've taken Theo and he'll need to call a pack meeting. We have to find them!" *Listen to me being all calm and rational. I'm usually the rambling mess in an emergency.*

Unwilling to let Dominick die, I walk over and put my wrist towards his mouth, only to have his female vampire push it away. "You're a werewolf. He can't feed from you. You're alpha won't allow it. He'll retaliate with war."

"That alpha is my mate. He'll understand my decision."

"You are the 'saviour' he talks about? You taste too good and he won't be able to stop. He'll end up draining you. He'll never forgive himself, or me."

"You said he'll die if he doesn't get fed. Your compulsion

won't work in here and no one is willing to offer. You won't be able to drag anyone off the street in through those wards. Their hearts will give up before you get them in. I'm not letting him die so I'll have to take the risk of him draining me." I put my wrist to his mouth but he's so far gone that he doesn't do anything. He needs to taste the blood before he'll drink.

I shove my wrist into the female vampire's face. "Bite me so he can taste the blood."

She looks uncertain for a split second but she leans forward and I feel her fangs pierce my skin. *Fuck it hurts!*

She's looking directly at me but isn't pulling away. She isn't drinking either. I look into her eyes. "Dominick will die you need to release my wrist. NOW!" She immediately follows my command.

I rest my wrist on Dominick's mouth once again. He's still not reacting to the blood. *Please, don't let it be too late.*

"Dominick. Come on babe you need to feed." I can't suppress my panic. "You're getting five star here. Feed dammit!"

My eyes fill with tears as I start to give up, when I suddenly feel his mouth close against my wrist and his fangs pierce the skin again. He starts to pull at the vein and as much as it hurts, it's the best thing I've ever felt because it means he's going to live. I'm not sure why him living bothers me so much because I don't really know him. I shouldn't care, but for some reason I do. He's only been feeding for a minute or two but I'm starting to feel dizzy!

Shit! She was right!

He is going to drain me!

"Dominick, you've had enough, you need to stop now!" I shove at his face with my free arm.

Fuck!

I have black spots dancing before my eyes, the spots are getting bigger by the second.

"Dominick, you greedy bastard. You're KILLING ME!" I scream. Managing to keep my eyes open long enough to see Dominick's eyes open. I catch a glimpse of recognition cross his face and I feel him release my arm as I fall to the floor.

"Rosabel, I'm so sorry." I can hear Dominick repeat it over and over, again his voice is getting more distant. Focusing solely on his voice pays off. It slowly becomes louder.

"Someone get her some orange juice," he demands. "She needs fluids and sugar."

I don't hear anyone move but when I open my eyes there is a glass of juice being held in front of my face. I sit up slowly leaning against someone's leg as the hand holding the glass carefully feeds me.

When I've drained the glass, I look up to see that it's Dominick's hand. He passes it back to the female vampire.

She takes it away and before I can blink she's back with the glass full once again.

Taking it in my hand this time I realise too late that I should've made him feed off my left wrist, the glass drops to the floor because my hand is drained and sore. As I watch the glass fall, I thank the gods I'm a quick-healing werewolf. I don't think a human would've survived that feed. I was too close to death.

Dominick catches the glass a second before it smashes on the floor.

"I am so sorry, Rosabel." I can see the regret in his eyes, hear it in the tone and feel it in his emotions. With vampires being dead, I would have never thought they would feel emotions like humans. I always thought emotions were for living things, but I guess I've just been proved wrong.

He points his finger at the female vampire. "You should have never let her feed me, Patsy. I nearly killed her and you should have known that was a strong possibility." He may be chastising her with his words but there's no conviction behind them. I think he blames himself more then he blames her.

"I told her not to—"

I quickly cut her off. "She tried to stop me. If anyone is to blame, it's me. No one else offered and I wasn't going to just stand by and watch you die."

"What? You were willing to die to save me?" He actually sounds touched.

"To be honest, not really. I didn't think you would actually drain me, especially if you knew it was me but you were so out of it, I couldn't make you see what you were doing. It was a close call."

Too damn close.

"You're not just a Lone Wolf anymore, you have a pack. You could've stood by and done nothing. Thank you for having enough faith in me to risk your life."

"I couldn't live with myself if I allowed someone to die if I could save them, but thanks for not killing me."

We are still sitting on the floor, directly in front of the door when Billy runs in and stumbles over us.

"What the hell? I left you for five minutes and you manage to get yourself in trouble?" he says, as he shakes his head.

I open my mouth to explain but he cuts me off before I can get a word out.

"There isn't time to explain. I've come to let you know that after I felt Theo's pain and left here, I followed his scent for five blocks, but the napper must've somehow managed to totally erase it after that point because it just stopped dead in the middle of the path. I couldn't pick it up again. So, what do you want me to do now?"

"Why are you asking me?" I ask, frowning.

"You're Theo's mate, which means you, my dear, are in charge until he gets back."

"Wesley is his second. Shouldn't he be in charge? He'll know better than me what to do," I retort back.

"No. Theo is just missing, which leaves you our alpha female and the highest ranking pack member. If he'd died, Wes would automatically become Alpha until someone challenges him for the position," Billy explains.

"But the Pack don't really know me. How can I expect them to take—or even respect—my orders?"

"They will do it for respect to Theo! What do we do now?" he asks.

How the hell should I know? I have never even been in a pack before, let alone led one.

"Misty has already called Wesley. I assume he will be organising a meeting to make a plan of action."

"Sounds like a good place to start to me," Billy praises me.

"If you could help organise that I'll get Dominick's side of the story and meet you there. I assume it'll be at Theo's still? If not, I'll need a lift because I won't be able to teleport there."

"Theo's place is pack headquarters. We'll all gather there. I'll check in with Wes and see what he needs me to do. Tell him to pull the pack together. I'll spread the news in here on my way out." He offers me his hand to stand, which I happily take because I've realised I'm still on the floor leaning against Dominick's leg and start to feel silly for being here.

"Catch you in a bit," I say.

I stand and look around for the first time since Dominick fell in. I suddenly notice everyone is frozen. "Wait a minute. Why is everyone frozen?"

Dominick, Patsy, and Billy all look around just as shocked as I am.

"I did it," says Misty, as she walks out from behind the bar. "I thought it would be better to freeze them, than having the werewolves trying to stop you feeding him," she adds, when none of us say anything.

"Good thinking," Dominick praises her with great sincerity. If she did it early enough no one will have seen him nearly kill me.

"That's a cool trick. What else have you got up your sleeve?" I joke, as Misty laughs she clicks her fingers and everyone unfreezes and acts like nothing happened. *I hope no one looks at their watch and wonders where the time went.*

"Okay. Now everyone is moving again. I'll go start organising things. See you in a little while." Billy doesn't wait for me to reply, he just walks off. I watch him tap a few people and lip read him saying three words. "Pack meeting now!" Once he's given the order, they immediately leave and he moves onto another pack member.

I feel bad for Misty. All her customers are leaving. Where are all the witches when you need them? Oh, that's right, there is one out there somewhere controlling the werewolves. I have no doubt about it being a witch now. Not one pack member would attack Theo unless they weren't in control of their own actions.

Dominick, Patsy, and I find an empty booth near the wall. Patsy gets in one side and Dominick sits next to her, leaving the seat opposite for me. Unfortunately, it leaves my back to most of the room. I shuffle into the corner and sit against the wall. I can see anyone approaching. Just as I get comfy, I spot Misty walking over with a bottle of bourbon in one hand and three glasses in the other.

"Hey. Thought ya might need this to calm ya nerves. It's on the house," she says, placing the bottle and glasses on the table.

"Well, thank you very much, Misty. Although, I'd rather you let me pay since you are losing your customers to a pack meeting," Dominick says, taking a couple of notes out of his pocket and tucking them into Misty's jeans pocket.

"Thank you, Dominick." She has a strange sparkle in her eye as she smiles at him, along with the flirtatious smile she gave Billy earlier; makes me think there's going to be a love triangle happening sometime soon. She heads back to the bar but when she gets a couple of steps away she glances back at Dominick over her shoulder.

We really don't have time for romance at the minute.

"Dominick. What happened outside?" I ask, making him tear his eyes away from Misty's direction.

He opens the bottle and fills all three glasses before answering me. "Well, as you know, Theo arranged to meet me. We were standing out the front and Theo was asking if I could send some of my men on the patrols with his wolves. I wasn't too keen because it would put my men in danger of attack. The wolves are getting taken but seem to be in good health. We hadn't been alone long; Billy left us to see you." He's staring off into the distance as if he is picturing the scene.

"He was trying his hardest to persuade me when we were ambushed. Neither of us fought back. Theo tried to command them to stop but he just couldn't get through. He didn't want to hurt them because he knew they weren't in control. It was then the lion jumped on me. I didn't see anything else. I had to fight back, it was me or him."

"Did you just say a lion jumped you?" There is only one lion I know of in town and that is Jared.

"Yes. It looks like he's controlling your friend too…Jared, wasn't it?"

I nod in agreement and take a mouthful of my drink as I let him carry on.

"Chomp sensed my distress and joined us in the fight. There was one fighting each of us but no matter how much I injured Jared he didn't act like he felt it. I don't know if it was just because they weren't in control, or if he's got some protection on them and they can't actually be injured. I never saw any blood on them. I'm Chomp's maker. When he died, I felt it. It was then that Jared left me, which turned out for the best because I wasn't far off death myself, as you saw. I just saw them drag Theo away. He looked like he was in a bad state. He wasn't moving. I can't tell you if he is dead or alive." He looked really concerned. "That's when Billy came out and I fell in."

"He's alive," is all the lump in my throat would allow me to say. He has to be alive. Besides, I would have felt it if he'd died.

Dominick pulls me away from my thoughts. "I guess we now need to come up with a plan to find them. Billy said the scent was gone so tracking is no good."

"*We* need to find out who is controlling them? I can tell a liar through my empathic ability but I can't interrogate every witch in town." I pause a second to think. "They have attacked you twice, so it's safe to say they want you dead. Do you know a witch that hates you enough to want you dead?"

Dominick laughs, spraying the table with the mouthful of bourbon he'd just had. "A number of people want me dead, Rosabel. Not everyone is as nice to me as you are."

"You saw for yourself that no one would offer to save him," Patsy adds.

"What if we set them up?" They look at each other then back to me, without saying a word. I explain the plan that just popped in my head. "It's safe to say they won't attack again tonight. He's got too much to deal with. Theo being injured is going to cause him some problems. If he was just another pack member he'd maybe be okay, but Theo is Alpha and no one can control an injured alpha. You need a stronger alpha or to lock him up until he starts to heal and calm down. He'll probably try again tomorrow night. Theo should be calmer by then. We need to set a trap."

They look at each other for a minute. It almost looks like they are having a silent conversation. *It's actually making me feel out of place.*

"What kind of trap?" I can tell from Dominick's emotions he's uncertain about something.

"We'll have to use you as bait." I look at Dominick hoping he doesn't disagree; he nods for me to carry on. *A good sign.*

"If you hang out in the back alley, make it look like you're meeting Wesley to plan what we're going to do next. I don't think he'll understand pack politics enough to know Wes isn't acting leader. Obviously we'll have pack members, and whichever of your men, there, watching from a safe distance—close enough to jump in when they attack, but far enough away to not be spotted beforehand. Paddy, Alyssa, and Jared shouldn't be able to pick up any scents because they're not in control of their own actions. They won't be thinking anything but what the controller is telling them; which will be to kill you. The controller has to be at a good vantage point with a clear view so he can see what's happening. My guess is a roof or fire escape of one of the surrounding buildings. As soon as the controlled wolves arrive, we look for him. If we can't see him and they attack, we get you out." I leave it at that, hoping he agrees.

"What time and where do you want me?" he asks.

I'm too shocked to answer immediately. I stumble over my words. "I-I guess first dark. If you meet Wesley by the bins near the back door of the bar. Send your men in and I'll tell them where to go. In the meantime, I'll look for some good places to put everyone."

"I'll be there but my men won't be. I can't put them in danger—not after losing Chomp."

"I understand. That's not a problem. I'll make sure we have plenty of pack members."

Patsy looks scared. "He controls the weres. What's to say he won't take them all over in the back alley and kill you immediately?"

"We just have to hope we get him before he gets them," Dominick says, as he stands to leave. "Thank you for earlier. I'll be there at first dark," he says, addressing me.

I stand and lean in to kiss him on the cheek. "I won't let them kill you, I promise. Even if I die saving you."

He laughs as we break away, "I know you are my 'saviour' after all. I can feel the truth through our tie."

After a smile, I close my eyes and teleport to Theo's.

22.
CONTACT

ROSABEL

I appear in the drive, deciding that is the better choice because if I enter through the front door like the rest of the pack, they might respect me that bit more. They will probably all know about my druid blood by now. Chloe will, no doubt, be spreading the word hoping for more haters to join her hate-on-Bel group.

I walk up the steps to find my least favourite werewolf playing bouncer at the front door. I can hear numerous footsteps behind me leading me to think there are at least three or four pack members behind me. *Surely she won't make a scene in front of them.*

"Hi Chloe," I say politely, as I pass.

She deliberately plants her feet and stands in front of me, denying my entry. She smirks. "Pack only."

I really don't have time for a fight. I need to find Theo.

"Chloe, you know full well that Theo has claimed me for his mate and I've been introduced to the pack as alpha female. Let me in so we can plan how we are *all* going to help find Theo and the others."

She doesn't move.

I sigh. "I haven't forgotten about your challenge. I told Theo about it and he agreed. I do accept. As soon as he's back, we are good to go."

I glance over my shoulder and count at least eight pack members watching and waiting to get in.

It looks like they're going to get a show after all.

Deciding my only option is violence, I turn my body slightly. To Chloe, it might look like I'm going to just walk down the steps and leave but I'm not. I'm just getting momentum. I swing my body back around with as much force behind my right fist as possible. When it makes contact with her jaw, she flies backwards and smashes through one of the closed, beautiful front doors. *Great I'll have to pay a fortune to replace that. It's got to be custom-made.*

The small audience behind me gasps. I can feel a small amount of anger coming from them. To stand my ground, I turn to address them. "Does anyone else want to waste more time questioning my position?" No one says anything or makes any move in retaliation. I turn back to the doors. I start to step over Chloe, who is out cold on top of the door when I hear Wesley shouting.

"WHAT THE FUCK IS GOING ON HERE?" He catches sight of me and bows his head, probably in apology for his tone of voice. "Rosabel?" He questions as he glances down at Chloe, still on the floor.

"She wouldn't let me in. I told her once we find Theo we can deal with the challenge she offered me, but she wouldn't step aside."

"Whoa. Back up a minute! She's challenged you? When? Does Theo know?"

"Yes. Last night after I left you in your room. I assumed you must have heard with it being right outside your door. I told Theo. He agreed we need to duel."

"Okay. We'll deal with that another day. Are you ready to

sort this lot out?" he asks, gesturing with a sweep of his arm at the werewolves.

I step into the room and hope that is answer enough.

We head to the dining room. It has been arranged just like the first meeting I attended with the furniture pushed to the edges of the room. We get to the front of the room and stop in front of the three chairs.

"Wes, do we need to wait for Chloe to come around and join us before we start?" I whisper, hoping the rest of the chatting throughout the room covers my words. I don't want anyone else knowing I have no idea what I am doing here.

He shrugs. "No. She isn't of rank. She can join us when she's ready. It serves her right if she misses out on knowing the plan."

I nod in agreement.

I turn and face the crowd, looking at each pack member standing before me. There are a number of faces I recognise. Darryl and Phil, who Billy had picked for his patrol tonight— the one that got cancelled the second Theo went missing. I have no idea how to start this meeting? *How does Theo start them?*

I force a friendly smile on my face. "Hi."

They all immediately stop chatting and nod in unison. They remind me of freaky programmed robots.

Wesley gives me a reassuring smile and Billy moves next to me, reaching out to stroke my arm in comfort.

I need to be honest with them. "I'm not sure how to start this, but I'll try to make it as quick and painless as possible."

There are a couple of friendly chuckles through the crowd. It helps to relax me; if just a little.

"First things first. I've spoken to Dominick and he's told me everything that he saw happen earlier tonight. He's also agreed to act as bait since he has been attacked twice now. I'm assuming that's the reason the kidnapper is taking pack members. He can control animals so that is his best weapon to kill a vampire! He's controlling a were-lion too!"

A guy in the front of the crowd speaks up. He looks like a cowboy from the boots with spurs, to the jeans, checked shirt and hat. I bet he even wears chaps some days. "If he's controlling Theo, all hells going to break loose. There is no one who will win against him. He's too strong."

They all seem to stare at me awaiting my response.

"I thought that too, but Dominick said Theo was hurt, badly hurt, and only dragged away once he was unconscious. I can feel Theo's pain. I don't think he will be able to calm Theo enough to control him for at least another couple nights. He'll have him caged up or locked away somewhere until he can control him. If we can pull together a good trap, with Dominick as bait tomorrow night, we might come out of this alive."

Numerous voices throughout the crowd shout out. "Yes!" I watch as others nod their agreement.

"We'll come up with the details tonight, and then call those we will need tomorrow. I'm not sure who or how many of you we will need so don't make any plans," says Wesley.

I feel a wall of anger drift through the crowd. It takes me a second to spot her but the minute I see Chloe, I know the anger is coming from her and being aimed directly at me. *Lucky me.*

"NOT NOW CHLOE! Theo will be furious enough when he gets back and hears about you playing bouncer earlier. You'll be lucky if he doesn't kick you out of the pack for this," Wesley commands. He's very dominant, thinking back on my words to Theo last night. I'd bet on him to win if we fought.

Chloe looks from me to him. She immediately turns and leaves without a word.

The rest of the pack slowly file out of the house.

After the pack leaves, Billy, Wesley, and myself head to the lounge. It's like the meeting after the meeting. Billy goes straight for the kitchen to make the drinks; which makes me think that is his usual job. Wesley and I sit on the sofa.

"You did real good in there, Bel. Theo will be as proud as punch when he hears about it," Wes praises me.

"Thanks, Wes. I just hope this plan works and we get them all back soon. He's only been gone a couple of hours and I'm already feeling edgy. I don't know how you've managed to get through the two days Alyssa has been missing," I say truthfully. My wolf seems to be pacing constantly and there is no calming her.

"Neither do I. Just keep telling myself we'll get her back. We have to," he admits.

Billy comes in with three drinks. "We'll get them all back tomorrow, try not to worry." Wesley and I both smile at Billy's words. I have a feeling that none of us are as confident as Billy sounded right then. When there's a bunch of werewolves going against someone that can control werewolves, there are a number of things that can go wrong.

"Right. Let's get down to business. What did Dominick tell you about tonight?" Wesley asks.

I tell them everything about the fight; from when Billy left Theo and Dominick alone in front of Misty's, to when Billy returned after I saved Dominick. I take a sip of my coffee and look up to find Wesley looking livid.

"Did you just say Dominick fed from you again, *and* nearly drained you in the process?" he demands. I won't call him up on his demanding tone. He's concerned about his missing mate. He deserves some slack.

"Yes," I say cautiously. When he doesn't say anything and just stares at me, I feel the need to say more. "He did drain me, to the point that if I was human I don't think I'd be here now, but I'm alive and that's the main thing. It wasn't Dominick's fault. He was nearly dead himself and I taste good. Ask Paddy later, he'll agree—I'm hard to resist." I laugh nervously, unable to stop my rambling. "He couldn't stop, but thankfully he stopped in time. I didn't think he'd drain me, or even come close but he was so out of it…I was wrong."

"I'm glad I'm not the one who has to tell Theo when he gets back," Wes says, thankfully sounding slightly calmer.

Thinking about Theo being protective brings Ruby to my mind. "Oh my god! How is Ruby? Is she still here? Does she know what's happened?" I can't believe I had forgotten about Ruby. She must be so worried.

"Yes. I'm here and I know," says a voice from behind me.

I turn around to see her standing out from behind the sofa I'm sitting on. Her red eyes and wet cheeks tell me she's been crying for some time. How did none of us notice her? How long has she been there?

"What are you doing down here? I told you to stay upstairs." Oh great. Angry Wesley is back.

Ruby cowers slightly but stands her ground. "No one would tell me anything! I needed to know. Theo wasn't here," she points at Wes, "and you guys were holding a meeting and running around looking all worried. I knew something bad had happened." She breaks down into heaving sobs.

I get up, put my arm around her shoulders and bring her back to sit on the sofa. She shuffles into the corner of the cozy sofa.

"I'm Bel. I don't think we were introduced last night," I say.

"Yeah. I asked Ted about you after you left." She bursts into tears again and I stroke her knee for a second to comfort her. Weres are touchy feely creatures. We use touch to comfort each other. Sometimes we even sleep in piles. Being the outsider of the pride I had never been privy to one of these piles but I have heard plenty about them. Ruby is only human but having grown up around a pack, I'm sure she's used to touch and comfort as any were is.

"He'll be back tomorrow." I try to sound confident.

Wesley looks at me. "What did you and Dominick agree on as the plan for tomorrow night?" He still sounds mad but I can tell he's trying to sound calmer. He probably doesn't want to upset Ruby any more.

"We didn't come up with anything in great detail. Dominick will be in the alley out back of the bar and some of us will be hiding in the shadows to protect him when they attack. But before we jump in, we have to find the controller. He has to be somewhere with a view of the alley. He'll need a view of them to be controlling them as well as he is. He must be at a vantage point. I'd suggest a fire escape or the rooftop of one of the surrounding buildings. You two would be best to decide who and how many of us go. I think it would be safest if we make it look like you're meeting Dominick, Wes. As second to Theo, everyone except pack will think you're in charge. Do you think you'll be able to handle being in the line of fire when Alyssa attacks?" I hold my breath hoping his answer is what I want to hear.

"I'd actually prefer that over hiding. I'd want to run out when I see her so if I was meant to be hiding, I would ruin everything. That all sounds great. You are going to make a great alpha female," he says with a smile.

"Billy, you have a think about who you think is best for the job overnight. We can discuss your choices tomorrow and then start with the phone calls."

"No worries! I've been thinking already. The boss can communicate with the two of us when we are in wolf form. Do you think if we tried now he could tell us where he is and we could go get him?"

Wesley looks serious for a moment before a huge smile spreads across his face. "That might actually work. He's badly injured so he should still be in wolf form. Only problem is, we can't talk to him and he won't know to communicate with us if he doesn't hear us." His face is solemn but suddenly hope dances behind his eyes. "Bel, you're his mate. It should work between the two of you. Dammit! Why didn't I think of that sooner?"

"Do you really think that could work? I haven't even met his wolf yet." I knew that wasn't exactly true as soon as it left my mouth. I know his wolf. He's there with Theo all the time. He's part of him just like my wolf is part of me.

"Alyssa and I can do it and we're not true mates like you and Theo are. Your bond is one of the strongest bonds I've seen. Everyone in the pack can feel how much he loves you. When Theo falls, he falls hard." He rolls his eyes. "What have you got to lose? You might as well try it."

All three of them stare at me, hopeful. How could I let them down? Plus, if I can get Theo back tonight that would be wonderful.

"Okay. You'll need to talk me through it. Remember. I've never done this before."

"All you have to do is shift and talk to him in your head. If it's going to work he'll hear you and you'll hear him reply, his voice in your head…It's odd at first but you'll get used to it," Wes informs me.

Here goes nothing.

I stand up and crouch behind the sofa. I don't like the idea of getting naked in front of Wesley and Billy, let alone Theo's teenage sister, Ruby. I strip with great difficulty; the dress is the easy bit. It's the underwear that causes me trouble. You try taking undies off while crouching down!

Naked as the day I was born, I take a calming breath to relax. I don't even need to call my wolf to come forward. The instant my defences are down, she's there taking over my body. Her anxiety over Theo isn't helping my pain during the change. I can't stop myself from grunting. Once I feel the change is complete and the pain starts to ease, I open my eyes and see furry paws in front of me. I try to shake out the remaining tingles before I walk around the sofa into the view of Billy, Wesley, and Ruby.

A gasp comes from Ruby and I whine in response. I don't want her to be scared of me. Her gasp confuses me, being brought up with werewolves, surely she has seen plenty of them in the fur before.

"She won't hurt you, Ruby. You don't need to be scared," Wes calmly reassures her.

"I'm not scared."

She is telling the truth. I smell no fear. Billy and Wesley should sense that too.

I start to walk over to her slowly, so she can touch me if she wants to. That might make her feel more at ease.

She moves to sit forward on the chair and reaches out to stroke me, starting with my shoulders. "Theo hasn't let me be around you guys in wolf form for such a long time. It was a shock to be so close to the beauty of you," she says, as her stroking hand works its way behind my ears. She knows how to stroke a wolf. That's the best spot to scratch. She could scratch me there all day if she wanted to.

"Our Bel here is some beauty," Billy says. He's the sweetest, scary biker, werewolf I have ever met.

"Let's find Theo. Focus people." Wesley sounds anxious.

He's right!

I lie down on the floor in front of the sofa and close my eyes.

"Theo, can you hear me?" I ask in my head, feeling like an idiot. Nothing. I knew this wouldn't work.

"Theo...Theo...It's Bel."

"Bel...you're...here?" He gasps and grunts and pauses between each word, like it is taking a great effort to speak.

I'm suddenly hit by an immense wall of pain. Great. My empathy even works this way. I suppose it's all through telepathic connection in a way so I don't know why I am so surprised.

"I...can't...see...you." I feel his hope; no doubt at the thought of rescue. He must think I'm there and not realise I'm only in his head.

"No. I'm not in the room, Theo; I'm in your head, like when you communicate with Billy and Wesley in wolf form."

I feel him deflate as the hope in him vanishes in a split second.

"We're coming to get you. You just need to tell me where he's keeping you," I say quickly, hoping to lift his mood.

"Was unconscious, don't know," he stumbles.

"What can you see around you now?" I ask hoping he can pick something, anything, up.

"Black. No eyes," He's not making much sense.

I reach through the bond hoping to pick up something better, but I get the shock of my life, he's so close to death.

"Theo, baby, we have a plan—a trap for whoever has you. We'll have you back tomorrow night." I hope he can hang on until tomorrow.

"Danger. Can control pack. Can't confront him," he warns.

"It's okay. The Pack will be safe, I promise."

I hope!

"Why aren't you healing? You shouldn't be in this much pain now." He should have been healing. If anything, he feels like he's getting worse as I talk to him.

"Need meat." His anger hits me like a physical punch to the gut.

"What? He's not given you any?" I can't believe he'd starve an injured werewolf. He must be insane. Wolves are dangerous as it is but an injured wolf is even worse. All they can think about is healing and meat gives us the energy to heal.

"N..." I take that as a no.

"Please stay with me. Hang on until tomorrow night. We'll

come and get you. I need my Teddy bear to hug remember?"
Nothing.

Oh god, please!

"Babe, you're my mate. I've only just found you. Don't leave me now. I need you."

"Bel…I…love…you!"

"I love you, too. You're going to hang on for me, aren't you?" I beg.

"I'll try." He feels uncertain. "He's coming."

"Can you smell him?" I feel a sharp pain in my neck.

"Tran." He disappears. I can't feel him anymore.

Tran? Tran? Tranquilliser!

My anger and sadness fills me.

I open my eyes and the scene before me is really confusing. I am standing at the bottom of the stairs, growling at Billy and Wesley, who are guarding Ruby half way up those stairs.

Chloe barges through the door to the hall on my left shouting, "What is going on d…" the second she sees me, she changes her tone to a whisper, "Wes. What's happening?"

My attention instantly changes from the three on the stairs to Chloe. My wolf has been dying to tear her apart.

Wes doesn't answer her and addresses me instead. "Bel. Did you talk to Theo?" I can feel him coming back down the stairs.

I stalk closer to Chloe. She is backing up against the wall. The fear coming from her is making me enjoy this all the more. I growl at her.

The terrified scream behind me catches my attention.

Ruby.

"Bel. Where's Ted? Let's go get Ted." She sounds terrified.

Ted, my Teddy.

I instantly shift back to human. I'm naked in front of the four of them.

Wes grabs my clothes and brings them over warily.

"I'm sorry about all that. I didn't realise it was happening, I wasn't aware of the things here. I was with Theo. Did I hurt anyone?" I look at each of them inspecting for injuries.

They all stare at me in silence.

I can still feel Chloe frozen in fear behind me as I slip the dress over my head. I shift the position of my body slightly so that my back is to the sofa and Chloe is to my side; in case she decides to attack. She has her head down in a bow towards me.

"No, Bel. You just scared us for a minute, that's all." Ruby sounds shaken.

"Ruby. I'm sorry I didn't mean to scare you," I plead.

"It's okay."

"What made you so angry? Is Theo okay?" Wesley asks, even he sounds shaken.

I look at Ruby wondering what to say? How much can she take? It doesn't take her long to guess what I'm thinking.

"Just tell me. I need to know, even if he's dead. Please just tell me." I hope she really means what she's saying.

"He's not dead, but he's in a real bad way. I'm not sure he'll last the night."

The whole room fills with everyone's sadness.

"He wasn't making complete sense, but he knows we are coming for him tomorrow night and he said he'll try to fight, to hang on until then. He's not getting any meat and he isn't healing."

They are all listening in silence but their emotions are speaking loud and clear. They've all gone from sadness over his imminent death to raging anger over the controller not giving him any meat.

"He can't see anything. I don't know if his eyes are injured or he's blindfolded. He just said black, when I asked him what he could see. He was unconscious between Misty's and getting there so he doesn't have any idea where he is. The controller just shot him with a tranquilliser dart and that's when I lost contact with him."

They are still staring at me in silence, but the rage is speaking loud and clear.

Billy is the first to break the silence. "Fuck! I can see why you became so aggressive."

"Okay. So tonight's rescue mission is a no-go but we still have tomorrow's plan of attack." I think Wesley is trying to reassure us all so we keep our hopes up, but maybe he is just reassuring himself out loud.

"Since I know we're not being ambushed and the growling has finished, I'm going back to bed, good night." Chloe turns and leaves out the same door she just entered, shutting it behind her.

"I'm off to bed, too," I say. "We'll need as much energy as possible for tomorrow. It's going to be physically and emotionally draining. Billy. You're staying here the night, aren't you?"

Billy nods in response.

"Bel, you might as well stay, too. There are enough rooms. You're acting leader. It would probably be best to be where the Pack can get in touch with you," Wes suggests.

"Plus, the more weres in here the safer since someone broke the door and deemed it unlockable." A smarty-pants Billy adds, making us all laugh.

"I'm not sure. I need to eat." Shifting takes energy and makes me hungry. "I don't have any other clothes here and I can't really sleep in this," I say, gesturing towards my dress.

"Ted has heaps of food. He's always eating. I'm sure we can also find you a spare t-shirt and sweats. Please say you'll stay," Ruby begs, with an eager look on her face.

"Okay. I hope there is a lot of food because I'm going to be shifting a number of times over night to check in on Theo; remind him to hang in there. Where are you sleeping Ruby?"

"I'm in the room next to Ted's. You could sleep in the room on the other side of mine," she offers.

"Okay. Sounds like a plan," I agree, with a smile.

"I guess that means I'm your next door neighbour, hey?" Billy says, as he nudges Wes in the ribs.

"Ow, Billy. If you're scared of sleeping downstairs on your own, you can be my neighbour. I'm off now. Do you want me to walk with you, Billy, to keep you from getting scared?" Wes jokes making us all burst into laughter.

"Fuck off, mate," Billy says.

"We can ring the pack members we decide would be best for the job after breakfast; about ten o'clock. All three of us will need to be down here to discuss it at eight thirty," Wes says more seriously.

I frown. I'm not sure if it's the fact that Wes wants me in on the decision or if it's the fact that he was referring to eight thirty in the morning. I haven't seen that time of the day in years!

"Why do I need to be here that early? I wouldn't have a clue who would be good for the job." I complain.

"You need to ring and give the order to do the job. It comes with the role of the alpha's mate. Well in this situation, it does anyway."

"Then I can come down at nine forty-five," I suggest, more cheerful at that thought.

Billy starts to laugh. "Are you not a morning person by any chance, Wolfy?"

"Are you kidding? I've not seen that side of noon for the last two years," I say, shaking my head. *It's too bloody early.*

"Eight thirty," is all Wes says, as he opens the door leading to the hall.

Billy waves bye to us and follows Wes, closing the door behind him. Leaving me and Ruby alone in the lounge room.

23.

REUNION

THEO

Hearing Bel's voice gave me a boost. I don't know how she knew but I was desperate for something to cling on to—to make myself live. She reminded me that I have a pack, a mate, and my baby sister relying on me. I need to get through this. The tranquilliser wasn't fun, but it's wearing off now. I need to focus.

"Look, he's coming around." Is that Alyssa?

"Don't get too excited. He might be too out of it to recognise us. He might attack us." That is definitely Paddy.

He must have knocked me out so he could bring them in here.

"At least he might recognise you. I've only met him twice. He'll eat me first," says who I can only assume is, Jared. Since I saw his lion attacking Dominick earlier I know he's under the kidnapper's control.

I need to shift back to human. I can't exactly talk to them in my wolf form. They are right. An injured werewolf is dangerous. I rein the wolf in. He comes willingly, knowing it's the best thing for all of us. He may be injured but he knows I would never put us in danger while we're so vulnerable. It's one of the most painful changes I have ever made. The intensity of the pain takes my breath away. I lay as still as possible once I'm human, not wanting to irritate my already sensitive skin and nerves.

"Theo, it's Alyssa. Can you hear me?"

"Yes," is all I can manage. The shift took it out of me. I will heal better in wolf form. The sooner I can talk to them and get back, the better. I honestly don't feel like I am going to make it until tomorrow night.

Someone covers me with a blanket.

"Someone needs to take those bullets out of you. You're never going to heal if those stay in you," Alyssa says, rubbing at a sore spot on my upper arm.

"Bullets?" I ask, trying to inspect my arm.

"I'm betting silver by the way you're not healing," Jared says, as he steps closer.

I can't control the warning growl that comes out of my mouth.

He holds his hands up in surrender and takes a step back. "Sorry. You're injured and your wolf doesn't know me. I'll stay over here."

"I can smell your lion. My wolf doesn't like that you are a predator. I'm sorry. I'm not normally so grouchy."

"It's understandable. You have at least three silver bullets in you and numerous injuries that aren't healing," Jared admits.

"I have your blood on me. I can smell it. Did we do that to you?" Alyssa asks, sounding distraught.

I sit up, ignoring the pain that rolls through my body, and pull her into my arms. "Alyssa, you did not do this. You may have been the weapon but whoever has us was wielding that weapon. Do you hear me?" I command.

"Yes," she whispers against my chest.

I look over at Paddy and he must see the pain on my face. He walks over and pulls Alyssa against his own chest.

"Go sit with Jared whilst I try removing the bullets out of Theo," he says, guiding her towards Jared.

Paddy turns back towards me and starts poking at my arm. "If I could shift just my claws, I could probably dig them out, but I can't do that. They're too deep. I need something…" he says, as he looks around the room for anything that could be of use.

I look around, too. The room is sparse. Three camping beds against different bare walls and a bucket in the corner. I guess the kidnapper doesn't want us to find anything we can use as a weapon.

"Can you shift just your claws, Jared?" Paddy asks, as he looks at Jared.

"I can but Theo's wolf won't let me near him as it is. There is no chance in hell he will let me near him with my claws out," he says, from his seat on one of the beds, with Alyssa tucked into his side.

"It's okay. I'll be able to hang on until tomorrow night. I spoke with Bel before he knocked me out." I tap my forehead to clarify how I spoke to her. "They have a plan."

"Bel is always the one with the plan. You're a lucky man," Jared says.

I am feeling weaker by the second. The silver isn't doing me any favours. I need to get it out. I shift just my hands, hoping to be able to dig them out myself. I reach around to the one Paddy was poking at and I can just reach it. I cut a cross through the wound to make it bigger and then dig my claw into the newer larger hole. I feel the silver. Not only does the arm it's in sting like a bitch, but it stings the claw that touches it too. Trying to ignore the pain, I keep digging. I add another claw to the wound hoping to pincer it out. It works! I drag the bullet through the wound and drop it to the floor with a grunt.

Feeling slightly faint and nauseous, I give up any thought of removing the other bullets and lay down where I am sitting. "That will have to do. I can't do anymore."

"You did good, mate. I honestly don't think I could have done that if I was in your shoes," Jared praises. "If you shift, I will watch over your wolves whilst you sleep."

I don't even bother thanking him. I give my body over to my wolf and fall into a deep sleep.

24.

SEEKING CONTACT

ROSABEL

"Okay. First things first. Where's the food?" I ask Ruby, as my stomach grumbles in agreement.

Ruby leads me to the kitchen and starts pulling food out for a sandwich. I manage to stop myself from eating the ingredients before the sandwich is made. But once that sandwich is in my hands, I eat in total silence, enjoying every mouthful.

Once I'm finished we both head up to the bedrooms. Since I have to get up so early, I should get as much sleep as possible. I also need to ring Misty and Benji; he should be home and I haven't heard from him yet. I understand why he was so mad when I didn't ring him after arriving here.

We get to Ruby's room and say our goodnights before she enters and closes the door behind her.

My door is painted a lovely lavender colour. The bedroom is laid out the same as all the other rooms I've seen. There's a brass bed with the head against the far wall, which has bedside cabinets on either side. There is a dresser on the side wall that has a plant pot with a lavender plant in it. The other wall has two doors—I'm guessing an ensuite and a wardrobe. The room has a really calming feel to it. Not that it will help calm my wolf at all, she's too edgy. The only thing that will put her at ease is having our mate happy and healthy in front of us.

I take my phone from my clutch bag and call Benji. It rings for a long time making me think it's going to click over to voicemail.

I'm just about to disconnect the call when Aunt Lily answers.

"Hello. This is Benjamin's phone."

"Hi Aunt Lily. It's Rosabel. I'm just ringing to make sure he got home safely. Is Uncle Jack okay?"

"Jack is doing fine. He's complaining about being cooped up so it seems he is back to his normal self. Benjamin is trying to distract him with a game of chess at the moment, but you know Jack. He won't be fooled for long. Shall I get him to call you back?"

"It's getting late now. I'll try him again tomorrow. Thanks, Aunt Lily. Pass my love onto Uncle Jack and you take care."

"Thank you, Rosabel. Good night."

"Bye," I say, disconnecting the call.

I don't bother putting the phone away. Instead, I scroll through my contacts and call Misty.

"Hello?" she answers with a sleepy voice.

"Misty, it's Bel. Did I wake you up? I'm sorry."

"It's okay. I wasn't in bed. I dozed off on the sofa with the candle burning, so it's a good job ya called or the candle could have burnt the apartment down. How's the pack coping without Theo?" she asks, sounding more alert.

"They're doing as good as can be expected and surprisingly they're letting me lead them. I only had a little trouble from Chloe, but that wasn't anything new. She wouldn't let me in. I knocked her out and ended up breaking Theo's front door in the process." I'm still dreading the cost of that door.

"You knocked her out?" she asks, surprise clear in her voice.

"Yeah. In my defence I just wanted to get past and I did try asking first. We have a plan for tomorrow night. The only thing is, with me falling into the leader position it means I need to be there. Do you think Lucy will be able to cover for me?" I ask, dreading her answer. If she can't do it, I have no idea what I will do.

"I guessed ya'd need a few nights off. She said she can do the next three nights."

"Oh, Misty. You are a star! I'm so bloody unreliable. I'm surprised you haven't fired me yet," I say, only half joking.

"The reasons you've been unreliable have been through no fault of your own. I'm not firing you for that."

"Thanks anyway. I have to go now. Wesley wants me up at eight thirty. Can you believe it? I think he's mad. I'll try and pop in the bar before all hell breaks loose."

"No problem. Sleep tight. I'm glad I won't be up that early. He's definitely not sane," she jokes, before disconnecting the call. I didn't even get to remind her to blow out the candles.

I quickly type up a text before setting my alarm for eight thirty and placing my phone on the cabinet by the bed.

I head into the bathroom to clean up. I find a towel and a towelling robe hanging on the back of the door so I decide to take a shower. The hot water running down my body is calming and relaxing but I start to remember my last shower with Theo. Before I know it I have tears streaming down my face. I don't want Theo to be torn away from me before I really get to have him.

Once I'm dried with Theo fresh on my mind, I decide to drop in on him to check he is still okay. I close my eyes and pray he's there.

"Theo. It's Bel. Can you hear me?" I wait for a reply but it doesn't come. I try again.

"Teddy baby, keep fighting. I'm coming to get you." I still don't get a reply but I can faintly feel his hope. He must be in a deep sleep, hopefully healing. Either that or the tranquilliser hasn't worn off. I'll hope for the former.

I open the door of the bathroom to find Wesley sitting on my bed. Glad I decided to wear the robe; I pull the tie making sure it's secure.

"Oh. Hi Wes." To say I'm surprised to find him here is an understatement. The look on his face tells me how worried he is. I have no doubts it's about Alyssa.

"How's Theo? Is Alyssa with him?" He blurts out.

I make my way over and take a seat next to him. "I'm not sure. I couldn't get a response from him maybe the tranquilliser hasn't worn off. I think he heard me because I could feel his hope, faintly. The good news is he's still alive. Sorry if I woke you up. I didn't think I'd be noisy."

"No. It's okay. At least we all know it's just you and we're not under attack. You need to keep checking on them to make sure they're all okay." His voice trembles as he speaks. I don't blame him.

I'm worried and I haven't been mated anywhere near as long as he has. I'm surprised he hasn't tried communicating with her since she's been missing. "Did Theo order you not to try and communicate with Alyssa?"

He tilts his head to the side with a stern look on his face. "Yes. He said I'd get lost in the communication and wouldn't leave her. It's been killing me knowing I could talk to her but I'm not allowed. I know he's right but it's still hard." He turns his eyes back to the floor before standing and making a move for the door. "I suppose I better let you get to sleep before you want to contact Theo again."

"I'm not sure I'll be able to sleep," I admit.

"I know," he says as he closes the door behind him. Just before it shuts he sticks his head back in. "Thank you."

I smile in return, but it's too late I'm left staring at a closed door. Getting into bed is easy. Laying there and trying to fall asleep is harder than I expected. I can't stop thinking about Theo and how if he hadn't been taken we would probably be in his room right now, snuggling up in bed amongst other things. Thinking about snuggling with Theo makes me crave his scent. I quickly pull on the robe and go to his room.

I open the door to Theodore's room and see Ruby sitting on the bed with her back against the head board, cuddling one of the pillows in a death grip. If that pillow was a person they would be struggling to breathe. The room looks different from how it looked last night and I can't quite place what's causing the change.

"I'm sorry. I didn't think anyone would be here. I'll leave you to it." She looks up at me in shock like she hadn't even heard me enter.

"No. Stay." She pats the bed next to her in a gesture for me to join her. "You miss him too. You need to be here just as much as I do." That's what's different; the bed has fresh sheets on it. A deep blood red satin set is replacing the black set from last night.

I sit on the bed next to her and we both slide down under the covers and sniff the sheet at the same time trying to breathe in Theo's scent. We look at each other and laugh.

"I know it doesn't even smell of him because I helped him put them on fresh this afternoon. How stupid am I?"

"As stupid as me because I know they were black sheets last night." We both chuckle in unison.

"Do you like the red? He put them on especially for you. He said red is the colour of passion. It reminds me more of blood than passion but, hey, that's my opinion," she says with a shrug.

"Well to be honest, I thought of blood, too, but don't tell Theo I said that. I do like it though, now I know what he meant by it." I admit.

"I heard you growling not long ago. Were you talking to him? How is he?" All the happiness she just had in her face vanishes with her words. I can feel nothing but sadness coming from her.

"He's still in a deep sleep. I didn't get a reply from him but I could feel him. He's still alive," I say cheerily, hoping to give her something to cling on to. "Will you tell me about him? I haven't known him for that long; I'd love to hear some stories," I add. Hearing about him will make me feel closer to him, and hopefully talking about him should do the same for Ruby.

25.

ONE TRACK MIND

ROSABEL

"*R*osabel! Wake up!" Wesley's shout wakes me up. It sounds like he's pounding on the bedroom door, the one I was meant to be staying in anyway.

"I'm coming in," I hear him announce.

I stifle my laugh; he's not going to find me in there.

"DAMN IT," he yells.

I stay quiet. He can wait for me to get dressed. He sounds mad and I don't really fancy facing a stressed out, angry werewolf first thing in a morning.

Ruby and I talked for most of last night. She told me about their upbringing, which sounded just as hard as mine but for different reasons. Their mother and father split up when Theodore was nine years old, and his mother was pregnant with Ruby. Their dad was high up in the pack. He couldn't divide himself equally between family and pack. Ruby mentioned another brother called Cain, who is two years younger than Theo. Apparently he's a lone wolf, who doesn't get in touch often. The werewolf gene skipped Ruby; which she finds disappointing.

Unfortunately, just because you have a were as a parent, does not mean you will be a were, too. They have human genes, as well. It's just luck of the draw. I'm not sure where the luck lies though. Are you lucky if you do become were or you don't? I suppose that is up to the individual really.

Once Theo changed for the first time when he was sixteen, his father took him under his wing and introduced him into the pack. Doing the same thing with Cain two years later. With Ruby being human, their father wasn't interested in her.

Ruby turned up on Theo's doorstep because her mother's latest boyfriend is a sleaze ball—Ruby's words. He came on to her and when she turned him down, he told her mother she came on to him. Her mother hit her and threw her out. I don't know how a mother could do something like that to her daughter.

Once the sun came up we decided we needed to go to sleep before we lost the chance for sleep altogether. We ended up sleeping next to each other in Theo's bed.

"ROSABEL! Where the hell are you? You better not have teleported home to get more sleep!" Wesley sounds like he's ready to tear my head off. I better face him now before he actually does tear it off.

"I'm coming, keep your hair on." I didn't bother shouting. He'd be able to hear my voice downstairs with his hearing. Only Ruby wouldn't be able to hear anything out of the room she's in, being the only pure human in the house.

Wes storms into the room and takes in the scene before him. He looks mortified at the sight of us both in bed.

"You don't seriously think…" I can't even finish the question. I know what he is thinking. I can't believe he's jumping to that conclusion.

Ruby must catch onto our train of thought because she burst out laughing. "Look at his face," she manages to get out, before another fit of laughter takes over.

"Have you managed to wake sleeping beauty up yet? I thought you might need a prince to do it." We can hear Billy taking the stairs two at a time. He must have felt Wesley's horror because he suddenly becomes very serious. "Wes. What's wrong mate?" He walks around Wesley to see what he is looking at. Us! "No way!" He sounds excited. He seems to be taking the scene better than Wesley had, but he's jumped to the same wrong conclusion. He seems more excited than I'd like; especially since Ruby is involved. She is only seventeen. Too young for him to be thinking about like that.

"You are not serious." Ruby sounds astonished by two guys coming to the same conclusion after seeing two girls in the same bed.

"Ruby. You must know by now, especially since you hang out with Theo's pack a fair bit," I say, as I get out the bed in my underwear—they've already seen me in my birthday suit, underwear is a step up. I walk over to Theo's chest of draws. I start raking through it to find something to wear. "Men have a one-track mind. Especially when faced with two women in bed together, no matter how wrong they are."

I find some t-shirts in the top drawer and take one out. It's the one with the werewolf howling at the moon, that he'd been wearing the first night I saw him. I find some sweatpants in the third drawer and pull out a grey pair.

"Do you think Theo will mind if I borrow these?" Billy is still staring at me; Wesley's eyes are averted to the floor, with bright red cheeks. I stand waving the clothes in the air but no one is answering me.

When I glance over at Ruby, she is getting out of bed and grabbing the robe off the foot of the bed to cover herself, being careful not to flash her underwear to us.

"Billy, what are you staring at?" I ask, hoping to keep his eyes on me.

"Sorry, but you were both in there in just your underwear!" he says, as if we don't already know.

"Yes. We both had the same idea of being close to Theo by

being in here. We talked for a while and went to sleep when the sun came up," I clarify.

"Together!" Wesley still sounds stunned.

"I'm going to use the bathroom now. That's if I'm allowed?" I don't wait for an answer. Instead, I go straight in to the bathroom and lock the door, hoping Ruby can manage to escape without a Spanish inquisition.

Before I even bother getting dressed, I shift, calling my wolf forward so we can check on Theo again. "Theo. Can you hear me?"

"Bel. You're okay? I was worried the tranquilliser had hurt you when he shot me." It's great to hear his voice.

I can't help but giggle at his words. "You're the one on deaths door, and yet you're worried about me? I'm fine. I tried to communicate with you again before I went to bed, but you were out cold. I could feel you faintly so I knew you were still with us," I explain.

"I'm glad you're okay." I feel him relax through our mating bond.

"Has he given you any meat yet? You sound and feel much better."

"Yes. He gave us some meat during the night. It won't keep me going long. It was enough to let me draw some energy from the pack. It should keep me going until you get here, later."

"Ruby and Wesley will be glad to hear you're better. You said us. Are you with the others?"

"Yes. They were in the room when I came around from the tranquilliser. They're both well. Alyssa was a little distraught at the thought of having hurt me but I think I managed to talk her out of that. Jared is here too. How is Dominick and Chomp? They were both in big trouble when I fell unconscious?" He asks.

"Chomp is dead, well dead dead; you know what I mean. Dominick wasn't far from following him but I donated a bit of blood, and he's fine now." I hold my breath as I wait for his reply, wondering how he will take the news about Dominick feeding from me.

"I bet he enjoyed that, the donation. So that means we have a tie to break again when I get back. That could be fun." His cheery reply helps me relax.

"Hey, cheeky. You might not be up to it." I can hear the laughter through our connection. But feeling through the bond, I can tell he's been pretending to feel better than he actually is. He feels extremely tired and he's struggling to keep up the act. "Theo. You can't fool me. I'm an empath and your mate. I can feel how tired you are."

"What? Your empathy works even like this?" He sounds as shocked as I was when I discovered it too.

"Yes. You're feeling guilty now for lying to me. Actually, you're probably only feeling guilty because I found out. You didn't feel guilty when you were actually lying."

"Sorry. I'm just trying not to worry you." I can feel the truth to his words.

"I know you're going to hang on for us, no matter how bad you feel. You're not one to give up. I better go before Wesley rips my head off."

"He better not." He sounds mad; his anger flowing through the bond confirms it. I'll take it as a good sign that he has the energy to spare on emotions like that.

"Oh, he's mad because he told me I had to be up, ready and downstairs by eight thirty. Have you heard of such a stupid idea? That is way too early for me to get up. He had to come in the bedroom and wake me up just before I came to talk to you. I'm only guessing because I haven't seen a clock yet, but it feels like lunchtime, but that could just be the hunger from all these changes confusing my biological clock," I try to explain.

"He can't give you orders," Theo demands. Did he even listen the rest of what I had said?

"I know. I had to lead a pack meeting last night. That was so fun." Sarcasm at its best.

"Did you have any trouble?" he asks, sounding nervous.

I really shouldn't worry him, but he'll be able to tell if I keep it from him. "Not really, except I owe you a new set of front doors. Don't worry. It's secure enough with all the top dogs staying there," I joke, hoping he doesn't ask for more details.

"Oh great. I dread to think what else can get broken before I get back tonight," he says with a laugh.

"I better go rally the troops so we can prepare for your rescue."

"I love you, Bel." It isn't just words. I feel the love being sent through the bond.

"And I love you, Theo." I could spend all day talking to him but I know I can't so I tear myself away by pulling my wolf back.

I get dressed as quickly as I can.

I head down the stairs and in my haste I lose my footing about halfway down. I reach out trying to grab the wall or something to stop my fall but there is nothing I can grip.

"SHIT!" I scream as I fall head first down the stairs.

Billy appears out of nowhere, at the bottom of the stairs, stopping my decent before my face smashes into the slate floor. "Jesus, Bel. Are you okay?"

"Oh my god, Bel!" Ruby cries, her voice sounding closer as she gets nearer.

"You caught me just in time, thanks Billy. You appeared out of nowhere. How did you know?" I ask.

"I felt you through the pack bond, not to mention heard you thudding down the stairs. I'm a werewolf. I've got good speed. I'm just glad I was quick enough. We can't have you damaging that beautiful face of yours." He leans to kiss me on the head but Ruby pushes him off me trying to help me up; which would be easier if my feet weren't still halfway up the stairs.

If Ruby had just left it to Billy to help me up, he would've been able to support my weight no problem. Hell, he'd be able to bench press a car, one-handed at that. That's a good bonus to being a were, super strength, and like Billy already said, speed. Unfortunately, Ruby doesn't have the strength of a were.

After watching us struggle for a second, not to mention seeing my face almost hit the floor once or twice, Billy barges Ruby out of the way. "Move it, Rubes, I'll get her. You go make Bel a coffee. I have a feeling she needs one to function in the morning."

Ruby disappears into the kitchen, hopefully to make that coffee. Billy is right. I'm ready for one.

Billy picks me up without a problem and carries me across the room to the sofa.

"Thanks Billy," I say, as he sets me down on the sofa.

Wesley is sitting opposite me with a face like thunder. *Thanks for your concern.*

"Sorry it took me a while to get down here, but I checked in on Theo while I was in the bathroom."

"We heard you. How is he?"

Ruby passes me a mug of coffee and it smells perfect. I take a sip, burning my tongue; I do that so often you would think I'd learn my lesson and wait for it to cool before drinking it, but the smell draws me in every time. I set the mug down on the coffee table before I do it again, as Ruby takes he seat next to me.

All three of them watch me with anticipation written over their faces.

"He's okay. He didn't realise my empathy worked through the connection so he tried to pretend he was better than he is by acting all happy and normal, but I could feel how tired he was. He became a bit more truthful after I called him out on it. He's keeping his hopes up and knows we'll be there soon. He said he's been taking energy from the pack, which is helping him."

"So that's why you have been so grumpy, Wes." Billy nudges him in the ribs playfully.

"I thought Wes was always grumpy." giggles Ruby.

"Well there is my excuse. Now tell us the rest." He tries to give me an order.

I don't know what comes over me but I'm not standing for it.

I stare him in the eyes, I wouldn't normally stare a werewolf down unless I know I could kill them in a fight, like Chloe for instance. Because if you won't back down and they won't back down that is what a stare contest will lead to—a death match. Wesley is really dominant and so am I. I'm honestly not sure who would come out alive between the two of us. Since I'm Theo's mate, I'm pack leader in his absence so the orders should be coming from me alone, not Wesley. I can hold my wolf back and only show the dominance I am willing to show. I'm not really sure how I do it and I've never heard of anyone else that can do it. But I made the mistake of showing my full dominance to Jared's pack and I have learnt not to do that again. I usually try to make it so I sit in the middle of a pack, not too dominant to be considered a threat and not too weak to be abused. There is only Wesley and Billy here, so I pull out my dominance to make Wes come to his senses and back down.

As I strip down emotionally to bare my animal, I feel Chloe come in the room. Her fear starts to grow along with my dominance.

Neither Wesley nor I look away from each other. It goes on for what feels like a long time, neither of us wanting to give in. Thinking on it, I don't even think he really meant it as an order in the first place, but I am not backing down and Wesley obviously feels the need to stand his ground too.

"Come on guys, there's no need for this." Billy tries to stop us.

"Billy, keep out of it!" I order with every bit of dominance I have. I guess my point gets across because he doesn't speak again.

My order must make Wesley realise something too because he looks down to the floor before dropping to his hands and knees and crawling over to me. He stops before me and turns his head, baring his neck. It's an animal thing, to offer a vulnerable body part in apology to the more dominant giving them the choice to rip you apart or chastise you.

I choose the latter by leaning forward and biting his throat, not hard enough to draw blood or even hurt; a nip more than a bite. But it's a chastisement, which is needed. As weird as it feels, I know I have to do it, it comes with the job. Maybe it was Theo's anger over Wes and his orders still residing in me that caused me to stand my ground.

We both sit back in our seats without another word.

By now Chloe has joined us, sitting on the floor at Billy's feet. She's dressed extremely conservatively for Chloe; wearing a fuchsia pink hoodie and sweatpants, with hardly any flesh showing at all. I guess Theo isn't here to impress.

They all look at me in silence, waiting for me to carry on.

Before I can open my mouth, Ruby breaks the silence. "Does someone want to explain what just happened?"

Billy looks at me questioningly.

I nod allowing him to answer.

"Dominance games. Pack stuff, sweetie." He smiles at her reassuringly.

"But she bit him," she says, sounding astounded.

Wesley turns his neck to show her that there is no wound, just a pink mark which will fade to nothing in five minutes. "It wasn't hard," he admits.

She shrugs dismissively.

Billy is watching me. I can feel through his emotions that my dominance arouses him. I don't know whether to feel flattered or creeped out by that.

Chloe has fear rolling off her in waves. I'm not the only one who can feel it. Billy reaches out and rubs her shoulder in comfort.

Wesley is concerned, no doubt about Alyssa.

"Theo said the others are safe and well. They were all together after he came around from the tranquilliser," I say, realising I have made them wait long enough.

They all stare at me in silence so I speak again, hoping we can get back to more normal conditions. It's all too tense after the stare down. "So who are we taking tonight?"

Wesley hands me a piece of paper over the coffee table. "Billy and I picked a few guys we think will be best for the job. Their names and numbers are on there," he says, pointing at the piece of paper in my hand. "Obviously, if you think someone is better for the job, by all means change it."

"No. It's okay, Wesley. You both know the pack members better than me. You know who is right for the job." I glance over the list and notice Chloe's name isn't on it. Theo had told me she was one of the most dominant, and a good fighter, which made me think she'd be pretty useful. "How come Chloe's not on there? She is one of the strongest in the pack."

Chloe looks at me, gobsmacked.

I tried to sound as friendly as I can but I'm still showing too much dominance for my liking, with me shifting so much recently, I'm finding it hard to push it back into hiding. My wolf likes being out at full strength.

"Yeah. We were going to put Chloe on but we thought she'd be better staying here with Ruby. We know how good you are, Chloe," says Wesley. He sounds a lot calmer. We might be getting back to normality now.

"I don't need a babysitter, I'm seventeen," Ruby complains.

"No. She's not staying to babysit you. Think of it as more like a bodyguard. Especially, with the front doors in the mess they are in. Theo left you with me when he went out and I can't let anything happen to you while you're in my care," Wesley says.

"Fine," Ruby snaps back, clearly not happy but willing to let it slide.

I pick up the phone from the coffee table and call the guys on the list. They all listened to my instructions silently with no arguments—just like the three wolves in the room with me. Each of them assured me they would be at Misty's on time.

Billy manages to get us all joking and laughing in no time. He's got a heart of gold that one. He soon takes Ruby and Chloe in to the kitchen to help him make sandwiches for lunch, leaving me and Wesley alone in the lounge. I think he did it on purpose since there is still a little bit of tension between us. Maybe he hoped we'd be able to sort it out in private.

Wesley speaks up first. "About what happened earlier, I didn't mean it as an order. I was just grumpy and didn't think before I spoke."

"I know. I don't know what came over me, I think it might be something Theo said to me," I admit.

"You had every right. I shouldn't be giving you orders."

I feel the need to explain. "Theo said that too. I think with his words fresh in my mind and my wolf close to the surface with all these changes I have been doing, my animal instincts took over."

"How did you become so dominant and then just let it disappear again? You only feel mid-pack dominant now, but you were a hell of a lot more a minute ago?" He asks.

"To be honest. I'm not sure how I do it, or what I do. The best way to describe it is that I bury my dominance deep inside me and only leave a mid-level amount on show. When I was younger I had it all on show and had so much trouble with

Jared's pride feeling threatened. I was always being challenged. That was probably just as much to do with being a wolf and didn't belong with the lions, as it was to do with my high dominance. One day it just happened. I could hide it, not that it helped with the lions. They already knew my full strength. I don't ever want to be treated like that again, so I keep it under wraps now."

"I never realised it would be hard being a lone wolf. Does Theo know about your strength?"

"I've never let it out since I originally hid it a couple of years ago. I don't think he knows, unless he has a way of feeling it without me showing it," I say, with a shrug.

The others come back with three big plates full of sandwiches and mugs of fresh coffee.

"I can't believe you two thought me and Bel were, you know…this morning," Ruby says, between bites of her sandwich.

"Come on. You were in bed together," Wesley says, grabbing a sandwich.

"And only in your underwear," Billy adds.

"What were we meant to think?" Wesley finishes.

"Chloe. What would you think if you saw me and Ruby just waking up in Theo's bed together?" I ask, just to prove a point.

"That you both needed to feel close to him," she answers, proving my point perfectly. *Men!*

"What? You wouldn't think they'd been together? Not even if they got out in just their bras and undies?" Billy seems astonished that she hadn't jumped to the same conclusion he and Wesley had.

"No. I guess it's a girl thing. My best friend and I used to sit and talk to each other while we had baths when we were growing up. Hell. We still do if we are getting ready for a night out together," She informs him, rendering Billy speechless.

"Besides. Rosabel is mated to Theo, and you both know I've

had a crush on Paddy and Eddie, for like forever," Ruby says, blushing as she realises me and Chloe had no idea.

"Aw, Paddy is a sweetheart. Eddie is a player, I'm not sure he's suitable for you Ruby," I say, getting nothing but an eye roll from her.

"Yes. Stay away from Ed. He'll end up breaking your heart," Wes warns Ruby. "I bet you weren't calling Paddy sweet when he was trying to make you his meal not so long ago," he says to me, with a smirk.

Ruby glances from Wes to me with a worried look on her face; probably concerned that her crush might have a habit of eating people. "*What?*"

"It wasn't really his fault. I was bleeding my delicious blood all over the place, right in front of him two days before the full moon. What did I expect?" I say, making everyone laugh at the thought.

26.

UNEXPECTED GUEST

ROSABEL

"Hubby. I'm home," says a stranger's voice from the front of the house, followed by a really irritating cackle of a laugh.

"Oh. God help us. The bitch is back! That's the last thing we need right now," Billy announces, obviously recognising the voice or more likely the cackle. That cackle isn't one you will forget in a hurry.

A blonde walks through the door looking like she's raided Chloe's wardrobe. She's wearing a baby pink tank top and a denim mini skirt, or belt whatever you prefer to call it, she's matched it with black knee high boots to finish off the look. Her mannerisms are just like Chloe's. She's almost like a twin.

"Oh great," Ruby whispers, as she gets up and heads for the kitchen.

"Wesley. What are you lot doing in my house? Where's Theodore?" She sounds just like Chloe too.

I bloody hate women with an attitude.

"Ruby is living here now. Theo asked us to stay and look after her while he's away with business." That was quick-thinking Wes. Well done.

"What? All of you? There are four of you looking after a seventeen-year-old?" she asks, sounding slightly perplexed.

"Yes. Safety in numbers and all. As you probably noticed, the front door isn't quite intact," Chloe throws out there.

"Ok. I'm going to get changed. If Theodore isn't here, his room will be free. I'll go in there," she says, before heading for the stairs.

This strange woman is not sleeping in Theo's room. I don't care who she is. "No! That room is taken. Any of the downstairs rooms are free," I clarify.

I hear Billy chuckle and start to wonder what he's laughing at, until I catch a whiff of my bonding scent. Jealousy will do that to a girl.

"And who might you be?" she snaps at me with attitude that could give Chloe's a run for her money.

I look at Billy, who looks at Wesley, who looks back at me with a shrug.

Ruby comes back from the kitchen and perches next to me on the sofa. "That's Rosabel. She's Theo's girlfriend and that's why his room is taken."

"His girlfriend? Oh, well. I'll go in the baby pink room down the hall near the front door. My case is through that way. It saves me carrying it far," she says, sounding put out as she walks off. I don't feel one bit of guilt.

"Who is that?" I ask no one in particular.

"She's Theo's wife, Selena. They've been separated a year. She cheated on him," Wesley answers, clearly not wanting to.

I'm floored by his answer. No one has mentioned a wife to me. "His wife," I whisper to myself.

"Aw. Didn't he tell you he was married?" Chloe asks smugly. So much for thinking she was starting to like me.

"We've not really had a chance to have the getting to know you conversation, yet." That wipes the smug smile off her face; I don't need to tell her what we have done. She already knows.

I quickly dismiss Chloe and look at Wesley. "You said she cheated on him. Is she insane? He'd kill the guy."

Wes glances nervously in the direction Selena had disappeared. "She doesn't know about any of us."

"What? He married her without telling her what he is? Where did she think he went every full moon?" I whisper, so she doesn't hear me if she decides to come back—not that I couldn't feel or hear her coming. Sometimes when you know something is a secret, you can't help but whisper when talking about it.

"Exactly. She isn't really bright. She just believed he was away on business," he explains.

"Well, fuck," is all I can manage. I can't imagine Theo deceiving someone like that.

Selena comes back in the room, halting the conversation. She sits down and starts chatting to the others, as if she has never been away.

I manage to sneak off unnoticed and go back up to Theo's room, to get away from her. I need some time alone with my thoughts. I've got more than enough things to think about right now.

27.

EXECUTIONER

I am only alone for about half an hour before Wesley knocks on the door to tell me we should think about going to find the best places to hide in the alley behind Misty's. He's right, of course. I tell him I'll meet him there after teleporting to the apartment, so I can change into more suitable clothes.

When I open my eyes, I find myself in my bedroom at Misty's. I can't help but notice how strange it feels being here. I don't belong here anymore. I go through the few clothes I have, hunting for the black hoodie and matching pants I know are there. I quickly pull them on with the black Nikes I have from my uniform at 'the Chief,' glad I had thought to bring them; considering I never wear them. It looks like they'll be my mission sneakers now.

Walking through the house looking for Misty, I come up empty. She must have gone to the bar early knowing we will be heading that way early as well.

I take a slow stroll to the alley to meet Wesley and Billy. I take the fifteen minutes it takes to psych myself up. I'm nervous about giving orders to all these guys. They all seemed compliant on the phone but they could always change their minds when they are face-to-face. We all need to do everything we can to get Theo and the others back. I feel down our mate bond, hoping for an insight into his well-being. He's still there but I can't get much else from him. Maybe he's blocking me from feeling him again.

It doesn't take us long to scout out some good hiding places. We decide to head in and grab a drink while waiting for the other guys.

We have chosen five of the of the most dominant pack members, thinking or more like hoping, the controller will have more trouble taking over the more dominant members. The only problem with that way of thinking is he's controlling Jared and he's alpha material. Wesley is adamant Theo's pack has some of the strongest wolves in Australia.

They all turn up one after another, not one of them a second late. The first to walk in is Darren from Billy's patrol the night before. We told everyone to wear black so it would be easier to hide in the shadows. He's wearing a black skin tight tank top and black slacks with his steel-toe cap boots. I still can't believe how huge he is. He had to open both doors to get in the bar.

Phil is next to come in, the other guy from Billy's patrol. He's wearing a black shirt, slacks and shoes, not his sandals and socks like he had on the other day. Although he looks like he's dressed for a party rather than an ambush. When I asked Billy earlier why he picked him, his answer was that he's reliable, fast, and loyal. 'He's the one person I'd want at my back in a fight,' he told me. I'm still not sure what good he'll be if all hell breaks loose, he doesn't look like the fighting type. I suppose if the plan works, we won't need any of the guy's. The only reason they are here is for plan b! I suppose if all hell breaks loose he'll be able to run away, *Fast!*

Greg is the next. He's one of the older pack members. He looks like he's in his mid-forties, although looks aren't much to go by with weres. We age slower than humans so we could be a lot older than we look. That being said, a human could look ten years older than he is and be bitten at forty. He'd still only look forty. Were DNA could cure a disease you carry but it won't make you look younger. He's five foot six, or thereabouts, with dark greying hair and hazel eyes. His camouflage consists of black jeans and black t-shirt with white sneakers.

Our fourth man to enter is Eddie—again, in an all-black ensemble. He's only twenty-two; I say only, but that's just two years younger than me. I think I feel older then I am because I had to grow up quick without my parents. He's got ginger hair and freckles with bright sky blue eyes. He's a similar build to Theo, not big but not small. He's cute, too. I can see why Ruby has a crush on him.

Our fifth and final man to turn up is, Dave. I recognise him as the cowboy guy at the meeting, who spoke up about my plan. Only today he's minus the cowboy gear. I don't think I would have noticed it was him if he hadn't given me a really mean look as he walked in. It's funny how you can remember who doesn't like you more than you can the friendly or silent ones. Without his cowboy hat, I can see a blonde ponytail and brown eyes. He is easily six feet tall.

They all greet us with a nod and wait for instructions; except Eddie, who decides to barge past everyone, grab me by the waist and give me a wet, open-mouthed kiss on the cheek. I push at his chest to get him out of my personal space. "Hi beautiful. Where do you want me?" he says, with a wiggle of his eyebrows. Yep. I was right. He's too much of a player for Ruby.

"Stop flirting, Ed, or Theo will kill you," Wes admonishes.

"Theo isn't here," he says, as he follows my step back.

"He'll hear about it, whether he is here or not. Now stop messing around. We need to focus on getting our pack members back," I order, having had enough of him wasting time. I quickly follow up with everyone's instructions on where they need to be and what they need to do.

It doesn't take us long to assemble into our designated positions; leaving us to wait for full dark to arrive along with the vampires. I'm hiding in a shadow at the entrance of the alley. I can smell Dominick so he must be nearby.

"Are you all here?" his voice says in my head, just before he walks around the corner.

How the hell did he do that?

He tells me, with two words, "The tie."

Brilliant. What other tricks does he have up his sleeve, thanks to that bloody tie?

"I'm not too sure myself, yet, Bel," he replies in a serious tone.

I wasn't talking to you. I think it managed to come over as a yell in my thoughts—I hope it did anyway.

"Sorry." I even hear the chuckle in his voice. It doesn't take Dominick long to reach Wesley.

I have a great view of them. I picked this position for that reason, plus the werewolves will have to pass me before they reach Dominick. That's when I need to turn my attention on our surroundings for the controller. I have a pretty good view of most of the buildings, thanks to the alley being nice and wide.

I hear a thud behind me so I turn quickly, hoping we didn't get all this wrong and I'm the one under ambush in the shadows where no one can see me. But I don't find an ambush.

I find Patsy facing me with a satisfied smile. "I scared you!"

I look her up and down, stunned that she's not wearing her usual attire. She's got her hair tied back and she's wearing sweatpants with a hoodie identical to mine.

"Patsy. I wasn't expecting you." There is no way I'll tell a vampire they scared me, true or false. "Dominick said he didn't want any of you here being put in danger."

"I'm not good with rules and orders. Especially in this case. I can't sit back and wait around while he's in danger. I'm not letting him be killed." I can feel her anger creep over my skin.

"I won't let him get killed either Patsy. Dominick knows that. I'll put my own life in danger before allowing his death."

"Yes, Dominick trusts you. But I don't. You have druid in you and they are not all to be trusted."

Alyssa, Paddy, and Jared come into view; thankfully they are all still in human form. I suppose that's a good thing.

I wonder how that thing works between me and Dominick. Maybe I can warn him. I was only thinking before. "Domini—"

His voice in my head cuts me off before I can say anymore. *"I heard, thanks."*

I turn my thoughts to looking for the controller by focusing on the roofs of the surrounding buildings. I can't see anyone on any of them. Why did I assume he'd be on a roof? He could be in one of the buildings looking out a window. If he's in the dark, we have no hope of seeing him.

Shit!

Panic flows through my body. If that's the case all hell's going to break loose and we won't all make it out alive, especially if he manages to take over the others I brought when they come out of the shadows!

"Rosabel. Feel for his emotions; vengeance or anger." Dominick's voice brings me out of the panic.

Yes. Okay. Calm down, Bel. Use your senses!

I reach out to see what emotions I can pick out. Everyone's emotions have an individual feel to them. People I've met once or twice like the guys, I can start to recognise their individual feel. I can ignore those emotions coming from our guys like, Wesley's sadness and concern, most probably over the sight of Alyssa. I can feel strong anger bordering on rage, but that's coming from Patsy next to me. I'm not going to be able to feel anyone else's anger while she's so close to me.

"Patsy. You need to either get rid of the anger or move away from me. I need to sense his anger. Yours is blocking me from it," I practically yell at her. If I was thinking straight I would have maybe asked her a little calmer.

Understanding what I meant and not taking offence to my tone, she does as I ask. Her anger eases almost immediately and is replaced with pure happiness.

I wonder what she was thinking to get that happy so quick, from such a dark angry place.

Aha. Now we are getting somewhere! I can feel some anger and a lot of resentment coming from the building I'm standing next to. He must be directly above me. That's probably why I couldn't see him. I'm surprised Dave couldn't. He would have a good view from his hiding place.

Found him, Dominick. I think to alert him as I run around the corner to the fire escape we checked out earlier. We had made sure we knew each fire escape and where it led, since we had no idea which building he'd choose. Luckily, it's only a four-storey building.

I can feel Dominick and Wesley getting tense. The controlled weres must be ready to engage.

"Hurry. We won't be able to hold them off long without someone getting hurt." Dominick confirms my thoughts. A bit of pressure is always helpful to give you the power to get up four flights of stairs in seconds.

I pull myself onto the roof and can't believe what's in front of my eyes. I take a deep breath to catch his scent because I just can't trust what I'm seeing.

"Emmanuel, Why?" is all I can manage to say.

I must have startled him—he hasn't got senses like me. He spins around and glares at me with a shocked look on his face.

I'm hoping that means the action down below has stopped.

"They needed showing they're not better than us just

because they are stronger and faster," he spits out between clenched teeth.

"Who?"

He nods his head in the direction of the alleyway. "The werewolves and vampires. I took Stephen and Mary at first, thinking kidnapping the vampires would make a war break out between them, but for some reason Dominick never thought Theodore was behind it. Instead, he asked for his help. I couldn't control them, and I couldn't let them go because then Dominick would kill me. I had to kill them!"

Stephen and Mary. No one ever told me their names. Knowing them now makes them real people. Emmanuel killed them?

"Not long after that, I found out I could control domestic cats and dogs, just a freak accident. I found Paddy drunk one night leaving Misty's and thought 'what if?' And, it worked. I used him to attack Dominick. That way he'd have to blame Theodore. Paddy is one of Theo's wolves, after all. The opportunity came to take Alyssa, so I did. The more werewolves I could use, the more damage I could do."

"Jared? Why did you take him? He isn't Theodore's pack." It just doesn't make sense.

"After he caused you to change in front of the bar, I had to punish him. He seems like a person who likes to be in control and if he isn't, well that sounds like good punishment to me." He has a smirk on his face, which I'm not too keen on. The Emmanuel I'm looking at now isn't the Emmanuel I dated.

"Theo. Was that planned?"

"No. That night I thought God must be looking down on me because I was so lucky! If I could control the alpha, I might be able to control the whole pack. It will save me taking them one by one. But it didn't work. Theodore's too strong. He wouldn't succumb to my control." He pauses for a second staring off into the distance. I can feel his rage strengthening.

"With the alpha missing, the pack should have fallen apart, but Wesley took control making sure that didn't happen." The way he said Wesley's name was a concern. I think if he could cast a hex, poor Wesley would be in trouble right about now.

"It wasn't Wesley that led the pack. It was me! As Theo's mate that job fell on me. I'm highest in the pack, after Theo, of course," I admit, hoping to disperse some of that rage he's aiming at Wes.

I hear a noise behind me and watch as Emmanuel's eyes dart around behind me. I don't need to look; my nose is telling me it's Dominick and Billy.

Dominick chooses that moment to enter my head again. *"Rosabel, it's only Billy and I. You need to persuade him to release his control."*

"Emmanuel. You can't control them forever. Please let them go and tell us where Theo is so he can go home," I ask him in my most persuasive voice, while slowly and continuously walking towards him. I try to come across as friendly as I can in this situation. I'm not worried about him hurting me because I know Billy is behind me, and he's quick. If Emmanuel tries anything Billy would be there before Emmanuel could cause me any severe damage. Billy won't let anything happen to me. That fact, I'm certain of.

He looks at me sadly and shakes his head. "I can't. If I tell you where I'm keeping Theodore, he'll kill me. The only way I can stay alive is to keep him."

"You can't do that!" Billy and I both shout in unison.

"He's right! If he lets Theodore go, he'll be against a death sentence. He's attacked pack. Theodore has to retaliate, it's law," Dominick says out loud, directed at me. "But Emmanuel, you seem to have forgotten you killed Stephen and Mary; who were my people. Therefore, I can retaliate." I hear the smile in his voice.

Emmanuel steps back away from us all. "You can't. You'll never find Theodore if you kill me."

"That is none of my concern."

"WHAT?" I spin around and glare at Dominick and find Billy staring at him just as perplexed as I am.

Dominick doesn't say anything out loud, he just stares at me with pleading eyes while addressing me in my head. *"Rosabel. He'll have kept them in the same building, if not in the same room. He'll have had to have been close to them all. They'll be able to tell us where that is when he releases them."*

"So, you're playing bad cop?" I think back at him, wondering whether I should believe him. He is a vampire after all. Why would he care if we get Theo back or not?

"Trust me, Rosabel," he says in my head.

Billy is looking back and forth between the two of us; something on my face must be showing that we are having a conversation somehow. Dominick's face has shown no emotion the whole time, actually come to think of it; he very rarely shows emotion on his face at all.

I turn my attention back to Emmanuel to find Wesley standing next to him. He must have come up another fire escape somewhere behind Emmanuel. "Bel. You or Dominick need to kill him so we can get the others back. I would love to do it, but unfortunately it falls on you." He really did sound like he was disappointed that he couldn't do it.

I step up to Emmanuel, close enough so that I could kiss him, although what I am about to do is far worse than that. He has tears streaming down his cheeks. *I suppose imminent death could bring the strongest of men to tears.*

"I'm sorry, Bel. I wish it could have worked between us. You're the one for me."

I can't kill him!

"You have no choice. You're doing this for Theo!" Dominick

says out loud. I don't know if he is warning the others about what I was thinking or if he has forgotten to say it silently.

You might be used to killing people but I'm not a murderer!

"Any of us would make it a long and painful death. That is our nature. You cared for him; you can make it easier for him. You can make it quick." I've been staring into Emmanuel's eyes through this whole conversation and now I realise I have matching tears running down my face.

How do I kill him quick without a gun? That would the quickest way, I think to myself. I feel Dominick is about to answer me, so I jump in before he does. *Yes. I know what I have to do. You don't need to answer that.*

I lean to whisper in Emmanuel's ear. "I'm sorry," I say on a sob.

"Thank you, Rosabel," are his last words.

I place my hands around his neck and with a quick sharp twist, he drops slightly. I expect him to hit the floor with a thud because as soon as I heard the crack, I had to let go. I look around to find Wesley had caught him and is lowering him gently to the floor. I drop to my knees and place my head in my hands.

Someone lifts me up and walks me back towards the fire escape I came up. The voice that speaks belongs to Billy. "Let's get you out of here." He leads me down the steps but my legs are too shaky and I keep stumbling.

There is no way I'm going to make it down four flights, without falling!

Dominick appears next to me. There is only room for one on this fire escape so he must be levitating or something. He turns his back towards me. "Climb on," he commands.

I don't argue. He wouldn't offer if he couldn't do it, plus I have just murdered someone I was dating only a few days ago; if I fell to my death I probably deserve it.

I put my arms around his neck to hang on, trying not to

picture Emmanuel's neck and how easy it was to snap. Dominick is a vampire, so at least I can't snap his by accident. It will take a lot more than Emmanuel's did, plus I don't know if that would actually kill Dominick?

The shock starts to wear off as I find myself sitting in the back of an open van that wasn't here when I went up on the roof where I…*Oh god. Did I really just do what I think I did? Think about something else.*

The others are huddled together about five metres away. It's good to see Paddy and Jared back to themselves. I feel a lot of tension coming from them. I focus my hearing to hear what they are talking about.

It's Billy that is talking. He's rubbing his stubble on his head with his hand in a motion from back to front. It looks like an anxious habit he must have. "So you don't remember anything? None of you?"

I shoot off towards the van and barge through the group in a split second. I don't care who I'm shoving or what they are. If a human was watching, I don't even think they would pick my movement up. I would just vanish from the van and suddenly be with the group. The guys here might catch a blur with their supernatural eyesight but I'm not sure and I don't really care.

"Did I just hear that right? They don't know where they were kept?" I'm glaring at Dominick and ready to stake him right now. Even if that makes it my second murder within minutes of my first. I guess once a murderer always a murderer. A second won't really make much difference. He just made me kill the only person that knew where Theo is.

"I'm so sorry, Rosabel. I had no idea they were hypnotised. I thought they would remember everything." He is sorry. I can feel his regret. I can even see it on his face and in his eyes. I know I shouldn't look a vampire in the eyes because they can make you do things just by meeting their eyes, but I trust he won't try anything. I'm not sure why but I do. Even after seeing the regret in his eyes, I can't calm down.

"You're sorry? I just killed the only person who knew where he was. On your word, that they'd be able to tell us. How the hell are we going to find Theo, now?"

I can feel aggression run through the pack members in the alley at what I've just said.

"Angel. You need to calm down. We've all been worked up tonight. Your tension could make us all change and that won't be useful to the boss, will it?"

I look at Paddy and Eddie; both their eyes are no longer human. I don't need to look at any of the others to realise what Billy said was right.

"Okay, sorry," I say through gritted teeth, as I take a deep breath and reach out to find someone happy. I find Wesley and Alyssa, who must be in Misty's and pull their happiness into me. With that happiness clearing my head I get an idea.

"Dominick. Theo mentioned a census for all the supes in town. Does it contain home addresses and other property addresses?" I can feel the hope run through everyone—that my idea might actually lead somewhere.

"Yes. But there are a lot of us in town. It could take days to find Emmanuel's entry. I'll get Patsy on it straight away, but if you get one of your men on it too they can start at opposite ends. If someone knows his last name that will help." Patsy leaves immediately after he says her name.

I look at Billy, having no idea who would know where the census information is kept. "I'm on it. Darren, you take everyone to Theo's shed and give Doc Patel a call; best to get everyone checked over. Don't forget Selena. Don't let her see any of you. Dave, can you go let Wesley know what's happening and ask about for anyone in the bar who might know Emmanuel's address?"

"No. I'll do that. Dave you go with Darren. Emmanuel was

Misty's friend, I feel like I should break the news to her. I'll find out what she knows at the same time. Dominick, do you mind helping by asking about in the bar too?"

"It's the least I can do," Dominick says, as his guilt flows off him. I feel even guiltier now that I have just realised I killed one of Misty's friends.

"Rosabel, do you want me to stay and help you too?" Eddie asks. His eyes back to his human sky blue. Thank God!

"That will be great. Thanks, Eddie."

He beams at me in delight.

Everyone heads off in different directions. Billy is going for his bike. Darren, Dave, Phil, Paddy, and Jared all get in the van I found myself sitting in not long ago, leaving Dominick, Eddie, and myself in the alley.

I look up at the roof. *Is he still up there? Oh my god! What did I do?*

"Rosabel, he gave you no option. Greg has taken him to the morgue. He'll make sure everything is dealt with. Let's get inside and focus on finding Theo," Dominick says, making his way to the back door that Misty must have left propped open for us.

28

FACING DOWN THE WOLF

ROSABEL

We enter the bar to a round of applause. Wesley has already spread the news. Ignoring the applause, I immediately look around for Misty but only find Lucy behind the bar on her own; which is really unusual for a busy night like this one.

I lean over the bar and shout over the crowd, "Lucy. Where's Misty?"

"No idea. When Wesley announced that Emmanuel was dead, she ran off through the back. If you didn't see her outside, I'd guess she's in the toilets or office." I nod with a smile, to let her know I heard her over the rowdy crowd and turn to go find Misty.

I nearly fall over Eddie, who had been standing directly behind me. "Oh, Eddie. Will you do me a favour and ask about in here for an address? Let Wesley know what everyone else is doing, too."

As I look around the bar to make sure Wesley is still here, I see Dominick is already asking people questions.

"Yes. Consider it done," Ed says, slipping away into the crowd.

I go straight through the back hoping to find Misty. I check the toilets as I pass but she isn't there. I just hope she hasn't slipped out between us entering the bar and now. As I open the door to the office, I get hit by a wave of sadness. It doesn't do my guilt any favours. I killed one of her close friends.

"Misty. I'm so sorry." I have no idea what else I can say. Nothing will make her feel better.

"It's okay. Ya had no choice. Wesley explained everything. I just wish everyone wasn't so happy about it. I feel so guilty that I set ya up with him. I had no idea he was like that," she manages between sobs.

"I went on dates with him and I had no idea either. He hid that side of him well, but he wasn't all bad." I start to cry. "I actually cared for him and if Theo and I weren't true mates, who knows, I could have fallen in love with him. And yet I just killed him."

Misty comes over pulling me into a hug. "It's okay. Don't live ya life blaming ya-self, ya had no choice." she consoles me, making me giggle at the situation.

"I came in here to console you not the other way around. I need to ask you something, too. Do you know his address? He didn't tell us where Theo is and the others don't remember anything about what they've done, or where they've been," I ask, hoping for some good news.

"I'm sorry, no. We always met up away from our houses. He never knew where I lived until he walked ya home," she says frustrated. Probably because she can't help.

"It's okay. Patsy and Billy are both checking the census, and Dominick and Eddie are asking in the bar, too. I'm sure we'll find it soon." A shocked look washes over her face.

"Oh. Poor, Lucy. I left her alone and the bar is packed tonight." With those words she dashes out of the office, leaving me staring at the door as it closes behind her.

I look at the chair behind the desk and think how nice it would be just to sit down for two minutes. But I don't have the time. I need to find Theo and the only way I will do that is by finding an address. It's like finding a needle in a haystack.

I open the office door and walk straight into Eddie, again. "We'll have to stop doing this," I say, whilst rubbing my nose after bumping it on his rock hard chest.

"I don't know. I quite enjoy it," he says, with a cheeky grin.

"No one knows anything in there. We're going to have to wait on Patsy and Billy," Dominick announces as he walks up behind Ed. He doesn't sound happy at the prospect of waiting.

"I know this might sound obvious, but can't you just tele-port to him? Billy said you can just think of somewhere with your eyes shut and be there when you open your eyes," Ed enquires, sounding eager for his plan to work.

"I can do that, yes, but I need to be able to smell, see, and feel the place in my head to get there. Not knowing where exactly he is means I don't have those senses about the place. I've never seen him in his wolf form, so I can't even try and do it by looking at him," I say, furious at myself for not being able to do it. Eddie's eagerness fades within a split second.

"But you know his scent. If you focus on just that, it might work. What have you got to lose?" Dominick always seems to know just what to say. Eddie gives me the loveliest, encouraging smile. How can I say no to that? I guess it's worth a try.

"All right. I'll give it a try."

I close my eyes and focus on nothing except Theo's dark spicy scent, letting it surround me like a blanket. On opening my eyes I find myself in Theo's room with a shocked Ruby staring at me with her mouth dropped open.

"Sorry. I'll explain later," I say, before closing my eyes and trying again. I would rather keep looking for Theo than waste time explaining what I'd just done.

This time I open my eyes hoping with every ounce of my being to see Theo in front of me, only to find myself in his lounge. *Crap*! At least Selena isn't in here. I don't think I'd be able to escape without an explanation if she was.

I go back to the alley feeling totally defeated.

"Did it work?" Eddie was so excited at the thought of me actually finding Theo. It's such a shame to fill him with the disappointment I feel, too.

"No, sorry. I just ended up in his bedroom and his lounge. I scared poor Ruby half to death," I say, trying to lighten the disappointment by adding that bit about Ruby. "If only he'd not stood me up the day he was meant to take me on a run, I'd be able to picture him, too." Now I'm mad at Theo; which isn't really fair considering he's the one trapped alone somewhere that no one knows about.

"What colour fur does he have, Eddie?" Dominick asks.

"It's a rusty colour. Why?" We both eye Dominick with the same questioning look.

He answers me rather than Eddie, "Because if you picture a wolf with that colour fur while doing what you just did with his scent, you might find him."

I close my eyes and picture a rusty coloured wolf, just like Dominick suggested. I wrap Theo's dark spicy scent around me. I feel the swirl that I felt when Dominick called me to him that first time, and as I open my eyes hoping I'm not at Theo's house again. I find myself faced with a big rusty wolf. I did a good job with the colour. It's just as I imagined. It's just the size I was off on; he's easily double the size I imagined—absolutely huge! And he's growling at me. I didn't imagine that.

"Theo. It's me, Bel! I've come to take you home!" I approach him cautiously, but when I am about a foot away, I realise he's not here with me.

He's delirious. His fur is matted with blood; obstructing my view of any actual wounds. I reach deep into our mate bond hoping to get through to Theo.

The wolf before me pauses and weighs me up.

I don't move. I can't tell if he recognises me or if he is wondering if I taste good. It's much scarier being faced with Theo ready to eat me than it was being faced with Paddy. He's making a rumbling growl deep in his chest as he slowly starts to edge towards me. I hold my hand out for him to sniff and hope he recognises my scent.

It doesn't take him long. He's barely sniffed it when he drops to the floor with a whine. His whole persona changes. He's extremely weak. It must have taken so much out of him to pretend to be so fierce.

When I fall to my knees and reach out to feel for injuries, he doesn't protest. I rub my hands over his head and neck, which all feels normal. I find the first wound on his shoulder. He doesn't even flinch as my fingers probe it.

What the hell is wrong with him? He should at least be reacting to the pain.

"Jared just informed me that Theo has at least two silver bullets in him. He clawed one out himself last night." Dominick's voice answers the question I was asking myself. I don't complain this time.

Thanks.

In the blink of an eye, I shift my hand to claws and slice into his shoulder making the wound bigger, once I get it deep enough so that I can see the bullet, I shift my hand back and grab the bullet between my fingers. I grit my teeth against the burning on my fingers where the silver comes in contact with my flesh, and drop it to the floor the second it's out.

"Theo, one down. Let's see how many more you have in you," I say, running my hands over his body. I find numerous bites but I can't find another wound that looks remotely like a bullet. I'm about to give up when I find it lodged in his front leg. It's not too deep but I still need to use my claws again to make the wound big enough for me to get a grip on the bullet. I'm throwing that bullet across the room in no time.

"I think that's it, Theo. Now we could do with some meat to get your energy back up." I regret my words as soon as they leave my mouth.

Mentioning food to a hungry wolf. Clever idea, Bel!

His eyes flash from the black of his wolf's to emerald green. Theo must be fighting his wolf for control.

I slowly back away looking for an exit, catching sight of the reinforced steel door with no handle. I realise I have no chance getting out of that so I give the rest of the room a quick glance. All blank solid walls and not one window to be seen.

Brilliant! There isn't even a wardrobe I could lock myself in.

"Rosabel, don't worry. We're on our way. I can sense you," Dominick says through our link; the panic clear in his own voice.

I turn my full attention back to Theo. "They know where we are. They're on their way. Just hang on a little longer."

His eyes are fully black now; telling me his wolf is back in full control. I have to have faith that he won't harm his mate. Normally that wouldn't be a problem but he's been confined and left injured for twenty-four hours. To make things worse, I just pulled out two silver bullets that had been stopping him from healing and taking all his energy. He's not exactly in his right mind right now.

"We're two minutes away Rosabel!" Dominick tries to reassure me and fails miserably.

It won't take him that long to devour me.

"Calm down. The fear will make him want you all the more." Dominick suggests.

How helpful, Dominick. It's not like I already know that, being a wolf and all.

Shifting into my wolf would only serve to make Theo feel more threatened, therefore, pushing him to attack me. I find myself backed into the corner of the room; I must have been backing up whilst arguing with Dominick.

Theo is stalking me. He nuzzles his snout into my stomach trying to get to the soft flesh he could tear into. Thankfully my hoodie is in the way. I hear the material rip.

Nothing like jinxing myself.

His teeth brush against my skin as I am wracking my brain for something to say to stop, or distract him but I can't think of anything.

I hope you are bringing some fresh meat with you, Dominick.

At that moment, the door bursts open three feet away from me.

The noise is not distracting Theo one bit. There is no way I can get to the door. He has me pinned to the wall.

Dominick and Ed appear from around the door.

"Eddie. You need to get out of here, Theo is full wolf. It will force the change on you. We don't need two wolves in here!" Panic once again floods my body.

"It's okay, I can fight it. If I feel like I can't, I'll leave. Theo you need to leave Bel alone. Come to me. I have some meat for you." He throws a dead rabbit in the room. It's freshly killed and dripping with blood. God only knows how he got one so quick.

Theo doesn't even bat an eyelid. "Theodore. You don't want to hurt, Rosabel. I nearly killed her yesterday. I know what pain it would cause you if you killed her. You don't want to feel that pain."

Both Ed and I give Dominick a perplexed look.

Are you insane? That's only going to make him angrier, Dominick.

"*Yes. That is my plan. If we get Theodore mad enough, he might take control.*"

Yes. Control enough to want to kill YOU!

I look down at Theo. I have to find something to say to ease the situation. When I see Theo's emerald eyes looking at me my fear subsides and relief washes over me.

"Theo. Ed has lots of those rabbits for you. Please go eat them," I say, pointing to the dead rabbit on the floor. I'm hoping Ed has more, at least.

Theo rubs his head against my leg, probably in apology at almost eating me. He walks over to the rabbit and starts to devour it.

I walk by him, slowly, hoping not to make him feel like I'm trying to steal it from him. Animals get extremely territorial over food. Once I reach Dominick and Eddie in the doorway, I can't believe how much safer I feel now that I am standing next to another werewolf and a vampire.

The three of us stand there, watching Theo thoroughly clean up the rabbit. Once he starts licking the blood off the floor, I nudge Ed. He gets my hint and leads Theo to a van, which looks like the one from the alley earlier. The only difference, this one is blue not white. They both jump in the back with a mountain of rabbit bodies.

God knows where he got all of them from.

Dominick gets behind the wheel so I climb in the passenger side.

It doesn't take long to get to Theo's house. We drive around the back of his house where he's got a big shed on the land there. I call it a big shed but it's a huge eight-bay workshop. Eddie called it 'the shed.' I had to add big and that still isn't a good enough name to describe it.

I get out of the van and walk in to 'the shed,' leaving Ed and Dominick to help Theo out. The floor is covered in gym mats. There are a couple punching bags and a weight bench, with weights. He must use this as a training area. There is also a couple hospital beds on the far wall set up with what looks like up-to-date medical equipment around them. The training room doubles up as a medical room.

Jared is sitting on the edge of one bed, and Paddy is on the edge of the other.

Wesley is cuddling Alyssa in the corner of the room. I don't think he'll be letting her out of his sight for a while. Just like I won't be letting Theo out of my sight for a while either.

Billy is standing with a woman of Indian descent, whom I don't recognise. She has a black, chin-length bob, and wearing a white doctor's coat with a stethoscope hanging around her neck.

As I approach Billy, he turns his attention to me. "Hey, beauty. You did real good tonight," he says, pulling me into a quick side hug. "This is Dr Patel. Dr Patel this is Rosabel."

She reaches out and shakes my hand. "Call me, Zainab."

"Nice to meet you, Zainab. I'm Bel. How are these guys doing?" I ask, waving my hand, gesturing to the three that had been taken.

"I've just finished checking them over and they are all perfectly healthy."

"That's great news. We have one more patient for you to look at. He's not in as good a condition as these three though. He should be in any minute, now."

I turn to look at the door and see Eddie walking in with Theo trotting in alongside him. His eyes roam the room looking for something. When they land on me, he heads straight for me. He stops in front of me so I crouch down.

"Bel, be careful," Billy warns me.

Wesley appears next to me ready to protect me if he needs to.

"It's okay. He won't hurt me!" I say confidently, before putting my arms around his neck, cuddling into his fur and filling my lungs with his lovely scent. My wolf is itching to get out. I can't stop myself whimpering in his ear. "My wolf will join you when you've been checked over, if you want?" I think it was her telling him that not me.

A rumble comes from deep in his chest, which I take as yes, along with the excitement I feel emanating from him.

I stand up and Theo pads over to the empty bed that Jared had been on a few minutes ago.

Jared is now standing behind me in a protective stance.

I notice Dominick is missing. "Eddie. Where's Dominick?"

"I need an invite from Theo. He's not got the ability to give one at the minute." Dominick's voice says through our link. I turn and head for the door before Eddie could answer.

"He's outside. You seem to know that already. How?" His curiosity rushes over my skin.

"We've got a blood tie. He answered me before you did, in here," I say laughing, while pointing to my temple.

"What?" Jared's anger hits me like a wall. I thought he'd be jealous when any other guy is involved, but he's angry like he's concerned for my protection. But then again, why would he be jealous? Dominick is a vampire. He's dead. I don't think he'd be capable of love. I don't think I'd be able to fall in love with someone that is dead either.

"Am I?" Dominick asks in my head. I'm kind of getting sick of not being able to think without being interrupted.

"Can't you just listen to me when I'm actually talking to you? Rather than butting in on my personal thoughts. I can only hear what you want me to. How come?" I take a few steps out the door before Dominick walks into view from around the other side of the van.

He speaks out loud this time, "If you want to drink some of my blood, then you'll be able to listen in on my thoughts whenever you wish, too." He tilts his head in a gesture to offer his neck to me.

"Eww. No thanks." That thought totally grosses me out. *Although I'm not sure why? Because when I'm in wolf form I hunt and eat animals; fur, bones and all.* It's probably because Dominick's cold and dead that it freaks me out so much.

"I have blood running through my veins and a heartbeat. Am I really dead?" He grabs my hand and places it on his bare chest through the opening of his dress shirt, right over his heart. I feel the thud, thud. It's slightly out of time compared to a human's. It has an extra faster thud, thud in between the normal thud, thud. Werewolves run to a slightly different beat too.

I move my hand away and force myself not to wipe it on my sweats.

"I don't know," is the only answer I can give him.

"I must leave now, Rosabel." He kisses me on the forehead before I even have the chance to think about dodging it.

"Thanks for your help tonight," I say, pulling away.

He smiles. "We are even now." He disappears with a pop before my eyes. How come he can make noises if he wants?

I turn back to go inside, only to find Jared standing in the doorway. I feel his concern tickle against my skin. "I don't like you having this tie with him. I don't trust him."

"He's not too bad, if you didn't nearly kill him the other day. I wouldn't have had to donate my blood and I wouldn't have a tie at all."

His face drops into a look of sadness as his guilt brushes against my skin.

"I'm sorry, Jared. I shouldn't have said that. It wasn't you. It was Emmanuel." I lean in and give him a big hug and he squeezes me back hard. He was always great to hug.

"I miss you baby Bel, I really do." The truth of his words is evident in his emotions. His love is just as strong as it was when we first got together all those years ago.

"I know." I stay in the hug to hide that I am crying. I don't want him to get the wrong idea if he sees so it's a good job he seems happy enough to still be hugging me. We hear a fierce growl coming from inside the shed causing Jared and I to break apart and run inside.

I can't see a problem with the scene before my eyes, except Theo was looking directly at me, growling. I look back at the door. He would have seen me and Jared cuddling but I can't feel jealousy coming from him.

The room fills with his bonding scent.

"Jared. Stay there," I warn as I put my hand behind me to stop him coming any closer.

"Yeah. I get the point," he replies as Billy, Paddy, and Alyssa walk over to where we're standing. I head for Theo, who is still growling quietly.

"Come on. You need to get out of here," I hear Billy say to Jared behind me.

"But, Bel?" He's worried that I'm going to get hurt.

"It's not her he wants to hurt," Billy tells him as Theo pounces in front of me facing Jared, growling fiercely once again.

Jared puts his hands up above his head like you do to the police to show them you have no weapons. "It's okay mate. I'm going," he says, backing up and out the door.

I start taking my clothes off. Wesley has seen me naked and I'm sure Dr Patel has seen plenty of people naked before. I need to get into wolf form so we can communicate better.

I've just pulled the bra off my arm, to be fully naked, when Eddie emerges from the cupboard with what looks like some medical supplies in his hand, "Is this what..." he looks up midsentence, "...you. Wow."

I instantly smell his arousal and so does Theo.

He spins around and growls at Eddie in warning, just as the room fills even more with the bonding scent. For Eddie's sake this time.

Billy comes running back in as I finish the shift into my wolf form; *I guess he heard the growl.*

He takes in the scene. "Eddie. What have you said?"

"Oh, Eddie. For god's sake. You've seen plenty of naked people before." He must have caught on to the scent of Eddie's arousal.

I trot over to Theo and wiggle my behind at him in a flirty way to distract him. *"I'm all yours, Theo."* It seems to get his attention.

"I never doubted that. You were crying. Jared upset you." He was trying to protect me. I can't help but smile at that thought.

"No! He didn't upset me, not really. He was telling me he missed me. I could feel how much he loved me still and I cried because I can't return those feelings."

Theo rubs his head against the side of mine and I notice a mass of matted blood on the back of his neck, making me think there must be a serious wound there.

"Has Dr Patel looked at this wound on your neck?"

"Yes. It's all healed. I just need to wash the blood off my fur, that's all. There is one on my stomach, too. I'm healed enough to change back now, but I'd rather have you to myself like this for a while first, or maybe for the rest of the night. I'm sure the pack can cope without talking to me until morning." Theo strides over to the corner on the gym mats. He turns around a couple of times to get comfy.

I make the same move curling up next to him.

"I love you, more than I knew it was possible to love someone," he blurts. The love flowing through our bond. He meant it with all of his heart.

"Ditto."

I feel him chuckle in a wolfy way against my side. *"Has somebody been watching 'Ghost' too much?"*

"Sounds like I'm not the only one since you knew what I meant."

We both chuckle at that. It's great to feel him so happy, not to mention, healthy.

"Has anyone filled you in on who the controller was?" I ask him. I guess he should be told and since I was in charge. I should be the one to fill him in.

"No. Not yet. I guess I'll have to bring him to justice tomorrow. Where is he?" He sounds as though he hates that part of being alpha. *I don't blame him, I do too!*

"No. You won't. It was Emmanuel. He wanted to cause a war between the werewolves and the vampires."

"I know you dated him, Bel But I have to serve a death sentence. It's the law." He thinks I said no because I didn't want him to hurt Emmanuel.

I wish that was the case.

"No, it's already been done. I k-killed him." My voice cracks in my head and tears well in my eyes. I don't know if I'll ever get over killing someone I cared for. Killing the pride members that duelled with me was a completely different thing. It was them or me. I could live with that. Emmanuel, though. Emmanuel was different.

"Oh, Bel. I'm so sorry you had to do that. It must've been hard for you." I can feel his regret through our connection. He nuzzles his snout against my fur.

"It was. But I had no choice."

"Why didn't you just leave him to me?"

"He knew he had a death sentence. He wanted to hold you hostage so we wouldn't kill him."

"Thank you for taking over and coming to rescue me." He gives me a toothy snarl that I think is meant to be a smile. It's hard to tell on a wolf's face.

I snuggle into his fur, breathing in his scent. It's so relaxing after such a long twenty-four hours.

We both lift our heads as we hear the door open, to see Billy rushing in and closing the door behind him. "You guys need be quiet. Selena thinks we have a pack of wolves on the property. She's talking about setting traps." I start to giggle in my head. There is a pack of wolves on the property, well a quarter of a pack, not to mention the lion.

Theo changes into human in a second flat. "What is Selena doing here?" He's fuming. I don't need to be an empath to know that.

I quickly shift to human form while Theo strides to the

cupboard and pulls out some sweats and a t-shirt, yanking them on quickly. He wets a towel and rubs at the visible blood on his neck and face.

I quickly gather my clothes and throw them on.

"She turned up this afternoon. She hasn't said why. She just booked herself a room. Didn't Bel tell you?"

"No. Bel didn't tell me," he snaps, aiming his anger at me.

Now wait a minute. Why are you mad at me?

"It totally slipped my mind. I have had a lot on it tonight. I did just kill someone for god's sake. I'm terribly sorry she wasn't on the top of my list." Sarcasm at its best. On the defensive, I go.

"Sorry, I snapped. I'm mad at her not you. She has no right to just turn up." He comes and kisses me on the top of my head. "Come on. Let's go kick her out." Grabbing my hand and interlocking our fingers, he pulls me out of the shed after Billy.

Just as we step out the door, I pull his body back towards me. "One thing first." He turns to look at me.

I reach up and put my hand behind his neck and pull his head towards me, brushing my lips against his. He reciprocates by working his mouth over mine. I pull away and press our foreheads together as we both catch our breath.

Breath caught, we step away and find Billy standing nearby waiting for us. The three of us head for the house and enter through the glass doors in the lounge without a word. I'm too busy thinking about how great that kiss was to bother speaking.

"No wolves on the loose out there, but look who I found making out behind the bushes." I'm sure Billy added that last bit for Selena's sake.

"TED!" Ruby screams as she pounces on him, throwing her arms around his neck and her legs around his waist. "You're okay?" she adds as she drops her legs back down to the floor.

He gives her a squeeze before breaking away. "I'm

fine, Ruby."

Ruby turns to me pulling me into a hug. "Thank you so much, Bel."

"You're welcome." As soon as she lets me go, Theo grabs my hand again.

I look around the room for the first time since entering. It looks so small compared to normal. I realise that's probably because it's full of werewolves; Wesley, Alyssa, and Paddy are all squashed together on the sofa facing the stairs. Selena and Jared are on the other one, Ruby is next to Jared. Eddie and Chloe are sitting on the kitchen bench top leaving Greg, Darren, Phil, and Dave all standing around leaning against the walls through the room. Billy walks to the kitchen and leans against the side next to Chloe.

Everyone seems to give Theo a little nod. I think they all probably want to come over and welcome him back just like Ruby had, but I'm sure Selena would ask why everyone was so pleased to see him. Ruby's reaction looked suspicious enough! Ruby goes back to her spot on the sofa next to Jared, who ruffles her hair as she sits down. *Typical Jared.*

"Selena. What are you doing in my house? I thought I made it clear, you are not welcome anymore."

Theo. Just cut to the chase why don't you?

She stands up, walks up to us, and actually tries to cuddle him. Before she manages to get a hold of him, he takes a step backwards dragging me along with him.

"Can we talk in private?" she asks, giving me a pointed look.

"Anything you want to say, Selena, can be said in front of everyone here." He waves his hand around the room. She follows his hand with her eyes falling on everyone, one by one.

She stares down at her feet. I can see the contemplation on her face, deciding whether she should tell everyone her business. She must have decided to go with it because she opens her mouth to speak; only nothing comes out for a second while she lifts her eyes and looks at Theo. "I thought we could give our marriage another go."

Theo sighs shaking his head "You're too late. A couple months ago maybe I would've been stupid enough to take you back, but I'm with Bel now. I'm not giving up what we have, for you. If that's all you wanted, you can get your stuff together and leave."

Tears fill her eyes, but she doesn't move. She takes a deep breath. "I'm pregnant! The dad chucked me out. I thought you..." She doesn't finish her sentence.

Theo's body goes tense next to me before I hear Eddie's whisper.

"Oh, fuck." If I had human ears, I wouldn't have heard it.

Theo squeezes my hand, too hard. I'm actually glad I have super strength or he might have broken something. Then again, if he carries on squeezing much longer he might just do that.

Selena is once again staring at the floor.

Theo glances at me with his wolf eyes as he releases my hand before storming up the stairs. We all hear the door slam behind him, leaving me to wonder if it's still going to be intact when I go up there.

"Theo?" Selena shouts as she makes a move to chase after him.

For the second time in a few minutes I find myself extremely grateful for being a were. I reach the bottom of the stairs first and manage to block her way. There is no way she wants to go up there when he's as angry as that.

"Just let him calm down. He'll come down when he's ready to talk," I say forcefully.

I watch the thoughts cross her face whilst she decides whether to tell me to get out of her way or just listen to me and wait. She chooses right, going for the latter; turning and sitting on the sofa without a word to me.

I sit down on the stairs, not wanting her to try and sneak up to him when I'm not paying attention. I don't know why he got so angry. His anger appeared before she mentioned the father so it can't be because he kicked her out. I'm so deep in thought that I jump a foot off the step as I feel someone's hand rubbing my knee. I look to my left to see Billy sitting on the step beside me.

"Penny for your thoughts?" he asks.

I shake my head and shrug. "Just wondering what got him so mad. It's still escalating, I can feel it."

"We all can. You should go talk to him. It might calm him down. Just be cautious," he warns me.

"Do you think he's that angry at Selena, that he might attack me?" *I really don't think he'd hurt me no matter how angry he is, not after he managed not to attack me tonight when he was so hungry and injured.*

"I don't have time to explain everything, Theo's mood is affecting everyone, and we can't risk exposing ourselves in front of Selena."

I look around the room at the others and he's right; everyone is tense. Paddy is really struggling at fighting off his wolf.

"The main cause of Theo and Selena's arguments were because he wanted kids like, yesterday, and she never wanted them. Now she turns up pregnant. The one thing he wanted from her, she gave to someone else."

I have a really bad feeling in my gut. "What are you trying to say, Billy?"

I finally place that look he had in his eyes before he ran upstairs. Regret.

"I honestly don't know. I just figured you deserved to have a heads up."

I quickly kiss him on the cheek. "Thanks Billy."

I race up the stairs needing to know what Theo is thinking

because my brain is coming up with too many scenarios I don't like.

Theo's door has a crack running right down the middle and the frame is loose, but it's intact enough to be serving its purpose. I knock on the door before opening, just to be courteous. He'll have been able to sense me coming, not to mention hearing my footsteps. I open the door before he has time to reply to my knock and close it behind me.

He's pacing back and forth across the room.

I decide to steal Billy's line. "Penny for your thoughts?"

He sighs and carries on pacing.

I sit on the edge of his bed ready to wait for him, but to my surprise he joins me, putting his head in his hands. We sit in a silence that I'm not willing to break. If he wants to talk, he can. He came up here to think and calm down. I haven't joined him to make him more tense, if that's even possible, by asking him stupid questions like, 'are you okay?' when it's blatantly obvious he's not.

He lifts his head out of his hands and stares at me with his beautiful emerald green eyes that are filled with nothing but love and regret. "Bel, I'm sorry," he says, giving me a bad feeling this is a conversation I don't want to be involved in.

"Billy is right, isn't he? You're going to take her back." It's a statement, not a question. There is no need for him to beat around the bush to tell me what Billy already has. There are tears running down my cheeks as I look at him making him a blur. I can't read what his eyes are saying, but I can feel his emotions loud and clear, the love, regret, and guilt.

He's made his decision.

"Bel. I…"

I don't need to listen to him tell me his decision, not when I can already feel it. I close my eyes so I can let my body take me wherever it wants to.

God only knows where I'll end up!

29.

PRIVATE CELEBRATION

THEO

I see Bel prepare herself to teleport whilst I'm mid-sentence. Her eyes close and her body relaxes slightly.

I am not letting her disappear on me.

"Don't you dare!" I yell, as I grab a hold of her, hoping to distract her enough to make her hear me out. Her eyes open as I'm kneeling before her and I quickly plead my case.

"He's wrong, Bel. How could you think I would do that to you? You are my true mate. You were made for me. I couldn't love anyone else, no matter what. You have my heart and it's not going anywhere. It belongs to you. Do you hear me?" I ask as I let my hands cup her face and roam around to her hair.

"But I felt your regret and guilt."

"Being an empath, you should know not to jump to conclusions about what people's emotions mean. I was feeling those things because I was planning on asking you if we could help Selena out, give her a roof for a while. I felt bad for even thinking about putting you in that situation," I explain.

"Oh," she says clearly embarrassed. "I thought—"

I don't give her a chance to finish her sentence. I take her mouth in a searing kiss, full of my passion for her. She relaxes into the kiss, I lay her back on the bed.

"What about everyone downstairs? They'll want to celebrate with you," she says as our mouths part.

"We can all celebrate together, tomorrow." I pause to peck her pretty pink lips. "Tonight, I'm celebrating with my mate," I say, before showing her exactly how I plan to celebrate.

EXCERPT

Please turn the page for an excerpt of

Forever, Young and Beautiful, book 2 of The Mount Roxby Series.

Available to purchase now.

BLACKNESS DESCENDS

RUBY

We walk out of the movies giggling at how I managed to trip up the stairs and face plant on the floor, while dashing back from a bathroom break. I can never get through a movie without having to dash to the bathroom. I blame the Coke.

"Ruby. One second…you were there, the next…you were gone," Bel manages to spit out between fits of laughter. "I thought you'd turned vamp or gained a druid's power of teleporting in and out whenever and wherever they want. Until I heard the grunt as you got up." The laughter starts again.

"If only that was the case!" I say, hating the embarrassed feeling I have. I can't help but wish I was a werewolf like Bel. She is so graceful and has such good instincts, she would never have fallen so stupidly. It isn't the first time I've found myself dreaming of being a werewolf. With two werewolf brothers, I have yearned not to be the human of the family. The ugly duckling.

"I better get home before Theo sends someone after me," I say. "He's more like a prison guard than a brother," I add.

"He just worries about his baby sister, so don't be too hard on him."

"Fine. I'll try to be nice," I offer. "You're going to do more packing aren't you?"

Bel nods. "Yes. Tell him, I'll be home soon. I love that I've moved in with him, but I hate this packing business," Bel says, hugging me goodbye. I watch as she dematerialises before my eyes. That druid blood she recently discovered she has comes in pretty handy at times.

Having parked my car at the other end of the main road means I have a good ten minute walk ahead of me.

I start walking at a fast pace, hearing nothing but the click clack of my heels on the pavement.

Click clack...

Click clack...

Click clack...

The hairs on the back of my neck stand on end and a shiver runs down my back.

I freeze on the spot and dart my eyes around, having no idea what I expect to see. I don't have the sense of smell a werewolf has or the hearing of a vampire, but I do have gut instinct of a human and mine is speaking to me right now—telling me to get the hell out of there. I do just that.

I run across the road not even looking for passing traffic. Luckily, it's clear.

Once my feet touch the pavement, I notice all the feeling of worry has gone. I look around again and could have slapped myself upside the head. I'd been so distracted that I hadn't noticed during our giggles, we had crossed the road and ended up outside Misty's—a bar that caters only for Supes.

It's owned by a witch who puts wards on it that scare the bejesus out of humans, so they don't, won't, can't enter. It's impossible. What if a Supe carried them over the threshold kicking and screaming? I hear you ask. A human's heart would just stop. Dead. Misty has been known to drop it enough that a human could be carried in but only for a few special people.

I start walking again, laughing at my stupidity; letting a silly horror movie distract me enough to not notice Misty's. I know my car wasn't far up the road. Another five minutes at the most. I start listening to the click clack of my heels again.

Click clack...

Click clack...

Click click clack clack.

I hear double footsteps in quick succession. Knowing I'm not walking fast enough to warrant that means only one thing —someone is following me.

"You might as well come out. I know you're there," I say into the darkness, not bothering to raise my voice knowing which ever wolf my brother has sent would have no trouble hearing me even if I whispered. But I get no response.

I stop and turn to face behind me to where they must be hiding in a shadow or eave of a building because I can't see anyone, but I speak up anyway.

"I won't tell Theo that you weren't covert enough." Were-wolves can move without being heard. This one was obviously being sloppy for a human to have heard them following me.

I still get no response so I give up and turn around, starting for my car again, at a much quicker pace. I can see it across the road, when I'm suddenly grabbed from behind. An arm around my waist, the other hand over my mouth mutes my screams. The person holding me drags me into a dark alley between the shops.

I'm pinned against the wall face first. All I can see is the bare red bricks on the wall.

The hand over my mouth pulls my head to a side stretching my neck out, as the arm around my waist disappears.

I wriggle to get free but I'm still pinned in place by the body behind me, as hard and strong as the wall in front. I feel the hand that had been around my waist brush my long, blonde curls from my neck. He strokes over my thudding pulse with his rough fingers.

It's then that I realise I'm not just trapped by a psycho; I'm trapped by a vampire.

That recognition hits a second before the fingers disappear and sharp fangs pierce my neck. The pain's horrendous. I can feel my heartbeat rise with fear.

I bite down hard on the hand over my mouth trying to distract the vampire at my neck. I try to fight with my body, but I don't have the room to move. The only thing I'm succeeding in is raising my pulse, therefore, giving the vampire a faster and easier meal.

My mind starts to become sluggish, listening to the vampire moan as he sucks my veins dry makes me push the fog back and try to think of a way out of this. If I don't do something quick, I won't survive this.

If I was a werewolf, I'd have the strength to get away, is the last thought that runs through my mind, before blackness descends…

ACKNOWLEDGMENTS

Boys, thank you for being mummy's #1 fans. Love you to bits.

Mam, the best friend and role model a girl could ever have. Love you. Thanks for being the first person to read this and giving me your blunt honesty.

Dad, you will always be the hero for me.

Kimberley, you are incredibly generous and I can never thank you enough for the editing you did.

Sloan Johnson, you did a fabulous job redesigning the cover. I am so happy with it.

Heidi Hafner, I wouldn't have written this if you didn't talk me into it. Thank you for the push. I promise I will keep kicking your butt to make sure you get your book finished.

Gemma Walker-Smith, you have been a world of information. I really appreciate all the questions you answered and all the help you gave me. You are a wonderful author, thank you for setting the high standard for me to strive for.

ABOUT THE AUTHOR

Aimie Jennison is a Yorkshire lass living in Australia. She is a mother to three boisterous boys, two of which are teenagers who drive her crazy on a daily basis.

Aimie loves to people watch, it's her favourite way to come up with new characters and stories. So next time a stranger is staring at you in the street, don't panic, they could be an author basing a character on you.

Aimie has always loved to read and write. Paranormal, gay romance and crime/thrillers being her favourite genres. Her characters talk the loudest when she's at the beach or climbing a mountain.

Aimie would love to hear from you so don't shy away from contacting her.

For more information:

www.aimiejennison.com

aimiejennison@gmail.com

ALSO BY
AIMIE JENNISON

Pride to Pack (Mount Roxby #1)

Forever Young and Beautiful (Mount Roxby #2)

Releasing the Wolf (Rossi Pack #1)

Haunted by Love: An Anthology